THE
COUNSELORS

ALSO BY JESSICA GOODMAN

They Wish They Were Us

They'll Never Catch Us

THE
COUNSELORS

JESSICA GOODMAN

RAZORBILL

RAZORBILL

An imprint of Penguin Random House LLC, New York

First published in the United States of America by Razorbill,
an imprint of Penguin Random House LLC, 2022

Copyright © 2022 by Jessica Goodman

Visit us online at penguinrandomhouse.com.

LIBRARY OF CONGRESS CATALOGING-IN-PUBLICATION DATA
Names: Goodman, Jessica, author.
Title: The counselors / Jessica Goodman.
Description: New York : Razorbill, 2022. | Audience: Ages 14 and up.
Summary: After a traumatic school year, camp counselor Goldie Easton is excited to reunite with her two best friends at an elite summer camp, but when a local boy is found dead on the grounds, all three must reveal a dark secret to find the murderer.
Identifiers: LCCN 2021061889 | ISBN 9780593524220 (hardcover)
ISBN 9780593524244 (trade paperback) | ISBN 9780593524237 (ebook)
Subjects: CYAC: Camps—Fiction. | Best friends—Fiction.
Friendship—Fiction. | Secrets—Fiction. | LCGFT: Novels.
Classification: LCC PZ7.1.G6542 Co 2022 | DDC [Fic]—dc23
LC record available at https://lccn.loc.gov/2021061889

Book manufactured in Canada

ISBN 9780593524220 (HARDCOVER)
1 3 5 7 9 10 8 6 4 2

ISBN 9780593527504 (INTERNATIONAL EDITION)
1 3 5 7 9 10 8 6 4 2

FRI

Design by Rebecca Aidlin
Text set in Granjon LT Std

To Grandma Belle, Grandpa Herbie,
Pop Siegel, and Supergrandma,
for passing down the love of camp
from generation to generation

PROLOGUE

Evil doesn't exist at Camp Alpine Lake. Not inside the wrought-iron gate that separates camp from the town of Roxwood, and not at the waterfront, where far-out buoys keep us isolated from the rest of New England. Everything here is safe. The tennis courts. The arts and crafts shed. The cabins. The Lodge. Camp is a bubble, made for bonfires and sing-alongs and friendships formed under the beam of a flashlight.

Even when I was eight and the group leaders would huddle us together on the man-made beach in neat little rows so we could watch the lifeguards line up in the water to practice safety drills, we knew they were all for show. We were never in danger. Not here.

We'd watch the lifeguards dive in unison, touching the ground beneath the surface, even if it was eleven or twelve feet below. They'd come up with nothing, handfuls of dirt. No harmed child, no limp arm. They'd do this over and over until they reached the end of the boundaries, never screaming in horror. Never fearful that a precious camper was gone.

Even when I became a counselor and was tasked with keeping the children alive, healthy, and well fed, I knew there was never any real danger here. Not on the edges of the forest up by the cliffs where loose rocks threatened to fall silently into the abyss. Not along the ropes course where harnesses always stayed buckled. And certainly not in the lake, where I wore my red lifeguard suit like a superhero's costume.

But that was before I knew what kind of dark secrets were hidden in the corners of Camp Alpine Lake, out of sight of campers, counselors, and lifers like me, who would give everything we had to keep this place whole.

That was before we learned the truth. About Ava, Imogen, and me—and how far we'd go to protect each other even after we had been exposed.

Before this summer, Camp Alpine Lake was a haven. An escape from what I could not face back home in Roxwood, only a few miles outside the gate.

But now Camp Alpine Lake is another place where I'll never feel safe.

CHAPTER 1

Now

The summer will begin like it always does, with me wandering the grounds of Camp Alpine Lake alone. It's the first day of maintenance week, when all the counselors arrive to get the place ready for campers. But I'm the only one who can come early.

No one else gets to experience how the cabins smell like cedar and lemon when they're empty, not yet filled with other counselors or twelve-year-old boys who don't know about deodorant. How the sun bounces off the lake when there aren't any swimmers bobbing in the lap lanes. Or how you can stand at the edge of Creepy Cliff and scream, loud and long, listening to your voice echo all across New England.

"This place is your home, too, Goldie," Mellie has always said. I've heard the words enough times to believe them, even though my *actual* home is right down the road from Truly's, the dive bar we go to on nights off.

But this summer is different. And Stu and Mellie are the only people at Alpine Lake who know why.

Mom and Dad insist I shouldn't break tradition. "You can't let what happened ruin every single thing you love," Dad says, gripping the steering wheel of our old Subaru as we pull up to the gate. "You deserve to have fun. We'll see you later at orientation."

Mom turns around from the passenger seat and squeezes my bare knee. "You're going to be okay."

I nod, unable to find words, but I know she's right. This place has always calmed me. Always washed away whatever sorrow I held on to at the beginning of the summer. If anything can heal me, it's a summer at Camp Alpine Lake with Ava and Imogen, who have been my best friends for a decade. I may not have told them about my school year, but eight weeks with them will erase the damage and the pain. Even if we've barely spoken in the past few months. They always make everything better.

I get out of the car with shaky legs and heave my duffel over my shoulder. I walk through the gate and inhale deeply, smelling freshly cut grass and woodchips. I'm home.

I make my way to the gazebo and sit down, pushing my sunglasses up on my head. The clock on the dining hall says it's only nine in the morning. I've still got an hour before Ava and Imogen arrive on the buses. They'll bring with them all the other former campers who are now counselors. The lifers. People I've known since I was eight years old. Later today, we'll meet the foreigners. The ones who fly from Argentina, South Africa, and Australia to experience eight weeks in America. There are always a handful of Brits, mostly teaching tennis or soccer. Men with silly accents who will offer you tallboys and cigarettes at bonfires. Women who order gin and tonics on nights off and sunburn easy. Some come back year after year and some we never see again.

"Goldie!" someone calls.

I swivel around to find Stu jogging toward me in a polo shirt and long khaki shorts, belted at the waist. An Alpine Lake baseball hat covers his bald head and he's holding a clipboard like it's an extension of his arm. For a second, my stomach cramps. *Does he regret how they helped me?*

"Hi, Stu," I say, my voice smaller than usual.

"There's our golden girl." I half expect him to ruffle my dark curly hair like he used to do when I was little. But he smiles at me, like nothing happened this year. Like he and his wife Mellie didn't save my life. "Do you want to know your cabin assignment early? Drop your stuff off before the buses pull in?"

I nod eagerly, pulling one knee up under my chin. There's no way Imogen, Ava, and I would be staffed in the same cabin since we're all going to be lifeguards, but hopefully we'll be in the same group so we have the same schedules. Last year was our first time on the staff side of things and we were all assigned cabins so far away from each other. It sucked. Nothing like the years we spent as campers. I wonder if that's when the gulf between us began to widen.

"Let's see," Stu says, tapping his clipboard with a pen. "Here you are, my dear. You're with the Ramblers. Nine-year-olds. And you'll be in Bloodroot. Best view of camp, but you know that already. Your bed was in the back left corner, right?"

That's the thing about Stu. He always remembers what cabins you were in, what your favorite activities were, and if you preferred chicken patties over wing dings. He knows my dad likes to stock the infirmary with neon-colored Band-Aids so the little ones can wear them like badges of honor, and that Mom blasts Queen in the woodworking shop to soundtrack the buzzsaws. Last year, he got her a vintage shirt from their Live Aid show for her birthday, and I swear it's her most prized possession.

I smile up at Stu, blocking the sun with my hand. "Any chance you can give me a hint about—"

"Ava and Imogen? I thought you'd never ask," he says with a wink. "Don't worry, they're with the Ramblers, too. Ava's in Ludlow and Imogen's in Ascutney. You're smack dab in the middle."

My shoulders relax and all I want to do is text them the good news, but I know there's no use. There's no service at Camp Alpine Lake. Barely any in the town of Roxwood at all.

"Why don't you get settled and we'll see you when everyone else gets here, okay?"

"Thanks, Stu. Holler if you need anything."

"You got it, golden girl."

He tips his hat in a playful way and heads toward the office. But as he walks off, his face falls, a furrow forming at his brow. For a second, I wonder if his worry is related to me. If he regrets letting me come back.

But I don't know what I would do if, after everything, I lost this place, too. The promise of spending the summer at Alpine Lake was the only thing that helped me get through the year. The stares. The whispers that echoed through the halls of Roxwood High. Whenever someone left a nasty note in my locker or shoved me hard in the shoulder, I would close my eyes and think of this place. Of the first day of camp. Of being reunited with Ava and Imogen.

They never treated me different even though I'm not like them. I'm a local—a *townie*. Someone who bypassed camp's exclusive admissions exam and five-digit price tag because my parents work here. But Ava and Imogen don't care about that. We're all the same—the kids who live ten months for two. That's all that matters.

I hope that's still true.

The walk from the gazebo to Bloodroot only takes a few minutes, but you can see just about everything. I pass the volleyball

court, the softball field, the upper picnic tables, and the first set of
tennis courts. My cabin is fourth in a row on a big hill and it's right
in the center of all the action. Everyone has to pass it on their way
down to the waterfront, so it always feels like you're at the center of
everything. Plus, like Stu said, killer views. You can see all the way
to the lake from the counselor room.

But I love Bloodroot for different reasons. Ava, Imogen, and I
lived here the first summer we were assigned the same cabin. The
previous year, when we were eight, we begged the counselors to
let us switch, but they never did. And then finally, a few weeks
before we were due to be Ramblers, Ava's mom called and worked
some fancy-person magic so we were not only assigned to the same
cabin, but also beds right next to each other in the far corner of the
room, right by the big window that faces the waterfront. Like Stu
remembered.

I push open the door, and as the metal springs squeak, tears prick
my eyes. *This* is my home. I dump my duffel on a top bunk in the
counselor room and walk slowly through the main cabin, running
my fingertips along the wooden bed frames, the rafters overhead,
and the cubbies that will soon be crowded with little girls' linens.

I stop at the entrance and look up at the plaques. There's one
commemorating each year that camp's been open, with the names
of those who lived here painted in dramatic fashion. I recognize so
many names. Girls who fell in love with each other, who formed
friendships you can only make at a place like this. I search the
plaques until I find ours.

There we are, along the bottom. Three lines of the same phrase,
repeated over and over with our names signed below. *Sisters by
choice*. Our handwriting still looks the same. Mine, neat and tiny,

like I'm trying to fit as many letters as possible. Imogen's loopy and bubbly, and Ava's a quick scrawl.

I close my eyes and hold my breath, keeping this feeling in my lungs. It's the first time since before the accident that I feel free. That I feel like *me*. But I can't think about that too much because I'll break into tears, and if I do, Ava and Imogen will know as soon as they see me. They always know. And then I'd have to tell them the truth.

They don't need to know yet. Maybe ever. It won't do me any good. I'll still be Goldie Easton, the most hated girl in Roxwood. I'll still have to repeat a semester of high school. And Dylan Adler will still never walk again.

I was lucky I didn't go to jail. That's what people said around town.

It's because she's associated with that camp.

Those directors saved her ass.

Stu and Mellie pulled some strings for her.

She should rot in hell.

What if Ava and Imogen think I'm a monster, like everyone else? We've shared everything with each other. Complaints about the bumps on our bikini lines, the jelly donuts Ava special orders around Hanukkah, the secret things that make our bodies hum alone in the dark. But not this. I don't want them to know about this.

It was easy to dodge their calls and the three-way FaceTimes right after the accident, and as the semester stretched on, they both became busier and busier, and their texts became less frequent. Now, six months later, I don't know how I would begin to explain that my whole life has changed without them even knowing.

Plus, Ava's got enough to worry about with her shitty investment banker dad who's happy to write checks for her Upper East Side prep school but refuses to visit from Palm Beach. And Imogen's busy with auditions after landing a cell phone commercial that plays before basically every YouTube video.

They never found out about the accident thanks to the fact that they never asked me about life up here. Well, and that Stu and Mellie made sure the news didn't hit the local paper. Whenever Ava and Imogen brought up our futures, I'd just say I couldn't wait to get out of this hellhole. No one expects anything else when you live someplace like Roxwood.

For now, I want to enjoy the summer. Eight magical weeks at Camp Alpine Lake. Nothing exists outside this place. Not even the past.

CHAPTER 2

Then

It was hard not to notice Heller McConnell at the haunted house orientation. There were nine of us, all seniors from Roxwood High, who had been cast to work the season at the old abandoned psych ward off Route 16, and Heller was the only athlete.

I was picking through a box of fangs when Heller walked over to inspect a roll of mummy wrapping. His dark curls swooped over one eye and a soft smile tugged at the corner of his red mouth.

"Didn't peg you as a vampire lover," Heller said, holding up a plastic knife.

His voice was low and smooth, the same way he sounded over the loudspeaker at school while making the morning announcements.

"I could get into it," I said. "A gender-swapped Dracula situation."

Heller laughed like he was impressed. "Goldie, right?"

My brows shot up in surprise and Heller snapped his mouth shut.

"Sorry, that's weird. It's . . ."

"We've been in the same class since kindergarten," I said. "It'd be weird if you *didn't* know my name."

A smile blossomed on his face, and I licked my lips, trying to ignore the warmth spreading through my chest.

In that moment, I wasn't Goldie Easton, the quiet girl who was always head down in her phone or an old mystery novel, never present. I was something new and sparkly, full of possibilities. I cleared my throat and hunted for something to say.

"Why are you here?" It was the wrong question. I knew it as soon as I saw Heller's face fall.

"College fund," he said. "Pays more than leading hayrides at the nursery."

"Dartmouth?" I'd heard their hockey coaches had been courting him since sophomore year. It was pretty much a miracle, a Roxwood kid going Ivy. I expected Heller to puff out his chest and be all aggro about it. But instead, he averted his eyes like he was embarrassed. It made me like him more.

"It's not a sure thing," he said, shrugging. "I still have to get in." Then he leaned forward into the bin of costumes and dug out a black pointy witch's hat, setting it on my head at an odd angle.

"Everyone said there was a reason no one took jobs here." Heller smiled right at me and took a step closer so the space between us almost disappeared, so I could smell him, all mint and flannel and firewood. "But I think I'm going to like it."

CHAPTER 3

Now

I hear the buses before I see them. Everything echoes up here in Roxwood, where the trees and the mountains create a canyon for sound to bounce through. It's especially loud at Camp Alpine Lake, where you have to climb up a huge hill to see the entrance. That drive is always the best. It makes your stomach buzz like you're on a roller coaster, and only when you reach the top of the hill do you see the massive banner welcoming you home, here.

I push open Bloodroot's front door and stand on the porch, squinting up toward the gazebo. A flash of yellow metal appears through the trees and my heart flutters. I make a break for it, rushing toward the buses, my friends.

I get there in time to see Mellie and Stu walk out from the office, wearing their matching striped senior staff shirts, the ones with the Alpine Lake logo stitched onto the chest. Mellie rubs her hands together and her dark ponytail bobs up and down. For the first time I notice a few gray streaks winding through her hair.

"This is the best part," she says, her shoulders rising to meet her ears. "It doesn't feel quite real until everyone is here. Right, sweetheart? You're all what makes this place so special."

She squeezes my hand and I resist the urge to rest my head on her shoulder. I shift my weight from foot to foot, trying to settle my nerves, to ignore the fact that I almost don't want this summer to start because then, of course, it will have to end. And I'll have to go back to Roxwood High.

The buses roar from right below the apex of the hill, and then all of a sudden, I see them peeking out, barreling toward us, the tops hitting the trees that canopy above.

"Here we go," Stu whispers. But he's not looking at the road. Instead, he's focused on some piece of paper stuck to his clipboard. "Damn Roxwood . . ." he mumbles.

But before he can say anything else, Mellie throws an elbow into his side. "Stu," she says with a singsong voice, as if he's a child. "My nervous husband. He's always worried on the first day, you know." Stu drops his arm and hides his clipboard behind his back.

"Sorry," he mumbles. "Forgot to eat breakfast."

Mellie gives him a sharp look. "Did you check—"

Stu pats his insulin pump, attached to his hip, and points down to his fanny pack, where everyone at Alpine Lake knows he keeps a little diabetes kit. Stuff like an extra insulin pen and glucose tabs just in case he or any of the diabetic kids have emergencies. Stu's always been super open about his pump, which is probably why parents who have diabetic kids like to send them here. In-a-pinch supplies are never far away, and Stu has a dedicated mini-fridge in the office for kids who need to store their insulin someplace safe. Plus, he actually knows how to help them out if their blood sugar gets low on a hike or at the lake.

Mellie huffs and shakes her head. It's obvious something is wrong. There's a tension in the air, something I know I'm not supposed to ask about. Not just because I'm only a second-year counselor, but because I'm not one of them. I didn't travel here from a cushy suburb, or talk about how when I'm older I'll donate a hundred grand to refurbish the stables. I'm the girl Stu and Mellie took pity on. The girl they look out for.

I straighten my spine and toss my hair behind my shoulders, willing confidence to come. Butterflies hum in my stomach as the first bus pulls around the traffic circle in front of the dining hall and comes to a stop. The doors make a hissing sound as they open and dozens of people pour out onto the front lawn. Smiling faces carrying backpacks and water bottles, wearing high-waisted denim shorts and tie-dyed shirts, fresh sneakers and bandanas knotted on top of their heads. Everyone's screaming and shouting and filling the air with their energy, their electricity. I bounce on my toes with anticipation and scan the faces for Ava and Imogen, anxious for their hugs, their love, their reassurance. It dawns on me for the first time in ten years that I'm nervous to see them. But they're not on the first bus.

The second one pulls in and I move toward it, waving to people as they call my name, screaming their hellos. I'm a given. Part of the scenery. Goldie Easton. Another fixture of Camp Alpine Lake. As present as the rock climbing wall or the chocolate fountain at Sunday brunch.

Finally, I spot them and my stomach lurches. There's Ava, the tall, striking white girl with chestnut roots and long platinum hair, piled high into a messy bun. Her limbs are like ropes that extend to forever. Imogen stands next to her, shielding her eyes from the sun. She's half Japanese, half white, with dark hair twisted into two French braids, dyed neon pink at the ends. Shorter than Ava, but with poise that makes her seem grand. They're searching the crowd and my heart skips knowing they're looking for me, too.

Imogen sees me first and her mouth forms a wide smile. "Goldie!" she shrieks. Ava turns and they both rush toward me. Within seconds, they tackle me to the ground and we tumble to the soft dirt.

Ava squeals and plants wet, sloppy kisses on my forehead and my cheeks while Imogen squeezes me to her chest. I hold them tight, feeling their bodies mold around mine, remembering how much we've grown since we first met. My stomach settles. Nothing has changed.

They release me in a fit of giggles and Ava cups my chin with both her hands. "I've never been happier to see you, my golden girl," she says. Her blue eyes are bright and her cheekbones are high. Her mom wanted her to model, but Ava always said she'd rather die than spend her free time hanging out with a bunch of handsy old guys looking at her every fold. When we finally disentangle ourselves, I notice a crowd is standing around us, watching.

"Never could break these three up!" a woman says in a British accent. I look up to find Meg, who taught archery last summer, rolling her eyes. She has pale, ruddy skin and a tiny gap between her front teeth, which you can only see when she's laughing for real, like she's doing right now. Meg's a few years older than us and was our counselor in our final year as campers. She quickly became my favorite since she shared the Welsh cakes her grandmother sent over from the UK and never told on us when we snuck out for a midnight raid to the boys' cabins.

Last summer, she was on-again, off-again with Ray Levin, the guy who runs the waterfront, and at the end of camp, she moved to New York to be with him and work at a startup. But last I heard, they broke up and she had to head back home to a shitty bartending job where London financiers grabbed her ass without permission.

"Easton, I'm in Bloodroot with you!" Meg says, throwing her bag over her shoulder. "Got promoted to group leader this year, so that makes me your boss." She sticks out her tongue and wiggles it in my direction.

Imogen grabs my hand. "Wait, you're in Bloodroot? Jealous!"

"Got any intel about us?" Ava asks.

"Ramblers," I say, almost breathless. "We're all next to each other."

"I knew they'd make it work." Ava pushes herself to stand. She reaches out her hands and we both take them, pulling ourselves up. "I mean, they had to, after I put in a phone call last month."

"You did not." Imogen laughs. I follow them to the bag drop and pick up Ava's sleek black trunk and Imogen's bright yellow leather backpack. Together we walk toward the cabins as the rest of the counselors stream by, frenetic energy pumping through the air.

"Ava, what did you do?" I ask, almost not wanting to know.

She shrugs. "I mean, there's only so much they can deny a girl whose parents were enmeshed in a truly tragic, high-stakes divorce that dominated the New York gossip blogs for almost a decade, right?" Ava turns her head to the sun. She looks amused, with a smirk and a casual hair toss, but her voice is hollow, and Imogen gives me a look that says *don't say anything*. So I don't. "It's not my fault that they desperately wanted Mark Cantor to send his precious *new* babies to Camp Alpine Lake this summer. He was always going to, obviously. But it doesn't hurt to remind them that there are other options."

"You did *not*," I say, blushing at her nerve.

"It's not like he was ever going to ship those little monsters off to some random camp in Maine where they don't even have electricity. They'd be laughed out of that stuck-up Palm Beach country club." She lowers her voice and leans in toward us. "Get this, Mom told me the twins almost didn't pass the entrance exam."

Imogen's eyes go wide in shock.

"I know," Ava says. "But I guess that didn't matter. Privilege's a bitch."

My skin prickles and I try to readjust the weight in my arms. Ava's always been blunt. She calls it *New York realness*. But her flippancy irks me. Doesn't she know that not everyone at Alpine Lake gets special treatment like that? That not all of us can pull the rich donor daddy card to get what we want?

Ava dips her designer sunglasses so they're low on the bridge of her nose. "At least my shithole pops came in handy." She bumps her butt in both of our directions and Imogen offers a sympathetic look.

"Worked in our favor this time," Imogen says, and Ava gives her a grateful smile, one that's intimate and knowing. It throws me off for a sec.

Ava and Imogen have always seemed to speak their own language, one forged out of living an hour away from one another—Ava in Manhattan and Imogen in New Jersey. When we were little, they would call me from one of their houses, saying they were having an impromptu sleepover and they wished I could have come, too, even though Roxwood is a six-hour drive from the tristate area. As we got older, it became obvious they'd merged their friend groups. Ava would share photos from suburban house parties, posing with the cast of whatever play Imogen was starring in, and Imogen would text me updates from Central Park picnics with Ava's prep school classmates. I started visiting as often as I could, a few times a year. But that didn't compare to the way they blended their summer worlds with their real ones. I was left up here, wondering what my life would be like if I was one of them.

If I had grown up in Manhattan, would I still have disappeared into the background of class photos, my head peeking out above pretty girls with shiny hair? Or would I be placed in the front, smiling next to Ava? If I had gone to school with Imogen, who lived in the best public district in the northeast, would I still have felt unmotivated? Or would I have been inspired to excel, earn honors, and gobble up extracurriculars like all of those ambitious, fresh-faced kids who think Big Ten universities are safety schools?

I'd never know, of course, because I had grown up in Roxwood, where the library hasn't been renovated since the sixties and the cafeteria smells like mildew because there's never a budget to fix the leaks. Where getting average grades means you're heading to community college, and the teachers spend more time figuring out how to get the district to pay for their printing costs than finding ways to inspire us. In Roxwood, you're either Heller McConnell, golden boy, or everyone else, lost cause. There is no in-between.

"God, it feels good to be here," Ava says, stretching her arms up above her head. "Like I can finally breathe."

"Seriously." Imogen pulls at one of her braids. "Mom and Dad have been up my *ass* about moving to LA. All I said was one year. That's all I need to see if I can make this whole *actress thing* work. And if it fails, I said I'd go to college. I already got into USC and deferred for a year. It was all they talked about while I was packing this week." She rolls her eyes and pouts. "Wait, Goldie, did you decide where you're going yet?"

I ignore the question, hoping they don't notice. "I didn't know you deferred," I say.

"I decided last week," she says like it's no big deal. "But you knew I was thinking about it forever."

Ava wiggles her fingers like jazz hands. "Our Imo! Trying to be a star. A queen! A viral sensation!"

"You're already a success, Im," I say, grateful they don't push the question of what I'll be up to come September.

Imogen nuzzles into my side. "God, I've missed you, Goldie. Your unbridled optimism."

Is that how they view me? Optimistic? For a second, I wonder if they know me at all—or if I've changed so much that I barely remember myself.

"Here we are." Ava drops her bag on the lawn in front of our three cabins. Other counselors are bustling in and out, and the screen doors slam with excitement. "Ah, maintenance week." She spins around. "No campers, no responsibilities, a full week of ridiculous fun."

"Ooh, I can't wait for the bonfires," Imogen says.

"And the nights off at Truly's," Ava says.

"Skinny-dipping in the lake!" Imogen shrieks.

Ava giggles and holds us tight to her. "It's gonna be a perfect summer."

Imogen nods. "Never needed it more."

Same, I want to say. But instead, I smile and grip their hands as tight as I can.

− − −

Ava pushes open the double doors to the cafeteria, which is buzzing with laughter and singing and clanking metal forks. She loops her arms in mine and Imogen's and saunters toward the tables, already filling up with counselors ready to kick off the first night of debauchery. During this one week before the kids arrive, anything goes.

But then Ava stops and squeals. "Willa!" she yells, throwing her arms around my mom as Imogen goes in for a bear hug from my dad. They swap and I stand off to the side, fitting my mouth into a smile.

"It is *so* good to see you girls," Mom says, clasping her hands together in front of her chest. She means it, too. Mom's been running the woodworking program here since before I was born and always likes to say that she never saw girls as close as us.

Dad runs a hand through his thick dark hair and smiles wide, showing all his teeth, even the crooked one on the bottom row. Imogen blushes and I remember the one time she told me he was a DILF, forcing me to fake vomit into the lake. Even though he *is* known as Hot Head Nurse, that doesn't mean I have to like it.

"Ready to have another incredible summer?" he asks.

"Eight perfect weeks before heading into the real world," Ava says.

Mom glances in my direction, a flash of realization crossing her face. She knows I haven't told them that college is still so far away for me. That I have one more semester in hell.

"Amen, Ava," Mom says, the smile reappearing on her face.

"Ooh, look. There's Tommy and Dale—let's grab seats with

them." Imogen points to one of the long tables in the middle of the room.

"We'll catch up with you girls later," Dad says. He squeezes my shoulder and I avoid his worried eyes as they head back over to the camp elders' table and dole out hugs to Ray Levin, the waterfront guy.

Ava cocks her head in Imogen's direction. "Just because Tommy Eisenstat went down on you at his after-prom doesn't mean you're going to ditch us for him all summer, right?"

"He *what*?" I didn't even know Imogen went to Tommy's prom. "How could you not tell me?"

"Well, I kinda tried," Imogen says, a little sheepish. "But you never called me back last month."

I rack my brain for a bunch of missed calls from Imogen. I think they came in right around what should have been my graduation. So that checks out.

"Sorry," I mumble. "You know how bad the service is up here."

Imogen loops her arm in mine, dispersing any tension. "So, he mooned us every single swim session when we were Scouts, but . . . I mean . . . he's hot these days, right?"

I look hard at Tommy as he offers us a cocky nod, his red hair lying flat over his oily forehead. A smattering of shiny pimples blankets his nose. He tosses a tater tot at Dale Franklin, sitting across the table.

"Sure," I say, laughing.

Imogen covers her face with her hand. "Oh no. Please don't judge me. He lives one town over. We have all the same friends back home."

Ava throws her head back and laughs. "Come on," she says,

pulling us toward Tommy. We climb over the benches and slide into our seats. Tommy nods at Imogen and she reddens before reaching for the bread basket in the center of the table.

"Hey, Goldie," Tommy says, flashing me a smile. I guess if I met him now, I might not remember that when we were ten years old, he always smelled of tuna fish. Or that he tried to pants Ava when we were twelve and she didn't speak to him for the whole summer. I guess if I met him now, I'd think he was kind of cute. *Kind of* being the key phrase.

I scan the rest of the table quickly to find it full of a bunch of other guys our year. Boys who had the honor of being witness to our first kisses, our first slow dances, our first games of spin the bottle. I know these boys in a way you only can from sharing something so special, so intimate, and in a way that makes you not really know them at all. I know who's a strong enough swimmer to pass their deep-water test, and who's better at tennis versus basketball. I know who can play acoustic guitar and who wore braces for six years or more. I know who cries every year at the end of camp.

But I don't *know* them, really. I don't know if they faked ADHD to get extra time on tests, or if they're assholes to their parents. I don't know if they call the smart girls *bossy* at school, or how they text.

I don't know them like the boys in Roxwood, the boys who drive trucks and shoot guns and think hockey is life. The boys who comforted Heller McConnell after the accident and told him things like "It's not your fault you were in the car. You did nothing wrong." The boys who taunted me and tortured me for the rest of the year. The boys whose disgust I can hear pulsing in my ears when I try to fall asleep.

Here, where the outside world doesn't exist, I can be whoever I want to. The boys at Alpine Lake know that.

I cram a forkful of pasta salad into my mouth as Stu and Mellie play their sleigh bells over the microphone. The entire room erupts in the announcement song without hesitation.

"Announcement, announcement, annooouuunce-ment! Stu and Mellie have an annouuuuncement!"

Stu chuckles into the microphone. "That never gets old," he says, shaking his head. Mellie beams next to him.

"We all wanted to wish you a hearty welcome—" He pauses.

"Or welcome back!" the room sings in unison.

"To Alpine Lake for another amazing summer."

The counselors cheer.

"By now you should all have settled into your cabins and met your group leader," Stu says. "The next few days will be a rollicking mess of getting this place ready for campers. You'll be broken into groups to focus on cleaning, decorating, and fieldwork. Lifeguards, the lake is now yours."

Ava, Imogen, and I nudge each other with our shoulders. Pride blooms in my chest. Everyone knows the lifeguarding gig is the most coveted job. I bet Tommy and Dale are stuck on baseball or soccer.

Mellie clears her throat and launches into a speech explaining some of the new changes around the grounds. Thanks to a few million-dollar donations from parents and alumni, they've renovated the Lodge where the summer musical takes place, added a new dance studio up by the arts and crafts shed, and hacked a new hiking path up by Creepy Cliff. They also purchased a fresh fleet of golf carts, a water trampoline, and will now have smoked salmon at Sunday brunch to go along with the bagels shipped up from New York.

"Guess they made that Cantor money go far," Ava mumbles under her breath.

"But now it's time for the not-so-fun part. The rules," Mellie continues. Everyone groans, another customary response, but she smiles even wider. "Remember, this is your *one* week without campers, so enjoy it!" The room cheers. We all know that maintenance week is *the* week to throw down. There will be dance party bonfires, water bottles filled with alcohol, and the beginnings of summer flings. We'll get one night off camp, where everyone will be deposited into the heart of Roxwood. At that thought, my stomach sinks.

Mellie starts mentioning all the major no-nos—drinking and smoking and hooking up when you're on duty—even though they often look the other way for those ones, especially if you're a lifer. She reminds us of the one rule that will actually get you fired—sneaking into their winter cabin without permission.

"When you leave camp to go into town, please know you are representing Alpine Lake," Mellie continues with her high-pitched voice. "That means no getting in trouble with the law, no drinking in public places, and no bringing non–Alpine Lakers back to camp. If you do . . ." She trails off and drags her finger across her throat in a slicing motion.

"Classic Dawn having to ruin it for everyone," Imogen mutters under her breath. "Did she really have to bring that loser back last year to screw near the stables?"

Ava covers her mouth to suppress a giggle, but my cheeks flush. Sure, Dawn Waterson was fired last year, but the guy she brought back was a few years older than me at Roxwood High. Stu and Mellie made his life hell after they found him here. They called the cops and forced them to give him a trespassing citation that came with a $3,000 fine and a court summons. He had been studying to get into nursing school but had to take on double shifts at the diner to pay it all off, just because Stu and Mellie didn't like that he was on their property.

But everyone here laughed it off, joking that Dawn would spend the rest of the summer tanning by her parents' pool before heading off to join a sorority at Indiana University in the fall. I bet she never thought of Roxwood again.

"Enough of the boring stuff," Mellie says, waving her hand in front of her face. "We're in for the best summer ever!"

The counselors bang their firsts and holler into the rafters. At our table, we pound so hard, our silverware and plates fly up into the air, clamoring back down with satisfying *thwack*s.

"Best summer ever!" the room chants. "Best summer ever!"

I have to believe it.

CHAPTER 4

Then

"Come with me," Heller said. His mummy costume was drooping off his shoulders and there was a smear of fake blood drawn across his cheek.

I handed him a makeup remover wipe. "Where?"

"Dylan Adler's," he said. "Annual Halloween party. You can't miss it."

I turned back to my cubby and hunted for my bag. "I missed it the past three years and seems like I survived."

"That was before you knew me," Heller said, holding out his hand.

I don't know if it was because we had downed a few nips of vodka in between guests or if it was because he was looking at me with those deep brown eyes, the ones that stayed focused on my smile, my mouth. But for whatever reason, I said yes.

"You made it, asswipe!" Dylan Adler slapped Heller on the back as he led me by the hand over to the bar, past a keg, a dart board, and a few beaten-up couches. Dylan wore his hockey uniform and a mullet wig that distracted from his pockmarked skin. I'd always been scared of him, thanks to his towering frame and his usual surly expression. But that night he clocked my hand wrapped in Heller's and nodded, friendly. "'Sup, Goldie."

I nodded, too, even though it was the first interaction we'd had since he cheated off my second-grade math test. "'Sup."

"You still working with those Alpine Lake snobs?" he asked.

Heller must have sensed my nerves because he held my palm tighter, rubbing his thumb against the back of my hand.

"Heading back this summer," I said.

"I guess it's good we have one of our own there," Dylan said. "Keep all the staff in line when they come into town. Piece of shit richies."

"Those assholes never tip." I swiveled my head to find Cal Drummond looking at me with curious eyes, peeking out from under a neon beanie. "That's what my dad says, at least. When the counselors come into the diner on days off."

His jawline had gotten more defined over the years, and his dark facial hair had grown in, coating the lower half of his face in a neat beard. He looked so much older, so different than he had when we were best friends in elementary school. Before his mom died of an overdose.

I knew I should defend the counselors—the lifers—but it was easier to nod and smile and agree by omission that yeah, the Alpine Lake staffers were leeches.

Heller leaned over and whispered in my ear. "Wanna dance?"

He didn't wait for an answer. Instead, he led me to the living room, which was dark and sweaty, pulsing with the heat, the need of my peers. He wrapped his arms around my waist and held me at a respectable distance.

But I was feeling bold, hungry.

As the music picked up and the lights stayed low, I pressed my body to his, ran my forefinger down the back of his neck. I sensed him smile, smelled his skin.

Heller closed the gap between us and I felt his mouth on mine, firm and still, and with such purpose, my legs shook.

Heller paused for a second as if to catch his breath. "Finally."

CHAPTER 5

Now

Ava's naked from the waist up, standing in front of the full-length mirror in the empty main room of Bloodroot. "Imo's sequined halter top or my linen sundress?" she asks, holding the two items in front of her.

"Sequined halter top," says Imogen. "Definitely."

I nod my agreement and sip on a too-strong rum and Coke, which Imogen mixed and poured into water bottles. It's day three of maintenance week and my muscles are sore from hours of threading buoys and cleaning the motors on the boats. Ava got stuck on kayak duty, while Imogen had to scrub the lifeguarding shack. But no one dares speak of exhaustion because day three also means it's our first night out.

Meg peeks her head out from the counselor room. "You lot never change, do you?" She laughs and shakes her head. "When you were fourteen, you'd do this whole *fashion show* thing for hours before the DJ socials."

I let out a laugh. As a camper, I adored Meg, not just because of the secret sweets, but because one night when Ava and I got into one of our big blow-out fights, Meg traded beds with me so I could sleep in the counselor room and cry into a pillow in private. She never asked me about it. Let me be.

"That's half the fun of coming here," Ava says. "Your wardrobe triples."

I look down at my threadbare tank top, which I plucked from Imogen's dresser an hour ago. "You have to wear it for our first night out," she said. "I got it at a sample sale in SoHo." That distinction meant nothing to me, but when I saw how excited she was to see me wear it, I knew I couldn't take it off.

"Sequined halter it is," Ava says, wriggling into the shirt. It fits snug around her chest and shows just a sliver of torso above her high-waisted denim skirt.

The loudspeaker crackles overhead and the first notes of Prince's "Little Red Corvette" begin to blare through the air.

"Ah," Imogen says. "Our signal."

"Chug on three?" Ava asks.

We all nod and I can hear Meg laughing at us in the counselor room.

"One," I say.

"Two," Ava calls.

"Three!" Imogen finishes. Together we throw our drinks back and set the water bottles down on the floor, erupting into a fit of laughter. When I can finally breathe again, I look at Ava and Imogen, the three of us huddled together in this empty cabin, our favorite cabin, wearing mascara and going-out tops, thick platform sandals strapped to our feet. This is what I always dreamed of. The three of us together, getting ready for a night off as counselors. I wish my insides weren't cramping from dread, that I could get excited about spending a few hours in Roxwood. But I can't. Not when I know most of the town hates me.

"Come on," Ava says. "Let's go."

We scramble to our feet and hold hands as we rush to the buses, waiting to deposit all the Alpine Lake counselors into Roxwood. Ava finds us a seat in the back near Dale and Tommy, who make whooping noises as we strut down the aisle.

Imogen sticks her tongue out at Tommy and grabs his baseball hat as she passes. She wears it backward as we cram into one seat. "Fight me for it, asshole."

"I'm gonna hit that later," Tommy says to whoever's listening.

"You wish!" Imogen calls.

Ava pushes her knees up against the seat in front of her and laughs in her deep, hearty voice. Then she looks up, her eyes alert. "Truly's?" she asks.

My stomach drops, but Imogen claps her hands in front of her face and bounces in the seat. "Yes yes yes yes yes!"

Tuesday nights off are for Truly's, the dive bar in town. And Thursdays are for West Lake, the questionable sushi place that serves sake bombs and doesn't card. The routine is tradition, which means it's sacred. But all I want to do is run.

Ava must see the reluctance on my face. "Oh, come on, Goldie. Don't pull that *Roxwood sucks* crap on us tonight."

"I know," I say. I roll the words around in my mouth, wondering how many ways I can say *I'm scared*. "I don't want to see all the losers from my high school tonight." I'm buzzed now, and I try to find an explanation. "What if camp were in New York and I was like, let's go to the one bar where all the dicks from your health class hang out? And you thought you never had to see them ever again, but, hey, you do! And it's on a night that's supposed to be fun, but then turns to shit. Huh?" Ava and Imogen stare at me with their mouths open. After a second, they break out into laughter.

"Oh my god, Goldie, you kill me," Ava says, wiping her hands across her face as the bus rolls out of camp. She waves a hand in the air. "As if we have *health* class at Excelsior Prep."

I elbow her side, which makes her laugh harder.

"This is totally different, though," Imogen says, draping her legs over my lap. She pulls our heads in toward one another. "This is camp."

I'm not going to win this one. Because in their minds Roxwood is an amusement park, a facsimile of a real town. Even after all this time, they don't get that this place is my whole world—and that I'd rather be anywhere else. Best to grit my teeth and sidle up to the Brits to get them to buy me drinks. To hide behind them and blend into the background, out of sight of whoever else is at the bar.

But as we careen toward Main Street, a bubble of hope forms in my chest. Maybe it'll be a good thing to show the people from Roxwood High that I fit in at a place like Alpine Lake, where, let's be real, they'd all *kill* to go if they could. I tilt my chin up and remind myself I'm not who they think I am. Not that anyone would believe that after New Year's Eve.

The bus deposits ninety-four Alpine Lake counselors in front of Town Hall at the end of Smith Street at 8:05 p.m. Everyone knows we have until midnight to get as loaded as possible. That's when the buses head back to camp. If you miss curfew, you either walk back or hitch a ride with Bart's Taxi Service, which every girl in town knows is a major no-no. As I step down from the bus, I'm reminded how much we stick out here in Roxwood.

The glitzy tops and platform heels that seemed totally appropriate for a night out back in Bloodroot are obvious and impractical here in the casual lakeside town. The people I grew up with only own T-shirts and flip-flops, fleeces and cargo pants. The international counselors' accents ring out loud as they take swigs from flasks. The older ones, Meg and her crew, head off to the marina, where they can rent a fishing boat for a few hours. The straight-edge counselors make their way to Grandee's for famous maple creemees. But everyone else, even those of us who are underage, walk the few blocks to Truly's.

There's a big wooden sign out front that displays the name in red script, set against silver and gold stars. The tables are sticky, the floor is coated in sawdust, and the walls are covered in New England memorabilia that makes it feel kitschy, like it's meant for tourists. Newspaper clippings proclaiming Roxwood's minimal greatness sit in chipped frames behind the bar. Every year, the Alpine Lake counselors compete to see who can leave the most ridiculous trinket in the place, tacked to the wall or hanging from the ceiling. Winner gets to drink for free on our final night off. That accolade went to Imogen last year when she pinned her rejection letter from Juilliard's summer program to the wall.

There are no bouncers here. No ID checks. Just a bunch of old dudes with silver beards and missing teeth pouring two-dollar beers and three-dollar well shots in plastic cups behind the bar. As long as you don't puke, they'll let you stay.

"I've been dreaming of this place for ten months," Imogen says, wobbling in her heels.

"No one in Manhattan knows how to make a proper vodka gimlet," Ava says.

"You're joking, right?" I say.

Ava looks at me with those wide blue eyes and plants her palms on my cheeks. "My golden girl, you cannot see the magic of this place like we can."

Imogen nods solemnly next to her, and I fight the urge to say something mean and bitter about what a shithole this place is in the winter, when everything freezes over and everyone takes their frustration out on the easiest punching bag. Or how that punching bag was me.

Ava drops my face and wraps me in a hug. "First round's on me!"

She leads us inside and I'm hit with a waft of cigarette smoke and stale beer. One of the bartenders mumbles something under his breath. No one else seems to hear, but I make out the words. "The interlopers are back."

I press my lips together in a tight line and watch Ava make her way to the bar. Imogen and I post up with Tommy, Dale, and two new counselors who sound like they're from Scotland, while the rest of the Alpine Lake crowd spreads out among the booths.

Suddenly, I'm desperate for a drink. For something to give me the excited feeling I had an hour ago and to make me forget where I am. I take a peek around the room and spot a few women who were seniors when I was a freshman, holding court in the back corner playing some sort of card game. Off near the bathrooms are a bunch of guys who work down on the dock. And over by the bar are a handful of teachers' aides from the library.

"Think if I give those townies a hundred bucks, they'll let me on the pool table?" Tommy asks, his words already slurred.

My face reddens and I can't tell if it's from the word *townies* or what he's implying—that he can buy his way around Roxwood. Which, to be fair, he probably could.

Imogen swats him on the shoulder and throws me a worried look. I shrug and watch the bar, willing Ava to come back.

"All I'm saying is those guys look like they could use a few extra," Tommy says. He nods over to the billiards area, and I follow his gaze to Cal Drummond laughing and holding a glass beer bottle by the neck. My whole body tenses.

He doesn't seem to notice me. Not yet.

Cal's with the usual crew. Guys from the hockey team who barely graduated, though I can't really talk shit about that. My heart quickens as I search the table looking for Heller, but he's not there. Dylan Adler's absent, too. Obviously. But his older brother, Jordan, hangs at the back of the group, rubbing chalk on a pool cue with a concentrated look on his face.

They're all huddled close, throwing their heads back in laughter as they lean against the felt-covered table to shoot another round. Cal runs a hand through his cropped hair and crosses his arms over his chest, revealing a cheesy barbed wire tattoo snaking around his bicep.

"Three vodka gimlets," Ava says, setting the plastic cups down on the sticky high-top. She holds hers up to cheers, and I remember where I am and who I'm with. It's going to be okay. Nothing bad will happen tonight. Not with Ava and Imogen by my side.

I take a long sip from my drink and perch on a stool, trying to hide behind Ava's height as Imogen starts talking about if she should live on the east or west side of Los Angeles in the fall. Ava scans the room and I watch her, wondering where she'll land. Who she'll set her sights on this year.

Last summer it was Scott Schroeder, a first-time general counselor from New Zealand who had a cute dimple on his left cheek and a habit of leaving hickeys on Ava's neck. The year before it was Joy Arlington, the soccer coach from Vancouver who spent the next six months begging Ava to visit her in Canada. They both fell in love with her, and were heartbroken when she dumped them, unscathed and detached.

Ever since her parents' divorce, Ava has detested relationships, said they could only drive us apart from one another. We were her true loves. Everyone else was a distraction, a story to tell at parties, a way to pass the lazy hours of the day. I wonder which Alpine Lake employee she'll go for this year.

But then her eyes land on Cal.

"Who's that?" she asks, nodding her head in his direction.

"Ava," I warn. "No."

"Aw, come on. What if I want to mix it up with some Roxwood ass this year?"

I bite my lip and try to figure out how much to share. "That's Cal Drummond."

"You know him?" Ava asks.

"There are 7,569 people in Roxwood. Yeah, I know him."

"Feisty, G," she says, tapping me on the nose with her straw. "What's he like?"

I sip my drink slowly. I guess I could tell her about when we were little, how he would come over and play dress-up with me, fighting fairies and killing dragons on my parents' lawn. Or I could tell her that when his mother died, he slept in a sleeping bag on my bedroom floor for a week since his father didn't want him to see him so distraught. Or maybe she'll want to know that when we got to high school, he called me a *dumb bitch* because I didn't want to do whippits in the alley behind the community pool.

Of course, I could tell her how he encouraged the hockey team to torment me after the accident, that he laughed along with everyone else when his friends spat on my locker. Or that she actually met him once before, dismissed him as trash.

If I was a different version of me—if I was brave—I could tell Ava the *real* truth, that he was the only person to see me get into the car with Heller McConnell that night—and that Heller was the one in the driver's seat. I could explain how Cal never pulled me aside and asked why *I* took the blame when he knew Heller was the one at the wheel.

Instead, I turn to Ava and say, "He's nobody."

Ava rolls her eyes. "No help." Then her focus moves above my shoulder and I turn around to see what she's looking at.

Fuck.

"Okay, now *that's* more appealing. Dish." Ava eyes track Heller as he leaves the bathroom, walking straight to Cal.

Even now, Heller has the power to make my stomach spasm, a lump form in my throat. He's wearing a nearly see-through Roxwood varsity hockey T-shirt and navy shorts that hang low on his hips. His jaw is a hard square, all edges and straight lines. He bows his head, laughing with confidence as his curls flop messily to one side. If I look closely, I think I can see his silver necklace dangling against his chest, a lightning bolt charm tucked between his skin and the thin cotton fabric. He never takes it off.

I squeeze my eyes shut and remember his touch, how soft his

finger pads were as they grazed the tender area of my stomach and how his palm was warm and assuring, rubbing my back as I drifted off to sleep in the back seat of his truck. If I block out the whole bar, I can still hear him whisper in my ear, *"Finally."*

"Heller McConnell," I say, my voice raw like a scab. "He's another loser."

"Maybe I can fuck with *loser* this summer." Ava downs the rest of her drink and steps toward them.

"Wait," I say, grabbing on to her elbow. Panic rises in my throat. "You can't even bring him back to camp. It's not worth it." *It would also break my heart.*

"Aw, come on," Ava says, yanking her arm away. "Let me have my fun."

I look to Imogen for backup, but she rolls her eyes and turns to Tommy. We both know how hard it is to talk Ava out of something she wants.

"Come with," Ava says, and tosses her hair over her shoulder.

I try to protest, but Ava grabs my wrist and yanks me with her over to the pool table. I clench my fists as Ava juts her hip out.

"Who's willing to let me whoop their ass?" she says. The boys turn to us and I try not to crawl out of my skin as they look to Ava.

"You tryna play?" Cal asks her, a playful smile forming on his lips.

Ava smirks. "You gonna let me?"

I glance at Heller to find him looking down, his eyes hidden behind his curls. I wonder if he realizes *this* is Ava Cantor, that Imogen Wexler's around here, too. I take a step back, hoping to retreat, but I should have known better than to make any sudden moves.

"Not if you're with this one," Cal says, nodding in my direction.

Ava throws her arm around my shoulder, holding me close so I can't escape. "Aw, you guys are jealous of our Alpine Lake night off, I see." She smiles, but the boys don't.

"That explains it," Dylan's brother, Jordan, says, looking Ava up and down with eyes I want to gauge out.

"What?" Ava asks, her focus on Heller.

"Why you'd hang out with Goldie." Jordan shakes his head and crosses his arms over his chest.

Cal laughs and someone else slaps Jordan's back in encouragement. Heller takes a sip of beer and lifts his gaze, but it doesn't land on me. Instead, he's drinking Ava in with the same look he used to give me.

My cheeks burn and I crack my knuckles. "Let's go back to Imogen," I say, tugging on her hand. Heller lifts his head fast, almost with concern. Or maybe intrigue. I confirmed his suspicion, that the stunning, sophisticated girl standing next to me is indeed Ava. He always asked questions about her. Imogen, too. Was bitter that I hadn't told my camp friends about him. There were reasons. They seem so silly now.

Ava's planted firmly in place. She hugs me to her even tighter and I know she's going to defend me, which will make everything worse.

"Oh my god, there is no way you actually think you're hot shit. You know that, right?" Ava's heated now. "When was the last time you even left Vermont?"

Jordan looks at Ava like he wants to break her in half.

"We don't fuck with Goldie," Cal says. "Plain and simple."

Ava looks confused, but I'm not. I know this game. I've been playing it for months.

"Why don't you two go back over there?" Heller says, his voice soft but stern. It sends a shiver down my spine, so familiar it hurts. But still, he doesn't look at me. His eyes stay locked on Ava. The other guys shut up. They know Heller's in charge. Always has been.

"Well, fuck you, too," Ava says, her mouth curled in a smile. "Come on, Goldie." She spins on her heel, and I follow her back to Imogen and the rest of the Alpine Lake crew, my heart beating so fast I think my chest will explode.

Ava sets her drink down on our table hard. "Goldie has some enemies, you guys!" she calls out, like it's the most hilarious thing in the world. "What did you do, break their hearts or something?"

My limbs are like jelly and all I want to do is go home, back to Bloodroot, and crawl into bed for days. But I force myself to perch on a stool and grip the edge of the table so hard my knuckles turn white. "Something like that." I laugh. A deep hearty chuckle that sounds real. I hope.

Ava throws her arms around me again and kisses the top of my head. "Fuck 'em!" she shouts, holding her glass up into the air.

The rest of the table chimes in. "Fuck 'em!"

I know this should make me feel comforted, like I belong. But I can feel the Roxwood boys staring, judging, furious that I'm out here at a bar, enjoying myself. I hunch over the table and try to disappear.

The conversation changes and I check the clock to see how much longer we have to stay here. But then Heller, Cal, and the others start pushing their barstools back against the sticky wooden floor. They pile their pool cues on the table.

"Let's get out of here," Cal says loudly. "Smells like the shit on the bottom of Alpine Lake anyway."

They laugh and I force myself to keep my eyes trained down, to focus on the conversation going on at my table, to not catch Heller's eye as he walks out the door.

Ava huddles close to me and I know it's for protection. She leans down, resting her elbows on the table. "What was that about?" she asks, her tone quiet and understanding.

It's a different Ava, tender and caring. The version of Ava I met when we were eight, before her parents divorced and before she grew nearly a foot. She would spend hours brushing my hair and twisting it into various updos, held in place with rhinestone barrettes, to make me feel pretty—or play the card game Bullshit, spitting out the word in a British accent because she knew it made me laugh.

She was loyal and sensitive, even after the divorce, when we both had grown breasts and leg hair and had body odor. That's when she would go through her yearbook, metallic and hardcover, and draw devil horns on the people who called her dad a *cheater*, who snapped her bra straps during field hockey practice. *Dead to me*, she wrote next to Gina Flute, who told the whole class Mark Cantor skipped town with a mistress because Ava wasn't smart enough.

That was when my life was still fascinating to her, so different than hers in New York. She wanted to do the same with my yearbooks, for me to show her who I was friends with, who I hated, who I wanted to kiss. But I always made up excuses. The Roxwood yearbooks were more like pamphlets, designed with Microsoft Word clip art, copied at the printer's in town. The kids looked undercooked compared to Ava's friends. We didn't wear designer outfits on picture day. We didn't get blowouts or professional faces of makeup.

Plus, I didn't want to admit to her that I had no one to circle, no one to call out. After Cal, there were no best friends, no enemies, no crushes. Not until senior year, not until Heller. For most of my life, I was a shadow in Roxwood. Someone who was there, but barely, counting down the days until I could visit Ava and Imogen, or head back to Alpine Lake.

At camp I could be free. I could be special. Talented. Alive. I was desired and loved and welcomed. Why would I want Ava and Imogen to know that in my real life—in the world outside the Alpine Lake bubble—I was not?

Ava asks again, her eyes concerned. "What happened, Goldie?"

I shake my head. "Nothing."

CHAPTER 6

Then

I didn't mean to keep Heller a secret from Ava and Imogen. That wasn't my intention, not really. The day after we kissed, I planned to tell them during our weekly video chat. But before our scheduled call, Ava's name flashed across my screen.

"You're early," I said, propping the phone up against my laptop so I could paint my toes sky blue while we spoke.

But when her face came into focus, my stomach dropped. Her usually perfect skin was splotchy and her hair was frizzy in the front, matted on the sides. "Ava . . ." I started.

That's when she lost it, her sobs loud and heaving as her shoulders shook.

"Whatever it is, it's going to be okay," I said, quiet. I wanted to reach through the screen and rub her back like I had so many times before.

Ava held her face in her hands and after a few seconds, her breathing steadied and she finally started to speak.

"He's sending them to Alpine Lake," she said. "My dad."

"The twins?"

Ava nodded. "Camp is *mine* and he's sending them there."

Part of me wanted to roll my eyes and tell her *who the fuck cares?* But Ava had barely met the girls. To her, they were symbols of her dad's infidelity—of all the ways people who are supposed to love you can betray you. His decision to send them to Alpine Lake may as well have been a knife through her heart.

"It's going to be okay. There's no way Mellie and Stu would make you their counselor."

Ava hiccupped as she tried to catch her breath. "But knowing they're there loving the things that I love . . . it's too much. It's going to ruin the summer."

"No way. Right after graduation? Not a care in the world?" I scoffed. "Come on, how can it *not* be incredible?"

Ava groaned. "How can you know that?"

I shrugged. "Roxwood Spidey senses."

Ava laughed then and fell back against a bunch of pillows on her bed. "I wish I had your outlook on life."

"Get out of that city life for a weekend. Come on up and smell the fresh air."

"We could sneak into camp in the middle of the night and swim in the lake."

I could picture it, how I'd introduce her to Heller and bring her to one of his hockey parties, how I could finally show her off. Ava would dazzle them all like she dazzled me, proving maybe there *is* something special about being one of the Alpine Lakers. That they're not all leeches, sucking Roxwood dry of its resources.

"How about Thanksgiving weekend?" I said, hope pooling in my voice. "Come up the Friday after?"

Ava winced. "Excelsior Prep has a big alumni gala thing that night. Another time, though, yeah?"

All traces of tears had disappeared from her pretty face, but my heart dropped. I had cheered her up, but still, even in her darkest moment, she didn't want to come to Roxwood. "Yeah," I said. "Another time."

"Promise me you won't ditch me for some loser this summer? I don't think I could stand it. Having to share you and Imo with a couple of douches? Not when the brats are running around camp."

I laughed and wondered if she could tell my voice was hollow, that I was holding something back. It would have been so easy to slip in a mention of Heller. To tell her about our kiss and ease her in to the fact that my heart was changing and growing and turning toward someone else's. But I pushed him out of my mind, worried that if I did tell her about Heller, she would assume I was betraying her, too.

Both our phones buzzed and Ava sat up. "Ah, there's Imo."

Imogen's face appeared on the screen, zombie makeup still smudged from whatever Halloween party she had been to the night before. But before she could say hello, Ava launched into a monologue.

"You'll never guess who my garbage can of a father is sending to Alpine Lake . . ."

Imogen listened intently and I continued swiping polish on my toes, tasting Heller's name on the tip of my tongue.

CHAPTER 7

Now

It's 7:45 a.m. and I wake up to the sound of reveille blaring over the loudspeakers. I groan, pulling my pillow over my face. My ears ring as the trumpets blare through camp.

"Morning, buggers," Meg says from her bunk beneath mine. I glance at her with one open eye to see she's already showered, dressed, and spraying herself down with sunscreen.

"How are you even awake right now?" Ava asks. She's curled up against my back, spooning me into cozy oblivion.

Meg laughs. "I'm on breakfast duty. Leaving Advil for you." She tosses the plastic bottle up onto my bunk. "You two look like you need it."

"You're a hero," I call after her as she darts out of the cabin.

Ava sits up and leans back against the wall, draping her legs over mine. The air is thick with humidity and our skin sticks together.

"I'm gonna miss cuddling with you when all these annoying campers get here," Ava says, reaching for a water bottle. She throws back two Advil and chugs. "Especially since those little goobers will be here in Bloodroot."

I grimace. "Maybe they'll be cool?" I ask, taking the water bottle from her and swallowing the pills. But we both know her twin half sisters will probably be the worst kinds of campers—needy and spoiled, furious they have to change their own sheets and sweep their own floors. Ava and Imo were never like that. But we had a few in our cabin. Cindy Hall, who told the counselors her parents weren't paying her tuition so she could wipe down shower stalls for Sunday inspection. Lora Jenkins, who only ate food her private chef shipped up from Manhattan. Ashley Nevins, who had her own horse brought in on Mondays to ride.

We ignored those girls, rolling our eyes at them from our bunk beds. But I could see shades of my friends in them, in the way they never broke eye contact with authority figures and walked with confidence. In moments of doubt, I wondered if Ava and Imogen *were* like them—that they were better at hiding those parts of themselves from me.

Ava shrugs and we're both silent for a second, listening to Stu read the morning announcements and the weather for the day. When he finishes, we chime in for the final line he says every morning. "It's going to be an amazing Alpine Lake day!"

Ava smiles thinly. "Not with this hangover."

I nudge her with my foot. "It'll go away by the time we head down to the waterfront."

"Always looking on the bright side." Ava pushes herself to the edge of my bed and peers over the edge. "Bombs away," she says, launching off my top bunk, so she lands on the floor below. I dangle my legs over the side and she grabs on to my ankles, moving them up and down like I'm a doll.

"Hey, you okay after last night?" Ava asks, resting her chin on my knees.

"Yep," I say, trying to ignore my own dragon breath and the

memory of those boys looking at me in disgust, of Ava realizing not everyone sees me the way she does.

Ava turns around and gathers her hair in a ponytail. Her skin is slick with a morning sheen, but she still looks so much more comfortable in her own body than I ever could be. "Musta done a number on you, huh?" she asks.

"What?"

"I've never seen you as freaked out as you were last night with those guys," she says, turning back to me with a furrowed brow. "What happened?"

I look at her pretty face, the one I've known for so long and have seen shift and grow and change. I could tell her the story that everyone in Roxwood thinks is true. But I know things would change, that she and Imogen would look at me differently. The way my parents do. Sometimes when they think I'm not paying attention, I can see it in their eyes, how they can't believe their daughter is a monster. That she hurt someone so badly.

Telling her the real truth isn't an option. Not after the deal we made, the NDA Heller's dad slid in front of me and asked me to sign with a shaking hand. So instead, I say nothing at all.

Ava sighs. "Look, I know I've got my own shit going on with my fucked-up family and everything. And I know we didn't really talk that much this year."

We're both quiet, the reality settling between us. She *was* MIA in the beginning of the year, so caught up with her world of black-tie functions and long weekends in Paris that she rarely returned my texts with more than a one-word answer. There was that one visit over homecoming, but even that was tense. And then after I ditched them on New Year's, we both stopped trying. I sent her and Imogen to voice mail. I responded to our group chats with single words instead of full thoughts. It became clear they were texting more and more without me. It was all for the best, I figured. If I couldn't tell them the truth, I couldn't tell them anything at all.

Ava looks at me square in the face. "I want you to know that no matter what, I'm here for you. We're a team, you, me, and Imo. Nothing will change that." Before I can respond, she steps up onto Meg's mattress and wraps her arms around my neck, planting a sticky kiss on my cheek.

"You're never getting rid of me, golden girl," she says. "I know you like I know myself." Then she opens her mouth wide and sticks out her tongue, breathing heavily in my face.

"Ugh, gross," I feign. I've always known that being in Ava's morning breath orbit is worth it. When she shines her spotlight on you, it's like standing in the sun.

"Meet you out front in five," she says. "I need six plates of hash browns to get me through today."

I climb down from the top bunk and make the bed from the ladder. When I pull the sheets back to tuck in tight hospital corners, I can still smell Ava and her blueberry-scented shampoo. She's used it for years, like it's her own natural perfume. Rich and vibrant. It's a scent that lingers, marking what's hers.

"French toast sticks!" Imogen squeals as we approach the dining hall. Today's menu is written on the chalkboard in a loopy scrawl, and my stomach growls when I see chicken patties are for lunch.

"It's like Christina *knew* we'd need hangover fuel after the first night out," Ava says, tossing her hair over her shoulder. "Come on."

Ava pushes through the screen doors, and the room is bright, sun streaming through the windows. There's a buzz in the air, an ease that has set in now that all the counselors are comfortable with one another, familiar within days. I inhale deeply and remind myself, *You are home.*

Imogen nods toward the breakfast queue and we line up behind one another. Ava rests her chin on Imo's shoulder.

"That bad, huh?" Imogen asks, reaching back to pet her like a puppy.

Ava groans and buries her face in Imogen's neck.

The line starts to move and I grab a warm plate from the dish rack as we enter the kitchen. There's a clicking of silverware, and steam rises from the hot water trays full of French toast sticks, shiny syrup, and bright yellow scrambled eggs. I try to imagine what these heaps of food would look like to an outsider, someone who didn't know that the head chef, Christina, has been here for thirty-one years, loves to drink whiskey, and plays the banjo on her nights off. Or that she always makes buttered noodles on the side for the picky kids who hate anything that isn't beige. Or that she lost her own son in a ski accident one winter and came back the following summer divorced and hollow.

When it's my turn, I look up to see Christina spooning eggs, her kind eyes and her graying hair pulled back under a hairnet. "Goldie, girl, what a delight!" She gives me double with a wink. "I was telling your folks how excited I was to see you. I missed you all spring." Christina also runs the cafeteria at Roxwood High. But I avoided that place after New Year's.

"Yeah, well, you know . . ." I say quietly, grateful that Ava and Imogen have already moved through the line and are now filling their mugs with coffee.

"If you ever need to talk, dear—" Christina starts to say. But I cut her off with a big smile.

"I gotta get going. Line's backing up."

Christina takes the hint. "You got it, doll." She winks again, one of her big green eyes disappearing for a second.

I shuffle away from Christina, grab my own mug of coffee, and make my way to the table right in the middle of the room, where Ava and Imogen have set up shop. I slide into my seat and house a French toast stick.

"So good, right?" Ava's eyes practically roll into the back of her head. "I need all the carbs I can get today."

But I barely register her comments because when I look up from my plate, I see Stu and Mellie talking closely with a tall, older white man with curly dark hair and khakis. His arms are crossed over his chest and he looks frustrated and uncomfortable. He scans the room and I hold my breath, waiting for him to see me. When he does, his eyes stop.

Judah McConnell.

Heller's father.

I force myself to look down, but now the eggs on my plate resemble a pile of vomit. Judah's wearing his McConnell Landscapers jacket with dirt stains on the elbows. I didn't notice him this morning, tending to the sports fields, but he must have been here, making sure the vast expanses of grass were manicured to perfection before

51

the kids arrive. Landing the Alpine Lake contract this year was the best thing that happened to the McConnells, Judah told me once.

His frown deepens and he turns back to Stu. They're talking quietly, but Stu's brow narrows and he lifts a hand, extending his pointer finger directly at Judah's chest. Judah takes a step toward Stu, his mouth forming a snarl.

"The check's late, Stu," he says, his voice carrying throughout the dining hall. "Really fucking late." But before he can keep going, Mellie stands and puts her hand on Stu's shoulder. In an instant, Stu's demeanor changes. He straightens his back and the muscles in his face relax. He says something under his breath, and Judah shakes his head and throws up his hands. Like he's mad he has to be here, like he'd rather be off fly-fishing with Heller and his buddies, cracking open cans of beer and planning their next backpacking trip.

"That the new landscaper dude?" Imogen asks loudly, waving a French toast stick in the air.

"Yep."

"Stu looks pissed," Imogen says. "Probably because he's been messing up the grass."

"What?" I ask. Maybe I misheard Judah.

Imogen shrugs. "The baseball field's super long and uneven. Tommy was bitching about it, saying the kids are gonna get ticks."

"He kinda looks like that guy from the bar," Ava says.

"That's his dad," I say.

"Strange." Imogen turns back to her plate, not waiting to see Judah storm off, the side screen door slamming behind him.

I whip my head around the room trying to find my parents. But they're not here yet. My chest tightens and I wonder for a split second if Judah's presence had something to do with me. But I know I'm being paranoid. They were probably arguing about how many coats of paint the sidelines on the soccer field need or the uneven grass. Judah is a perfectionist when it comes to his work, like his son. Maybe he hates being told he messed up. Also like his son.

A paper straw wrapper hits me in the forehead. "Hellooo," Ava says.

I turn back to her. "Sorry, what did you say?"

She rolls her eyes. "I *said* are you ready to set up the docks today? My arms are *still* sore from yesterday's manual labor." Ava massages her biceps and pouts.

I nod and look down at the puddle of sticky syrup spreading across my plate. "Ready for anything," I say. I have to be.

CHAPTER 8

Then

Being chosen by Heller was like being given a key to a secret version of Roxwood I didn't know existed. Saturdays that I had previously spent studying and catching up with Imogen and Ava were now packed with plans—hockey games, bonfires, hikes in the Green Mountains.

There were after-school pancake runs to the diner with the hockey team and sunsets seen from his inflatable gray dinghy, powered in circles around the lake. There were meals at the McConnell kitchen table, where Heller's dad, Judah, would ask me about working for Stu and Mellie and muse about how if he had only gotten the landscaping contract earlier, Heller could have gone to Alpine Lake, too. There were knowing winks from Heller's mom as she filled up the wineglass in front of my plate and sent me home with doggy bags full of leftovers.

There were lazy evenings with my family, where Heller would twirl my mom around to Queen in the living room. Where he would politely ignore the fact that we kept the house at a cool sixty-five degrees to avoid astronomical heating bills, and pretend not to hear Dad on the phone with the bank, whispering in hushed tones about overdraw fees and bounced checks.

There were Sunday strolls to Café Cloud, where Heller would

buy me fudge brownies because he knew they were my favorite, and tell me about his part-time job at the clerk's office where he had worked since he was thirteen years old, filing paperwork for the town. There were sloppy, desperate kisses near our lockers, even when he knew his friends were looking. And there were frigid nights where we lay naked under a handmade quilt, our bodies pressed together, eager and hopeful, our whole lives stretched before us.

CHAPTER 9

Now

There's nothing better than being a lifeguard—pulling on the red one-piece with the white cross on the chest and throwing on a pair of plastic sunglasses that say *Alpine Lake* along the side. It's a sign you made it, that you pushed your body to the brink taking the dreaded lifeguard test. Only half of us from last summer passed again. Being a lifeguard means you're disciplined and strong, respected and worthy. All the things I wasn't at Roxwood High.

But it also means you get to skip out on things like kitchen cleanup duty and laundry shifts. Instead, you have unfettered access to the waterfront.

After announcements, the head guard, Ray Levin, hands us each a set of keys that unlock the swim hut, the motorboats, and a special set of lifeguard golf carts. The counselors who run tennis and special events barely get sheds for their equipment. We get the world.

Imogen spreads sunscreen across my back and pats me gently when she's done. "My turn."

I take the bottle from her hand and repeat the motions, looking out over the waterfront, our domain. It's hot now, the afternoon sun beating down on us after a few hours spent threading the buoys for the lap lanes in the shallow end. But now it's time to anchor the docks, the most arduous task of waterfront setup.

"Goldie, you're on the left dock today," Levin calls. He's got a few worry lines etched into his face, but he's still as chiseled and muscley as he was back when I first met him a decade ago. I totally get why Meg's into him. I'd guess he's twenty-five, but he always pretends to be older, especially since he became head guard. Levin's a lifer. Started coming here when he was eight, back when Mellie had no gray hairs and the state-of-the-art Lodge was only a construction site. Rumor has it he was a good kid—not the kind to go on midnight raids or participate in senior pranks. He became the kind of counselor you could go to when you were homesick, but not one you'd ask to pick you up a slushie on his night off.

Last summer when they were on-again, Meg told me snippets about him, how his father was Jewish and his mother was Hindu, and how he was still figuring out if religion was a *thing* he was into, especially since they split up a few years back. Every week, his mother sent him care packages full of fennel candies from the Indian markets she frequented in New Jersey, and he'd share them with Meg under the stars. He spoke of bringing her to Chennai to meet his cousins and aunties, and his dreams of becoming a principal at the private school in Westchester where he teaches during the school year. He loves the job because it means he can keep coming back to camp. He's one of the only lifers who keeps doing so, shrugging off prospects of med school and Wall Street internships. Levin cares about this place as much as Stu and Mellie do. As much as I do.

"Imogen. Ava. Get after the dock with Goldie," Levin calls.

They groan, but we each grab a side of the massive white platform that's sitting on the sand.

"Use that core, bitches," Ava says, bending over.

Imogen grunts. "I hate this shit." Her voice carries over the water.

"But you love it!" a handful of the lifeguards yell back to us. Another classic Alpine Lake call-and-response. I look toward the deep end, and there are four guards hanging off the right dock, which they've just set up. They cheer us on from their post. One of them, Aaron Jacobson, is clearly looking right at Ava.

"Aaron's checking you out," I say through stilted breath as we shuffle the dock toward the water.

"Oh yeah?" Ava asks.

Imogen nods. "Please don't make me speak while we're carrying a million pounds." We're at the edge of the water and it's now or never.

"Ready?" I say with a huff. "Two-six-hut!" Our muscles tense as we push the dock into the lake. Then we climb in, the cold a sudden shock, and start swimming, pushing the dock farther into the deep end.

"I mean, I guess I could go for Aaron this summer," Ava says. The three of us are shoulder to shoulder now, our arms braced against the dock as we flutter our legs behind us. "Eh, he's a nice guy though, right?"

"Pre-med at Cornell," Imogen says.

Ava rolls her eyes. "Pass."

Levin blows his whistle long and loud from the head lifeguard chair at the base of the waterfront. A signal the dock is finally in place. We pause and tread water, grasping on to the sides. "Rock paper scissors for anchor duty?" Imogen suggests.

"Loser gets winners' canteen?" Ava asks.

Imogen and I nod, and I'm comforted by another ritual, another piece of shorthand only we understand. It's a tradition we've had since we were kids, when you could only get three pieces of candy at weekly canteen. Counselors take five, and lifeguards get as much as we want, but that never stopped us from gambling with it.

I lose. "Charleston Chew or bust, baby."

"When are you gonna realize that shit *ruins* your teeth?" Imogen says, splashing me with water.

She and Ava get into position to hold the dock still as I duck under it, looking for the metal chain that will connect to the anchor down below. My head bobs in the pocket of air between the dock and the surface of the water as I ready myself for the dive. All you have to do is swim down to the floor of the lake and hook the metal chain to the anchor below. Should be easy, if you've been keeping up your lifeguarding training all year. But I started slacking after New Year's.

I take a deep breath and go under, using the chain to guide me to the floor. When I finally get there, my head feels like it's about to explode and I know I need to find the anchor fast.

I grope around with my hands and find the metal circle. *Quick*, I think. *Hurry*. I grab the end of the chain and fumble a few times. I'm lightheaded now, wondering what Ava and Imogen are joking about up at the surface.

I fumble again, not able to thread the metal links. I try once more. One final time.

Click. Relief passes through me.

I let go of the chain and kick my legs harder than I ever have, pushing, pumping, rushing to the top. For air. For light.

I gasp when I reach the surface, sputtering.

A hand extends to me from on top of the dock and I look up to find Imogen leaning over the edge. "Iconic performance," she says, smiling wide. "Come on. Enjoy the fruits of your labor."

I take her hand and let her pull me up onto the dock, where I flop over onto my back like a dead fish. I turn my face to the sun and my chest heaves as I catch my breath.

"I did it."

"Yeah, you did." Imogen lies down next to me and we both enjoy the quiet laughter around us until I realize Ava's not there.

"Where'd she go?" I ask.

"Levin asked her to set up the flag on far right," Imogen says. She sits up and looks around. "There she is." She points to the dock where Aaron and his friends once were. But they're gone now. Instead, there's Ava, hanging a flag from the lifeguard chair, her body stretched out lean and long in the air.

But floating in the water beyond the buoys is an inflatable gray dinghy, powered by a small motor. When I see it, my heart stops. I'd know it anywhere. Heller sits inside the boat, shirtless and tan, sunglasses wrapped around his head. His lightning bolt necklace blinks with the sun. Heller's laugh bounces off the water and I shiver at its familiarity. Ava doesn't shoo him away.

"What . . ." I start to ask.

"Maybe she's giving him hell after last night," Imogen mumbles, frowning as she shields her eyes.

Ava steps off the lifeguarding chair and squats down so she's closer to eye level with him. Her mannerisms are nonchalant and my stomach seizes. *What is he saying? Why is he here?*

Something splashes in the water nearby and I hear the sound of swimming, of churning water and fluttering feet. Levin slices through the lake toward Ava, his red swim trunks bright under water.

Crap.

Ava takes notice. Her head jolts upright and something changes in her eyes, like she's remembering where she is and what the rules are, what her *best friend* might think about what she's doing. Heller smiles politely in his dinghy as Ava stands up straight.

Levin climbs on to Ava's dock. "Off." His voice is gruff and loud so we can hear it from here. Water rolls down his torso and he crosses his arms, stern.

"My bad," Ava says, tossing her long hair over her shoulder. She pushes out her chest a little. I know this move, but a small part of me is happy it won't work on Levin. She can't sweet-talk her way out of everything.

"You need to get off camp property," Levin says to Heller. "You gotta stay outside the buoys over there." He points to the magical boundary behind Ava.

Heller looks over his shoulder. "I live here, too. The water's free. Roxwood law."

I clench my fists, fighting the adrenaline surging in my body.

"Nice try, but you probably know as well as anyone this is *not* public property," Levin says. "Stay beyond the buoys or we're going to have to get Stu and Mellie down here."

Heller tries to keep cool but he flinches, and something shifts in his eyes at the camp directors' names. In one swift motion, he pushes off Ava's dock and paddles away. As soon as he's past the rope, Heller turns the motor on and starts off toward town. But not before glancing back at me, a look of worry forming on his face.

CHAPTER 10

Then

I said "I love you" first.

The words came out easy, a reflex, an instinct. Like riding a bike or flipping an egg.

Heller had driven to my house on Christmas morning and asked if he could take me for a ride, even though he knew we spent the day in the way so many Reform Jews do—with Chinese takeout and movie marathons. He smelled like cinnamon rolls and bacon and held my hand in the middle of the console as he drove me toward Camp Alpine Lake.

"What are you doing?" I asked. Everyone knew camp was forbidden property. Especially for kids in Roxwood.

But Heller squeezed my hand harder and kept his eyes on the road. We passed the entrance and he didn't slow.

"Come on, where are we going?"

A smile danced on his lips and he shook his head. Soon we came upon a dirt road, nearly hidden by naked branches. He made a quick left and kept going for a few miles. We bounced over rubble and rocks, and after a while I noticed a rusty sign, depicting a horse, deep within the trees.

"Are these the old Alpine Lake riding trails?"

Heller shrugged, but a smile tugging at the corner of his mouth gave him away. I'd heard rumors about these paths but never found them. Everyone said they were overgrown, impossible to traverse. Stu and Mellie had closed them for good before I got to camp because they were too dangerous. But the oldies said they led to the most beautiful vistas in Roxwood.

Heller parked at the top of a steep hill and cut the engine. When I looked out the windshield, I gasped. All of Vermont lay before us, snow-covered and so white, it was almost metallic.

He motioned for me to get out of the car, and when I stepped down, I saw he was setting up two chairs, spreading a runner out on a card table. He opened a tote bag and pulled out a box of my favorite fudge brownies from Café Cloud and a thermos of coffee.

"Heller . . ." I said, trying to find the words.

"I stumbled on this while cross-country skiing with Cal last week," he said. "I knew I had to show you."

I threw my arms around him, so grateful. We'd never talked about camp, not really, but he knew how much it meant to me. He'd seen my bedroom walls, covered in photos from color war, and old chore wheels I kept at the end of each summer to press into scrapbooks. He'd felt how soft my ratty camp T-shirts were thanks to hundreds of washes, knowing I could never walk around town in them.

I leaned up against his chest, like being with him was the easiest thing in the world, like my life wasn't about to change completely within a week's time.

"I love you, Heller McConnell." The words came out in one breath.

Before I could be embarrassed or regretful, I felt his heart race against my cheek, his head come down on top of mine.

"I love you, Goldie Easton."

CHAPTER 11

Now

I don't see Ava again until dinner. I make my way through the mess line, grabbing spaghetti and meatballs, and a whole bunch of steamed broccoli. I don't wait for Imogen or Meg or anyone before plopping down at an empty table in the middle of the room. My arms are still heavy from the weight of the dock, and I know sleep will come easy tonight.

After I take my first bite, Ava slides in next to me. Her hair is still wet from the shower and it tickles my arm when she gets close.

"Finally got a letter from my mom in the Hamptons," she says, dunking a piece of garlic bread in marinara sauce. "She spent about forty-five pages dissecting the housewarming gifts her fake friends brought to the new place. As if Waterford Crystal wasn't good enough."

Annoyance fills my stomach, but I keep my eyes forward. "That sucks," I say, the words clipped on my tongue. I hate being short with Ava, but I can't help it right now.

"It's like she doesn't even care about how I'm doing or the fact that *the twins* are only days away from ruining my summer."

"What else is new?" As soon as the words leave my lips, I know they're the wrong ones. Cutting and cruel. But I can't take them back.

Ava's bottom lip drops open and her eyes grow large with surprise. "Ouch, G. What's up with *you*?"

"Heller . . ." I say, trying to find the words. "What did he say to you at the lake?"

Ava looks down at her food. "He asked me if I was your best friend. That's it."

But there's something about her tone. It's the same one she uses when strangers ask about her dad, when she's trying to pretend like everything's *fine*. When Stu and Mellie demanded she rat out her senior raid coconspirators when we were campers. When we pretended to have our periods to get out of instructional swim when we were twelve. It's the tone that means she's lying.

But why?

"Ava—"

Her fork clatters against her plate and she tenses next to me. "Clearly you two have history. Wanna tell me what the hell happened?"

My face flushes as the words come up in my throat. But I can sense Ava turning, the judgmental, ruthless part of her bubbling to the surface. The dining hall buzzes around me, and suddenly I'm too aware of everything else here, the laughter, the clapping, the clanking of silverware. I can't tell Ava the truth. Not here. Not now.

Ava doesn't wait a second longer. She wipes her mouth on a thin paper napkin and flips her hair over her shoulder. "If you want me to fight your battles, the least you can do is tell me why." Her tone is icy and I know I've lost her, at least in this moment.

Tears prick my eyes. It's easy to forget Ava can be like this, cool and distant when she's on the defense. Selfish when she's wounded.

In the past, I've been able to get back in with an apology. A real one. She may get mad easily. But her rage doesn't last long. At least when it's been directed at me.

"It's complicated," I say.

"Everything is complicated," she snaps. "But *we* are not supposed to be complicated. World. Complicated. You. Me. Imogen. Not complicated."

"I know."

"We're supposed to tell each other everything."

"We do."

"Clearly that's not true." Ava picks up her plate and stands. "I'm here for you, Goldie," she says. "No matter what. All you have to do is believe me."

I want to respond, to grab her arm and plead with her to *trust me*, but Ava takes off, dumping the remnants of her spaghetti and meatballs into the trash and heading out through the swinging side doors. Something unlatches inside my chest, and all of a sudden, I want to tell her the whole story—about Heller and the accident and all the bullshit in between. I want to ignore the nondisclosure agreement and say *fuck it* for once. But when I do, everything will change. I squeeze my eyes shut and listen to the sounds of plates hitting the wooden tables, of laughter and Alpine Lake inside jokes. The noises that remind me of my friends, my home.

I'm home, I try to remember. *I'm home.*

CHAPTER 12

Then

Heller heard back from Dartmouth in the middle of December. We were in the ice fishing hut a quarter-mile behind his house. He had outfitted it with an old TV, a cooler, and a futon covered in blankets. We put on an old nineties movie and set a box of chocolate-covered raisins between us. But his brain was elsewhere as he held his phone with a clenched grip, periodically lifting it up to the rafters to get a better signal.

He fiddled with his necklace, the one shaped like a lightning bolt that he kept hidden, tucked beneath his ribbed undershirt, pressed close against his chest. He never laid it on top, never pressed his thumb behind it, thrusting it into people's faces. He let it hang, resting against his bare skin. A secret.

I ran my pointer finger along its edges, holding it to his flesh, so it would leave a faint mark.

"I wish there was a symbol for thunder," I said, trying to ease his anxiety. "I'd get that one."

He laughed and then got quiet. "I wish it were gold," he said. "Like you."

In that moment, I made a silent promise to myself that if we lasted until graduation, I would buy him one. A gold lightning bolt. Even if the threat of college, of the distance between us, broke us apart, at least he could carry some of me with him.

Suddenly, his body went still and he clasped my fingers tight, his eyes glued to his phone. He let out a whoosh of air and leaned his head back against the wall.

"I got in," he whispered.

"Heller!" I bounced on the cushion and threw my arms around his neck, feeling his heart beat hard through my sweatshirt.

"I know," he whispered. "Fuck."

I squeezed him tight to me and planted a soft kiss on his collarbone.

He pulled back then and pressed his forehead to mine. "Stay close, okay? Roxwood Community or UVM or something?"

We had never talked about where I would go, what my plans were—how there was no way my parents could scrape together anything resembling tuition money. But the answer was easy.

"Yeah," I said, and he relaxed, as if he had been worried, as if he had been waiting.

We stayed like that for a while as he sketched out our lives. He could study poli-sci and run for office right here in town. We'd come back to Roxwood and raise a little family deep within these woods. Make it a better place—something to be proud of.

I nodded along, while he traced my body with his forefinger, dipping into the valley of my stomach, the creases of my thighs. These were *his* dreams. He didn't wonder aloud what *I* would do. He didn't ask me if I wanted to come back to Roxwood.

But at the time, I was eager to be part of his plan. Because I didn't have one of my own. I only had Alpine Lake and a sketch of a future that, until Heller's, was blank.

CHAPTER 13

Now

"Clothes off, we're going skinny-dipping!" Imogen throws open the screen door to Bloodroot and is wearing only a beach towel, wrapped around her body. "Leaving in thirty seconds. Let's go!"

I peek out at the dark night sky behind her, and a million reasons why I should say no pass through my brain.

It's late.

My arms are sore.

Levin might catch us.

I fought with Ava.

Imo must sense my hesitation because she skips over to the counselor room and pulls down a towel, tossing it to me. "Come on," she says. "I'm not taking no for an answer."

"But—"

"No buts. I refuse to let you miss this."

"Where's Ava?" We left things unsettled at dinner, and I've got that same gutted feeling I had when we fought as kids, like I'm unmoored, floating into space. I don't know if it'd be better for her to be there or not.

"Can't find her, so I definitely need you." She taps her foot impatiently. "Ten for two, right?"

A smile spreads on my face. "Ten for two." I strip down and tie my towel tightly around my chest.

Imo ambles out the front door, where a golf cart waits for us. Inside are a few of the other lifeguards only wearing towels, too.

"Got her!" Imo calls. We hop on the back of the cart, and my stomach flips as we take off down to the waterfront, the wind whipping in my hair. I laugh hard as Imo throws an arm around my shoulder, her eyes bright and full of freedom.

This is it. What this whole summer is about. Feeling free.

When we get to the lake, we tumble out of the golf cart and devise a plan.

Our little group splits up to canvass the buildings and the trees, looking for the red blinking lights indicating that security footage is being recorded. Mellie and Stu installed the state-of-the-art system a few years back when they realized the old analog cameras did nothing to catch the counselors who took motorboats out for joyrides in the middle of the night. But now we all know how to get past their little booby traps. A simple reset will keep the cameras off for a few hours, then they'll turn back on by themselves. It's how we got away with all our after-hours swims last summer, too. Thankfully no one told Levin, and everyone assumed the cameras were sorta faulty. Unclear why they never replaced them, though no one wants to ask.

"Up there," I say, spotting a few on the swim hut. "And over by the kayak stand."

We spread out and hoist each other up to the cameras, tapping the reset buttons on the side while aiming our faces away from the lenses.

"They're gonna figure this out one day," Aaron Jacobson says. "But until then . . ." He drops his towel as a wide smile spreads on his face, free from any sign of embarrassment. "Guards assemble!"

Aaron takes off toward the water, his bare butt bright against the dark night. Everyone erupts in laughter and squeals, and soon I'm naked, too, running through the sand, splashing in the lake, the cold stinging my skin. I cut through the water and swim out to the far dock, where everyone's treading, laughing and not bothering to hide their bodies, sparkling in the moonlight.

Imo cannonballs off the dock and another counselor wraps himself in the Alpine Lake flag Ava hung earlier today. We race each other back and forth from the shallow to the deep end and gaze up at the sky, counting stars.

I puff my belly out and float on my back, listening to the sounds of laughter, of joy. We're only a few miles from Roxwood, but here in the lake, I feel so far away from the events of this year, as if they happened to someone else, not me. But I know if I flip over and take a peek toward town, reality will come crashing down. You can't see the main drag from here, only a hint of it—the bright pink neon sign from Grandee's, the glint of the drive-in movie theater—and for a second, I wonder what all those people are up to tonight, if they're looking up at this same dark sky, the smattering of stars that never seem to end.

Something splashes behind me and I feel someone nudge a foam floatie around my back and under my arms.

"At your service." I dip my head back to see Imo flutter kicking with a few red rescue tubes. I lean back against the one behind me and stick my legs out long. She comes in front of me and slides another one under my knees, then drapes her legs over it, too, so we're facing each other, creating a little circle of two. The gentle current pushes us, and we spin around slowly, creating gentle ripples in the water.

Our breasts peek out of the water as we look upward, quiet, our legs interlocked. I drag my hand through the lake, my skin bright in the darkness.

Imo clears her throat, breaking the silence. "What happened, Goldie?" I look to her and find Imo gazing at me with sad, understanding eyes. The parts of her hair that are dyed pink float in the water around her, expanding like lily pads.

"You seem older," she says. "Changed."

"We all do."

"You more." Imo presses her leg to mine. She opens her mouth like she wants to say something else.

I stop her before she can. "I'm okay, Imo."

"Are you?"

I nod, but my head feels heavy, like it's rejecting my movements.

"We don't keep secrets from each other," she says.

I nod again, lying like I did with Ava at dinner, and for a second, I wonder when we'll admit the truth, that no one tells each other everything. That even the best, oldest friends keep some things buried beneath the surface. Things that are too dark, too broken to share.

Imo drags her foot in the water. "I want you to know I'm here and I'm not going anywhere."

For a second, I want to blurt out everything. I want to unload on Imo and let her carry this burden for a moment until I can catch my breath and think straight for the first time in half a year. I wonder how it would feel to spit out the words, how they would sound coming out of my mouth and lingering in the air.

But I don't. I press my lips together and watch Imo lean her head back, dipping her hair in the water as she arches her body toward the sky.

"Maybe tomorrow," she says. "You can tell me tomorrow."

"Okay," I say. "Tomorrow."

CHAPTER 14

Then

There was nothing spectacular about Dylan Adler's New Year's Eve party. It was standard and ritualistic with thirty racks and garbage cans full of jungle juice. Because it was my first time spending New Year's with Heller, I stayed away from the booze, not wanting to forget a single moment, and clapped as he threw back shots with his teammates. When it neared midnight, he led me to the backyard to watch Cal and Dylan set off fireworks. They sent them up into the cold dark sky and I saw my breath form little clouds of warmth in front of me. Sparks exploded above us and I shrieked in delight, watching them fizzle into the night.

When midnight struck, everyone cheered, and Cal lit a round of sparklers. Heller spun me around and kissed me fiercely. He tasted sour, but I held his face in my gloved hands, grateful, grateful, grateful.

Around one in the morning, the party had begun to die down and Dylan was trying to motivate the rest of the hockey bros to make a McDonald's run. He was wearing a Roxwood hockey sweatshirt, going on and on about how he only had a few more weeks to go ham on fast food before coach made him buckle down for the back end of the season.

"Think your parents will care if you sleep at the ice fishing hut?" Heller whispered in my ear.

I shook my head. *No.*

We crept off to his pickup truck without saying goodbye. And when Heller climbed into the front seat even though I had seen him throw back a few Dixie cups of whiskey, I said nothing. He fiddled with the radio and settled on an old nineties station. I rubbed my hands for warmth.

"Perfect," he said as Britney Spears sang over the radio.

I laughed and swiveled my head to look out the window. That's when I saw Cal, coming out of the woods, zipping up his pants, a sophomore girl trailing behind him. He looked right at me in the passenger seat and held my gaze, his face unsmiling, unreadable.

Heller revved the engine right as my phone buzzed in my pocket. I saw a call from Ava and Imogen. The fourth of the night. It had been seven years since we spent New Year's apart. But I ignored it and reached for Heller's hand.

The drive was easy at first, even though the roads were dark and it had started to flurry. "Gonna take it slow," Heller said as he glanced at me and smiled. "You're my precious cargo."

I laughed and peered out the window even though there was nothing to see but darkness. Nothing except . . .

"Heller!" I screamed, but it was too late.

CHAPTER 15

Now

I have to tell them. That's all I can think about now, lying in my top bunk as the moon shines so damn bright, like a spotlight hovering in my window. I want to share the truth. The *real* truth. Despite the paperwork and the consequences and all that I could lose . . . I need to tell them.

Ava and Imogen would keep my secret. They wouldn't tell. It would be okay.

Except . . .

A sliver of doubt lines my stomach. Maybe they wouldn't understand. Maybe it wouldn't be okay.

But telling them is the only way my distance, my reactions will make sense. I'll do it tomorrow, I decide. Tomorrow. I'll pull them aside after breakfast, while we walk to the lake. They'll react like we did when Ava told us she skipped a period and we waited while she took a pregnancy test in the Truly's bathroom on a night off last summer. With hand squeezes and support when everything turned out to be okay. Or like when Imo told us she didn't get that premium cable show she auditioned for in the fall. With tight hugs and the reassurance that her life was not over.

If I can't trust them with this, I can't trust anyone at all. And I don't know if I can keep living that way.

I sigh and roll over, hoping not to wake Meg, who's conked out below me. Thank goodness she sleeps like the dead.

My hair is wet from the lake and sticks to my neck. I brush it away, searching for rest and reprieve. The clock on my nightstand says it's close to two. Six hours to reveille. I squeeze my eyes shut, praying for sleep. That's what Mom and Dad said I needed this year. Sleep. But it doesn't come. Not yet.

I push aside the flimsy curtain with my pointer finger and look out the window. It's a clear path to Ava's cabin and I can see the trail down to the waterfront. The night is dark and crisp. I wonder what Ava's dreaming about. What Imogen is plotting. I wish we were all together, huddled in one bed like we did when we were kids, whispering after flashlight time, never wanting to leave each other's sides. Maybe that's how I'd tell them, under the blankets far away from anyone else.

But then I hear the soft squeak of a wooden door creaking open. It comes from Ava's cabin. I lean closer to the window and see a tall figure, wearing all black, a hooded sweatshirt pulled up around their face. The person closes the door gently and shoves their hands in their pockets. When they turn around, there's no question. Big blue eyes shine in the night. A platinum lock of hair slips out of place. Ava.

My heart quickens.

She looks around and then starts running. The soft running we learned early, when the older kids taught us the secrets of sneaking out of the cabins. The kind where you press your whole foot to the ground to keep the sound away, to run like you're on a mission, fighting for your life. That's always what those middle-of-the-night raids felt like. A fight.

I sit up in bed and watch her path. It's a familiar one, down to the entrance to the lake, where we used to hide out when we were campers. It's a secret spot. One designed for smoking weed and making out in the dark.

I want to call out to her, but I can't. I don't.

Instead, I keep my face pressed against the screen window, waiting for her to return. And when sleep comes, I wonder for a split second if she was ever really there at all.

I don't hear the hinges of the door open in the main cabin, and I don't hear Ava push aside the hanging sheet that separates the counselor room from the main one. But even in my sleep, I feel her weight, her warmth, as she cocoons herself around me.

"Ava?" I whisper. But I don't have to turn around to know it's her. She smells like she always does, of expensive blueberry shampoo. Her long fine hair fans around my shoulders, against my bare skin. She wraps her arm around my waist and we lie like that for seconds, maybe minutes, before she whimpers into my T-shirt, stifling her own sobs.

"You okay?" I ask.

She nods silently, her head bobbing up and down behind me. I flip over and face her. There are tears streaming down her face and she's wearing all black.

"Ava," I say again, but she shakes her head.

"I love you, Goldie," she says. "I love you, okay?"

I nod, confused and drowsy. "I love you, too."

Ava turns around, facing outward and scoots herself toward me so we're packed tightly on my twin bed. I rub her back like I used to do when we were little, and soon her breathing grows slow and heavy, my hand stops moving in circular motions, and we both drift off into the night.

CHAPTER 16

Then

The crash was immediate and sharp, as Heller tried to slam on the brakes. I heard a thud and the screeching sounds of metal as the truck came to a halt. The smell of burnt rubber cut through the window. I gasped for air, tasted iron on my tongue, and my first thought was if Heller was okay.

I turned to him and saw he was gripping the steering wheel, his face frozen with shock. He read my mind and nodded. "I'm okay."

I surveyed my body, realizing I was fine, that everything worked, and I unbuckled my seat belt. I pushed the car door open, apprehension building in my stomach, willing what I saw to have been all in my head.

"Must have been a deer," Heller said from the front seat.

But his voice faded into the darkness when I realized I had been right.

There, in the middle of the road, was Dylan Adler, lying facedown on the pavement, his legs contorted at an awful angle. A paper bag with the McDonald's logo lay next to him, and French fries were scattered around, wilting with the falling snow.

Heller must have gotten out of the car, but I couldn't hear him. I could only see Dylan's back moving up and down, slowly, a sign he was still alive. I could only hear my screams, pulsing in my ears.

Heller wrapped his arms around me and pulled me back to the driver's side of the car.

"Call 9-1-1," I yelled. "Now!"

Heller looked at me with a terrified face. "We will," he said. "But, Goldie . . ." He paused, breathing out a puff of air. "Can we say it was you?"

"What?"

"I'm drunk," he said. "Dartmouth . . ." Heller shook his head, his hands gripping my shoulders. "Can we say it was you?"

I should have said no. I should have pushed him off me and screamed at him for even suggesting that my future was worth less than his. That's what Ava would have done. Imogen, too. But I'm not them.

Instead, I cupped his chin with my freezing fingers and said quietly into the darkness, "Yes."

CHAPTER 17

Now

When I wake, Ava is gone and my mouth is dry and scratchy. Meg grumbles below me, and for a second, I think reveille will start. But there are no horns to wake us, no Stu on the loudspeaker wishing us an amazing Alpine Lake day, no announcement about all the work that's got to get done before the kids arrive tomorrow.

"Oi," Meg says, kicking the bottom of my bed. "It's late, yeah?"

I fumble for my alarm clock, and when I see the time, I sit up straight. "Eight thirty." I lean over the bed so I can see Meg in her oversize T-shirt and cotton shorts. "What's going on?"

She shrugs. "I know as much as you do."

"No group leader alerts?"

Meg points to her bedhead. "Does it look like I got an alert?"

I pull back the curtain in my window, expecting rain or thunder or a natural disaster that would make it impossible for us to have a regular day starting with some undercooked waffles and a dip in the frigid lake. In all my years at Alpine Lake, we only had late wake-up when there was a storm. But when I look outside, it's bright and beautiful, the sun hanging high in the sky ready for us to come out and finish setting up camp.

Something isn't right.

Meg hops out of bed to get ready quickly.

I follow her lead, going through the motions of brushing my teeth and pulling on sweatpants, but my brain is spinning. Ava was here last night. No, wait. Ava was heading toward the lake, *then* she was here. And now something is wrong.

As I pull my hair into a high pony, Meg's walkie comes alive with a soft beep from the nightstand.

"Lodge to all staff. Lodge to all staff." Stu's voice crackles over the speaker. "Code dungaree," he says. "Over."

"Code dungaree? What the fuck is that?" Meg asks, half-amused. "This man, I swear . . ."

My throat is like sandpaper. "It means 9-1-1," I say. "We've got to get to the dining hall."

"Maybe it's a fire drill or something," Meg says.

"You're probably right." But when I look outside, I see other counselors pulling on hoodies and shoving their feet into flip-flops as they run to the dining hall with a sense of urgency only used for making sure you get the last bus back to camp on a night off. Meg senses it, too, and we follow everyone else. As we get closer to the action, there's a pit in my stomach, and I can feel Ava's breath on my neck from last night, her tears damp against my skin.

I'm halfway to the dining hall when I hear my name behind me. "Goldie!"

I turn and find Imogen hustling toward me, her tie-dyed sweatshirt half on and her eyes wide with confusion. "What the hell is going on?"

I shake my head. "I don't know."

"Have you seen Ava?"

I want to tell her about last night, but Stu bursts through the dining hall doors and motions for us to hustle inside. "Quickly," he barks, more gruff than usual.

Imogen grabs my hand. Whatever's going on, we'll face it together.

When the final counselors enter, Stu shuts the door and locks it, which sends a tingle into my stomach. They don't believe in locked doors here—only in the bathrooms.

Mellie is up front, pacing back and forth, her ponytail a little off-center and her skin grayer than it should be. Her polo shirt is neatly ironed and her khaki shorts are pleated in all the right places. But with dark circles under her eyes, it looks like she hasn't slept at all.

"There you are." Mom's voice is frantic and there's a little quiver when she speaks. She comes up behind me and squeezes my shoulder. Dad is right behind her, his shirt untucked and his lips pursed.

"What's happening?" I ask.

Mom opens her mouth to speak, but before she can, Stu taps the microphone.

"Thank you all for responding so quickly," he says, all joy gone from his usually sunny disposition. "There is no easy way to say this, but we wanted to tell you all as soon as possible." The room goes still and Mom grabs my free hand. *Where is Ava?*

"This morning we found the body of a young man down at the waterfront," Stu says. Gasps ring out nearby. "But please know, he was *not* affiliated with Camp Alpine Lake." Shoulders relax. Throats clear.

He wasn't one of us.

"He was a local boy and we have been dealing with the Roxwood police all morning to find out what happened," Stu continues. "Please note, his death looks like an accident. Drowning. This has nothing to do with the safety of our camp or our facilities. He was not horsing around on any of our equipment."

My mind spins. That's what he's worried about? That Alpine Lake has some dangerous *equipment*?

"Again, we are cooperating with the local authorities, but we want you to be aware of what we are dealing with as we continue to get ready for the campers, who are arriving tomorrow, no matter what." The room is silent as everyone tries to digest this information and what it means for the day—the summer.

But all I can think is *who*? The word forms in my mouth and before I can ask, Mellie speaks.

"The boy's name was Heller McConnell."

CHAPTER 18

Then

Heller disappeared from my life as quickly as he thundered through it.

Maybe *disappeared* isn't right. He didn't vanish. He continued being Roxwood's golden boy. Sitting at Dylan's bedside and holding fundraisers for his physical therapy. He walked through the halls like he always had, with his head held high and his backpack slung low.

He didn't ignore my texts. Not at first. After the NDA, he told me to "wait for things to blow over." He said he was sorry, that things would go back to normal soon.

But they never did.

Instead, I became Goldie Easton, the girl who ruined Dylan Adler's chances of playing hockey, of changing his lot in life. I took away his dream. I was Heller's ex, a mistake he had made. A lapse in judgment. And he continued to be the captain of the hockey team, the guy who held up the state trophy and yelled, "This one's for Dylan!"

For the rest of the year, I watched him from afar, waiting for him to realize what he had done. I couldn't stop believing that one day he would fix everything. Because no matter what he did, how far he drifted, how many lines he crossed, I couldn't deny the truth. I still loved Heller.

CHAPTER 19

Now

It's almost as if the entire room sighs with relief.

"Shit," someone says, breaking the silence. "That sucks."

"At least he wasn't an Alpine Laker," someone else mutters.

Their words shock me, but I can't think straight enough to respond. My mind swims with so many questions. Heller is dead.

I spin around, looking to Mom and Dad. They'll have answers. They must know something—anything—else. But Stu signals for them to approach for a senior staff meeting. Imogen tugs on my sweatshirt.

"Hey, you okay?" she asks. There's still a little sleep crusted in the corners of her eyes, and she looks concerned, her hand wrapped around my forearm. "That's the guy from yesterday, right? Talking to Ava?"

I nod, the only motion I can manage.

"Yeesh," Imogen says. "Must have been drunk on that boat or something. I'm so sorry you knew him."

Her words slice through the air, hovering between us. *Knew him.*

I did. At least, at one point.

I thought we'd have more time. I thought we'd come back to each other. I thought, one day, I'd open my front door and find him there with an apology and a heavy heart. I thought he'd come clean and clear my name. I thought he'd smile and whisper in my ear, *Finally*. I thought he still loved me. I thought . . . I thought we'd have more time.

"Goldie?" Imogen leans in.

I focus on her face, worried and puckered. "What?"

"I said do you want to get ready for the waterfront? Stu dismissed us."

"Oh," I say. "Yeah." I follow her out the swinging door and she loops her arm in mine.

"Geez," she says. "I can't believe it. Someone *dead* at Alpine Lake. Do you think they're gonna tell the kids when they get here? Oh my god, are they going to alert the parents?"

Kids.

I totally forgot in twenty-four hours we're going to have to care for *children*. I can't think about that now. I have to get through the hour, the day. I have to find Mom and Dad. I have to know what happened.

When we get to our cabins, Imo gives my arm a little squeeze and skips back to her bunk. I walk inside slowly, trying to focus on the tasks in front of me: Change into swimsuit. Go down to the waterfront. Clean the buoys. But the truth smacks me in the face. *Heller is dead.*

I pull on my bathing suit, shivering as a breeze comes through the window. I climb up onto my bed to close it, but when I do, I get a whiff of something.

Blueberry.

Ava.

She *was* here last night. Where is she now?

"Goldie!" Imo calls out from the porch. "Come on, let's go."

I pull on a hoodie and grab my towel, still wet from last night's skinny-dipping. When I push open the door, I see her standing on the grass, wrapped in an Alpine Lake sweatshirt, holding a Styrofoam cup of coffee from the 7-Eleven a few miles down the road.

"Where'd you get that?" I ask.

Imogen nods behind me. "Don't worry. She got one for you, too."

I turn around to see Ava standing there, dressed in a bathing suit and drawstring cotton shorts sitting low on her hips. A towel's wrapped around her neck like a scarf. She holds out a plastic to-go cup. "Iced vanilla with whole milk. Just the way you like it."

She looks untouched, unbothered, like nothing strange has happened. "Thanks," I say, taking the cup. "You went off campus this morning?"

Ava shrugs. "I was up early," she says. "Saw Aaron jogging and he let me take his Jeep."

Imo smiles, grateful, and takes a sip from her plastic cup. "I didn't know you drive stick," she says. "He's got that old Wrangler."

Ava nods. "Don't you?"

Imo shakes her head. "Nope."

I shrug. "Never learned."

Ava checks her watch. "Come on, we're gonna be late."

We start down the trail and I want to say something—anything. Less than twelve hours ago I decided to tell them the truth about Heller. But now . . . I don't even know where to start. Thankfully, there's no time because Imo asks about Ava's twin sisters, Jordie and Bianca, coming up from Palm Beach tomorrow.

"Little brats," Ava says. "Mom said I have to be nice to them, even though *they're* the reason my dad no longer has a 212 area code." She sighs and puts on a high voice, imitating her mother. "If you're not kind to Jordie and Bianca, then your father will *not* pay for Wesleyan and you *know* that *cannot* happen."

Imogen laughs, but it's hollow.

We all know why Ava loves camp so much. Here, she doesn't have to be a Cantor. Her family's reputation doesn't precede her like it did at Excelsior Prep, where there's a Cantor Library and a Cantor scholarship. She doesn't have to worry about seeing headlines about her parents' divorce settlement in *Page Six* or hear the Excelsior parents whispering about her stepmother at the nail salon. At Alpine Lake there is only Ava, the one Cantor in all of Vermont. Until now.

"Can't believe they're in Bloodroot," Imogen says.

"Maybe you can spy on them and tell me all the weird shit they do," Ava says, elbowing me in the stomach. "Or if they divulge any secrets about the evil stepbitch."

Ava wiggles her eyebrows, but for the first time, I can't read her. Not directly. Why is she pretending like she wasn't in my cabin last night? As if we didn't fight at dinner?

Imogen yawns but then snaps her mouth shut fast.

"Late night with Tommy?" Ava asks in a knowing voice.

Imogen groans. "Guilty. Found him after skinny-dipping."

"That's the third night this week." Ava pulls at the ends of her hair and it's obvious she's annoyed. "I thought he was a plaything."

"He *is*," Imogen insists. "It's just . . ."

"What?" Ava snaps. "Do you seriously think he's worth it? Gonna be the love of your freaking life? Be real, he's Tommy Eisenstat."

"Hey," I say. "Chill." I reach for Ava's arm, but she yanks it away.

"It's nothing serious," Imogen says quickly. "I'm having fun."

Ava snorts. "Sure, Imo." Her voice is hard this time.

After ten summers together, we all know what happens when one of us falls out of sync—the others get closer and the divide becomes greater. A random hookup here and there is *fine*, but sacrificing the eight languid, precious weeks to a full-blown crush, nightly sweaty makeout sessions, and some naked roll-arounds behind the rock wall can only mean disaster. It can only mean less time with each other.

We're all quiet for the final leg of the walk and I can tell Imogen is trying to hold back tears. Ava has that power over her. Over me, too. I give her hand a squeeze.

We reach the end of the trail where the concrete stops at a knee-high wall, meant for campers and counselors to drape their towels over. Levin's swim hut sits on one side of the man-made beach and the boat launch is over by the other. I gaze out at the water, expecting to find some sort of signal Heller was here—that his life ended *here*, maybe only hours ago. Yellow caution tape. That dumb dinghy. A detective crouching in the sand.

But there's nothing to indicate anything is out of the ordinary. Only tiny waves caught in the breeze. As if he was never here at all.

"Imo, you're needed on sailing," Aaron calls, his voice slicing through the air.

She tosses her towel on the wall and jogs over to him, leaving Ava and me alone.

When she's out of earshot, I turn to Ava. "That was kinda harsh."

"Oh, please," she says, barely looking at me.

We're both quiet, chatter buzzing around us. I decide to go for it.

"You heard about Heller McConnell?" I ask.

"So sad," she says with little affect. She checks her nails.

"Last night," I say. "Why'd you come in my cabin?"

Ava opens her mouth, as if she's going to respond, but then Aaron calls out to her, motioning for her to scrub the far dock. Ava nods and steps out of her cotton shorts, setting down her coffee.

She doesn't say anything, and instead I watch, incredulous, as Ava runs barefoot down to the lake and climbs into the water, swimming out to the docks, away from me and the questions she won't let me ask.

By the time I get to lunch, the mood has shifted. The dining hall is full of laughter and song, and I catch bits and pieces of conversations about campers arriving tomorrow. It's as if I'm the only person who remembers that the day started with a death. *Heller's* death.

"The Millers' trunks got here and I swear to god they each have four pairs of Gucci flip-flops."

"There aren't any New York bagels yet!"

"Mellie's saying the camp musical will be *Hamilton*!"

"One kid's preference sheet is fifteen pages long!"

My chest tightens and my lungs are on fire. I desperately want quiet. A moment alone. But that's the thing about camp—even when there aren't any kids here. You're never alone.

Most of the time that community, that camaraderie, that insistent togetherness—it's magical. Addictive. The whole point of being here. But in moments like these, of real confusion and terror and—fuck—grief, all I want is to shut the world out and be alone with my brain.

I'm good at being alone. I've had to be. I've learned to find friends in books and movies and all the adults who traipsed through our home with kind eyes and warm laughs. Mom always said I was good at bonding with their friends because I was an only child. But I liked their crew, a hodgepodge of community college professors and beekeepers, funky people of all ages, few of whom had children. They never babied me, never asked me to eat kid food, never dumbed their conversations down. They told me to pull up a chair and listen.

But camp was never about being with adults. Camp was about discarding the loneliness and leaning into the feeling of having your whole body, your whole personality up for grabs, and if you gave yourself over to camp completely, you would never be alone again. That was the promise of Alpine Lake. And it delivered.

But now, staring at the glossy sloppy joe on my plate, all I can think is that Heller is dead and I want to hide.

"There you are." Mom comes up behind me. Her voice is low and sad, and she grabs for my hand, squeezing it in her warm one. "C'mere."

She pulls me to stand and leads me to the screen door. When we step outside, I find my dad sitting on a picnic bench, his head in his hands. He looks up and the skin around his eyes is red. His bottom lip is trembling.

I've seen him cry so many times this year. When he came to get me at the police station. When Stu and Mellie made their offer. When the principal told him I wouldn't graduate. When the letter from University of Vermont came saying they were rescinding my acceptance. But the frequency doesn't make it easier.

"Oh, Goldie," Dad says, his voice shaking.

I let myself be hugged, sandwiching my body in between him and Mom. I let them envelop me and rest their heads on my shoulders and whisper sweet sounds into my ears.

After a moment, Dad lifts his head and rubs his face with both hands.

"What happened?" My voice sounds small, almost like it's not coming from me.

Mom holds me to her, her grip tight on my shoulders. "Levin found him in the lake at dawn."

That must have been why our boss wasn't at morning maintenance.

Dad shakes his head. "He drowned, Goldie."

My head snaps up. "That's not possible." Heller was an excellent swimmer. He'd had that dinghy since he was ten. His house was *on* the lake. He won an underwater breath-holding competition when we were eleven.

Dad sighs. "It's true. Spoke to some of the other nurses at the hospital a few hours ago."

"Aren't they going to investigate?" I ask. "To make sure?"

Dad shakes his head. "Stu and Mellie are dealing with the McConnells and the police. It was an accident."

"There's a vigil tonight. In town," Mom says. "We were going to go pay our respects."

"Can I come?" I don't know why I ask. The last place I should be is at an event that honors Heller McConnell. I know that everyone will stare and sneer and wonder out loud why I wasn't the one to die after all the pain I've caused. But I need to be there.

Mom and Dad exchange a look. "I don't know," Mom says. "Is that really the best idea? After everything that happened between you two . . ."

I hate that phrase. *Everything that happened.* As if she can't say "after he let you take the fall for hitting Dylan Adler." But I have to keep reminding myself that she doesn't know Heller was driving. Only Heller, Cal, and I do. And one of us just died.

I grit my teeth. "I have to go, Mom."

She snaps her mouth shut and tugs at her old concert T-shirt, worn and weathered, faded from years spent washing out sawdust from the woodworking shed.

"Fine," she says, her mouth a thin line. "I'll talk to Stu and Mellie."

"Wait, I'm sorry, but you're going to that douche's memorial service?" Imogen asks. I'm standing in her cabin, since she's the only person I know who would bring a black dress to camp in the middle of the summer. Even Ava says black is only for New York. Imo tosses me a simple sheath and I slip it over my head.

"I can't explain it," I say. "I . . . I need to be there."

"Do you want moral support?" she asks. "We can go with you."

I shake my head. For one, Mellie and Stu barely let me take the night off to go. There's still so much to do for the campers' arrival. Plus, they said, it wouldn't be good for me to be around all those people mourning Heller. But Mom told them I insisted and finally they relented. And the idea of Imogen and Ava spending any more time around Roxwood High people makes my skin crawl. I can't risk it.

The front door of the cabin squeaks open and Ava pops her head in. She's wearing a tie-dyed sweatsuit and a matching scrunchie, and looks totally unbothered by the weirdness between us at the waterfront earlier today.

"Wanna get seats for outdoor movie night?" she asks. But when she sees what I'm wearing, her face falls.

"Vigil," I say. "For Heller."

Ava steps inside the cabin and slumps down on one of the naked twin mattresses. "Thought you said he was a grade-A asshole."

"My thoughts exactly," Imogen says as she zips up the back of my dress.

"Now he's dead," I say.

Ava falls back against the bed. "Well, at least you look gorgeous," she says. "He was kind of cute. In another life, maybe you two could have been a *thing*." Her tone has an edge, almost like she's slinging an accusation, but I ignore the comment, suddenly eager to get out of the room.

Ava stands and heads to the door. "I'll save you a seat, Imo. Think you can ditch Tommy for one night?"

"Duh," Imogen says.

The screen door shuts behind Ava, and Imogen lets out a sigh.

"You know it's okay if you like Tommy, right? It's legal in all fifty states."

"Of course," Imo says. "But you know how she gets—and plus, it's the last summer before I move to LA. I'd rather spend it with you guys than him."

"Your loss," I say.

Imo laughs and hugs me from behind. "Anything else we can do for *you*?"

"Save me a chocolate chip cookie, okay? I'll be back in time for the bonfire."

I spin around and Imogen gives me a serious look like she knows that there's no greater task than saving one of Christina's famous cookies. Campers have been known to hide them in pillows for midnight snacks.

"You have my word."

CHAPTER 20

Then

Imogen called me on Valentine's Day when I didn't respond to forty-six messages in the group chat about what she should wear to some party.

I didn't mean to answer, but my finger slipped and I was too chicken to hang up when I heard her peppy voice.

"You're alive!" she yelled. "Which should I go with? Pink dress or red crop top?"

I chewed on my bottom lip. "Pink crop top," I said.

"Okay, that wasn't an option, but duly noted." When I didn't laugh, Imogen changed her tone. "You're not okay, are you?"

I shook my head even though she couldn't see. I let a little whimper escape out my mouth.

"Oh, Goldie," Imo said softly. "Whatever you're going through, please know there are only one hundred and twenty-five more days until camp, okay? Can you promise me you can make it one hundred and twenty-five days?"

Tears pricked my eyes. It was so classic Imo. She understood that whatever was going on was too deep to admit over the phone and that when we would finally be together it would all wash away. She knew that because I knew it, too. I believed it. Alpine Lake cured all. It always had.

"I promise," I said, my voice a whisper.

"Hugs, G."

"Hugs."

We hung up soon after and she kept texting, announcing the pink dress had won the wardrobe contest and that she loved us both, more than whatever Jersey loser she was hoping to mack it with that night. I waited for her to mention our call, to clue Ava in on the fact that we had sidebarred. She didn't though, and I was grateful.

But it was in this moment that I began to wonder if she was so good at keeping secrets that maybe she was hiding some of Ava's from me, too.

CHAPTER 21

Now

The ride from Camp Alpine Lake to town always looks different in the car than it does on the big yellow school bus that shepherds us around on nights off. The roads feel wider, more cavernous under the canopies of massive trees blocking the sun from streaming through. And if you roll the windows down you can smell the lake in the air, no matter where you are.

Mom, Dad, and I drive in silence, Queen floating softly from the speakers. They hold hands in the front seat, their clasped fingers resting on the console between them.

I clear my throat. "Have you heard anything else?" I ask, trying to keep my voice steady.

Mom turns around and shakes her head. "No, sweetie."

"So, it's an open-and-shut case? Heller drowned by accident?" I ask. That truth seems so unimaginable.

"I don't think you're going to get any more answers than we already have," Dad says, his eyes on the road. "At least not yet."

Mom looks to Dad with worried eyes. "I'm going to tell her, Lou."

Dad blows a raspberry but doesn't say anything else.

"There was alcohol in his system," Mom says softly, spinning around in the passenger seat. "He was drunk and took a fall into the lake."

Her words hit me square in the chest and fury takes hold. How could he have been so stupid? So careless? He had so much left to do. So many wrongs to right.

Dad makes a left and the beginning of Main Street comes into view. We drive a little while longer and I can see people I've known forever hustling by on the sidewalk. Shoulders hunched. Faces solemn. The independent bookstore owner is pulling the door shut, turning the lock. Café Cloud, the bakery that sells fresh sourdough and triple fudge brownies, has a CLOSED sign on it. And when we get farther into town, I see the flag at Town Hall is at half-mast. I suck in a breath and close my eyes, tears escaping down my cheeks. This is all for Heller.

Some kids are chosen at birth. Each town has them. Babies who come out all fresh and clean and start their lives with the subconscious understanding that, without a doubt, they will be special. Their lives will be easy. They will have wide smiles and long eyelashes, and they'll be able to talk to anyone. They will find it easy to make people laugh, to disarm new acquaintances, to charm. They will be magnetic. Electric. Explosive. They will have a *way* about them that pulls you close.

Heller was one of those kids. The only one in Roxwood. Chosen.

Back in kindergarten it became obvious he was destined to hold this town—the world—in the palm of his hand. That's when kids are plucked from obscurity in a place like Roxwood. It was as if everyone else on the playground had decided. Heller McConnell was special, he was the one who could get out of this town—do *something* with his life. And the fact that Heller picked me out of the cast at the haunted house and said *mine* . . . well, that made me special, too. For a moment.

Dad pulls the car into the high school parking lot, which is almost full. We find a spot at the end of a row and walk in silence toward the football field. I hear hundreds of people finding their places and greeting each other with the devastating sniffles and back claps that only come from mourners.

As we get closer, the sobs from the crowd get louder, and the cramps in my stomach get more intense. Mom must sense my fear, because she grabs my hand.

"We can go back to camp, you know," she whispers but I shake my head. I want to witness this. I have to.

Dad straightens his shoulders and continues leading us toward the crowd. He grabs an empty row in the bleachers near the back and I sit in between them, behind young kids and parents who look familiar. I let out a big exhale and squeeze my eyes shut.

Blend in. All you have to do is blend in.

From my seat, it looks like the whole town of Roxwood is here. Hordes of people of all ages sit clumped together in their T-shirts and shorts. There are so many Roxwood red baseball hats, turning the bleachers into a bloodstained sea. Even though I've lived here my whole life, I couldn't feel like more of an outsider.

I try to remember that I have a right to be here. I'm grieving, too. But no one here knows the truth about the accident. No one but Cal. I scan the crowd and see him sitting with the rest of the hockey team in the front row, down toward the sideline. Dylan is next to the team in his wheelchair, a crimson hat sitting on top of his head. A pang of shame shoots through my stomach.

Cal turns around in his seat and looks out over the crowd. His eyes are rimmed with red and his usually pale skin is all splotchy, like he's been crying. He has the same forlorn look to him that he did right after his mom died and he spent countless nights in a sleeping bag on my bedroom floor. A hitch catches in my throat and I wonder what's going on inside his head. I wish I could ask him.

Then, though, his eyes find mine and it's like all the air is gone from my chest.

"Are you okay?" Mom asks.

"Yeah," I say. "It's . . . a lot."

"We don't have to stay . . ." Mom says, a whisper.

"I need some space. I'll be back in a sec."

I stand up and scootch my way into the aisle, down the steps. I get to the bottom and make a hard turn. No one's under the bleachers. There's only darkness and shade and muffled sounds coming from above. I'm safe here and I can finally breathe.

And suddenly I'm overcome with the weight of it all, the significance, the horror. Something churns inside my stomach and before I can stop myself, I vomit onto the ground.

"What the fuck?" A hard male voice rises up behind me.

I spin around to find Jordan Adler, Dylan's older brother, staring at me with disgust. He was a hockey player in high school, too. Never good enough to go further, though. I think he took some classes at Roxwood Community College, but didn't make good enough grades to transfer to a four-year, thanks to a penchant for cheap beer, whiskey, and dirt bikes. It always creeped me out that he hung around at high school parties. Cal appears behind him with a few of the other guys from the hockey team, and my heart begins to pound fast.

I wipe my mouth on the back of my hand and stand up straight, searching for a response.

"What are you doing here?" Jordan asks, surprise in his voice.

"I'm sorry . . ." I start to say, but another one of his buddies cuts me off.

"Sorry? Are you fucking kidding, Goldie? Heller is *dead* and he died at *your* precious camp."

The tears are starting to come, and I take a step back. "They said it was an accident." My voice is a whisper, hoarse and raw.

"If you think this is some sort of fucked-up coincidence, then you're as dumb as we always thought you were," another one says. "*You* should have been the one who drowned. Not Heller." He takes a step closer to me and cracks his knuckles, like he's looking for a fight.

Before any of them can make a move, Heller's dad's voice cuts through the air, asking everyone to take their seats.

Cal motions toward the stands. "Come on, guys," he says without looking at me.

They all turn away to head back to the memorial to honor their friend, the boy I loved.

All except Jordan Adler.

He lingers a bit, waiting for the other guys to go. I brace myself, waiting for a punch, a shove, something that proves I'm as worthless as they made me feel.

But then Jordan steps toward me and looks at me with big, dark eyes. He reaches out and grabs my elbow hard.

"I know," he whispers.

Everything in my body tightens.

"That fucker got what he deserved."

Jordan releases me and walks back to the memorial, fast. When he disappears in the crowd, his words begin to make sense and I try to catch my breath. I text Mom with shaking fingers.

We need to leave.

I rush to the parking lot, my vision blurred from tears and snot. Mom and Dad appear with concerned eyes and shaking hands. They unlock the car and we throw ourselves into it, speeding out of the lot, back toward camp, toward safety.

But as the trees whip by through the window and I replay Jordan's words in my brain, I wonder for the first time if maybe camp *isn't* safe. Not anymore.

By the time we get back to Alpine Lake the sun is setting and the air is growing cold. I know there's a final staff bonfire tonight, the last one before all the kids arrive tomorrow, but all I want to do is curl up under the covers of my top bunk and forget everything.

I slam the cabin door behind me and Meg yelps from the counselor room.

"Oi!" she says. "A heads-up woulda been nice."

"Sorry," I mutter without making eye contact. I start to climb the bunk, but Meg tugs at my hand gently.

"You okay?"

"Not really." I step back on the floor, on solid ground, and Meg wraps me in a tight hug, her thick arms pressed against my back.

"Death's a bitch, babe," she says.

I snort out a laugh. A perfect Meg-ism. It's similar to what she told Ava when her dad never showed up to visiting day. "Divorce's a bitch, babe." Ava jokes about getting that line tattooed on her forehead.

"Come to the bonfire," Meg says when she releases me. "You think you're going to feel better hanging out here alone reading or some shit? I refuse to let you wallow."

I look at her then and notice she's wearing makeup on her usually bare face. Her lashes are coated in mascara and her lips are bubblegum pink. Her dirty blonde hair is different, too. Free from its usual ponytail, blown out with a little wave.

"Megan Marie Allen, do you have a *date*?" I ask.

Meg releases me and looks a little embarrassed. "I'm spending time with Levin," she says. running her fingers through her hair. "After . . . you know what he saw." She clucks her tongue. "We talked a lot today, that's all."

"Glad he has you," I say, and mean it. I don't want to imagine what it was like to find Heller. To hold his lifeless body and realize what had happened.

Levin must have been so scared.

But I can't think about that now or I'll lose it.

I peek out the window and see streams of counselors leaving their cabins, dressed in dark hoodies and sweatpants. They carry backpacks full of marshmallows and graham crackers, unmarked bottles, and portable speakers. Their laughter floats through the air and a calm settles over me.

I shrug off Jordan's comments, the taunting from the boys at the vigil. I know the truth: Camp is safe. It's where I belong. It will make everything better.

"I'll go to the bonfire."

"That's the golden girl I know. Come on then."

I unzip Imo's black dress and pull on sweats, shoving my head through my coziest Alpine Lake lifeguard hoodie. I stuff my feet in thick socks and sneakers and spray heavy-duty bug spray all over.

"Ready," I say.

Meg throws an arm around me and practically pushes me out of the cabin.

The air is cold and crisp and I can smell muck and algae and sand floating from the lake through the night wind. It mingles with smoke coming from the bonfire. It smells like possibilities. Like summer.

"Come on, now." Meg pulls me toward the boys' side of the camp, where the cabins are closer to each other, tightly packed beneath a grove of weeping willows. It's shadier over here, hidden. That's why we always went to the boys' cabins on raids. It was harder to get caught.

As we get closer, I can hear laughter breaking through the trees. Someone strums an acoustic guitar and there's a nervous, kinetic energy bouncing in the sky. It's the final night of maintenance week, the last night it's just us before the campers get here. Spirits are high. Everyone is on fire, light, like they've finally shed the skin they came with only days before. They don't care that a boy died on camp. They didn't know Heller.

I clench my jaw. I'm jealous of them all.

"There you are!" Imo bounces toward me and wraps me in a fierce, urgent hug, nuzzling her nose into my hair. "I practically had to fight off that group of Scots to save this for you." She presses one of Christina's cookies, wrapped in a napkin, into the pocket of my sweatshirt.

"Im," I say, choking on her name. Tears prick my eyes.

She pulls back and looks at me, her face worried. "That bad, huh?"

I nod.

"You're safe here," she says. "We got you." Then she turns around to the bonfire assembled in the middle of the group . "Who here loves Goldie Easton?" she yells, her voice lighter, higher.

A chorus of cheers rings through the night and people stand, holding out beer cans and plastic cups like they're making a toast. They all sit on logs arranged in a circle and the flames dance across their faces.

"Have a drink." Levin tosses me a slim can of cheap sparkling wine. His eyes are sunken into his head and his shoulders are hunched. Guess that's what happens when you find a dead body.

"Aren't you famously anti–underage drinking?" Last summer he had one of his counselors fired for coming back wasted and throwing up on one of the kids after a night off. Though . . . that was probably the right call.

Levin shrugs. "Don't think it really matters right now." He takes a swig from a red cup and smacks his lips. Levin doesn't say anything else, but he keeps looking at me, like he wants to.

There are so many questions I want to ask.

How did Heller look when you pulled him out of the water?

How did he feel?

What was he wearing?

Was there any life left in him at all?

I pop open the can of wine.

"Thanks."

Meg comes up beside me and reaches for Levin. He flinches but only slightly.

"Sorry," he says.

"Wanna go for a walk?" Meg's tender, like she's talking to a bullied camper.

Levin nods and starts to follow Meg toward the horse stables. But before he leaves, he looks at me again with those vacant eyes. He leans in, his mouth so close to my ear I can feel his breath.

"Whoever he was, he shouldn't have died like that," he whispers.

A shiver slinks up my spine as I watch Levin and Meg head into the darkness. *Like what?* I want to call after him. But there's nothing Levin could say that would make this horrible reality go away. I look around the ring and remind myself this is the place where I'm wanted. Where I'm safe, no matter what.

Imogen skips off toward the back of the bonfire, where Tommy's telling some dramatic story, talking with his hands. I look over to the basketball court and finally spot Ava, who's talking to Aaron Jacobson, their foreheads turned toward one another. But I can tell Ava's not really paying attention. She has that look in her eye that she always gets when she doesn't give a shit—like when her mom asked her to say hi to all her old great-aunts at her bat mitzvah or when the group leaders would tell her to share her black-and-white cookies from Zabar's after visiting day.

I take a sip of the wine, which is way too sweet. It burns as it slides down my throat. I watch Ava, waiting for her to turn to me, to ask me how the vigil was, to tell me why she was in my cabin last night.

She doesn't though. She stays aloof and unaware, tipping the contents of her drink into her mouth and swallowing in one big gulp. Then she stands and motions toward the grass behind the basketball shed, a signal everyone knows means *I'm going to pee*.

I chug the rest of my wine and follow her.

"You holding up okay, Goldie?" someone asks as I pass other counselors.

"Yeah," I mumble.

"Man, sorry to hear about that townie," someone else says.

My cheeks burn and I pull the hood of my sweatshirt up around my face until I reach the pee zone.

"Ava," I whisper in the direction of where she's currently squatting. "It's me. Can we talk?"

Ava grunts an acknowledgment but she doesn't say anything. Leaves crinkle under her feet as she shakes off and stands. She walks to me light like she's a dancer even though we both know she quit ballet after two lessons and spent every hip-hop workshop sitting in the corner eating fistfuls of Cheetos.

"Ava." Her face comes into view and her skin looks gray and ashen. She's drunk. I can tell by the way her eyes won't focus on me. Her head lolls to one side. She tries to walk past me, but I grab her wrist. "Why are you avoiding me?" I ask.

Finally, something snaps inside her, and Ava turns to face me, her hair falling around her cheeks. Her bottom lip quivers and her eyes flash fire. But then her face turns to stone again.

"I'm not avoiding you," she says.

"Where were you last night?"

"What do you mean? I was sleeping."

"You came into my cabin."

Ava gnaws at a cuticle. "I always do that."

"But where were you before? When Heller . . ."

Ava looks at me, concerned. "What are you asking me, Goldie?"

"I . . . I really want to know what happened to him. Did you see anything?"

Ava shakes her head, disgusted. "Honestly, it might be better if you didn't ask any more questions about this."

I take a step back, shocked at her words, but before I can press her, she waves to someone over my shoulder and heads back to the bonfire, leaving me in darkness next to a river of piss.

CHAPTER 22

Then

We were all together when Ava found out about her dad's new family. We were ten and it was the first time Mom had let me visit Ava in the city for a sleepover. She had driven me the whole way down, all six hours, and was staying with a friend in Brooklyn so she could take me home the next day.

Late that night, when we were snuggled up in Ava's queen-size bed, we heard her mom shout from the living room. "Motherfucker!"

Ava rolled her eyes and turned the volume up on the TV.

But that didn't drown out the sound of glass shattering. Ava winced and her body stiffened. "I'll be right back." She stepped out of bed, then tucked us back in. "You guys stay here, okay?"

Imo and I looked at each other but didn't say anything. She grabbed my hand under the blanket and squeezed hard as we tried to focus on the rom-com blaring in the room.

I don't remember drifting off to sleep or hearing Ava come back, but when we woke in the morning, Ava was sitting in the big armchair in the corner of her room, her cell phone in her hand. Her messy bun was askew and she had bitten her nails raw, so you could see blood.

"My dad's new wife had her babies," she said when she saw us stir. "Twins."

We knew better than to say anything resembling *congratulations*. Instead, Imogen climbed into the chair with Ava and I plopped down at her feet.

"Bianca and Jordie." She snorted. "Couldn't get much more ridiculous than that, huh?" Ava stood, not letting us respond. "I ordered bagels. Lox and whitefish and the whole deal."

Ava wrapped us both in hugs so tight I thought we might meld together for once, finally.

"Maybe you guys can stay another night," she said softly. "Call in sick to school. We could watch movies *all* day. The good nineties ones, too. Julia Roberts."

Imogen nodded eagerly, encouraging. "Maybe," she said.

"Yeah," I echoed.

We all knew that would never happen, but no one dared mention it, especially when it was clear that Ava's mom had left us to go to the gym, or a spa, or a boozy brunch somewhere downtown. When my mom came to pick me up, she hugged us all and hung out for a bit, eating half a bagel with schmear and lox and capers.

"I swear this tastes like the bagels we get at camp for Sunday brunch, don't you think, girls?"

Ava smiled at my mom. "I'm not supposed to tell anyone, but Stu and Mellie get them shipped from H&H," she said, then looked over at the window. "My dad worked it out. Back when I was a Rambler."

Mom smiled at Ava. "Well, isn't that nice."

Ava shrugged. "It was nicer when he wasn't cheating."

Mom set her bagel down and turned to me and Imo. "Imogen,

how about I drop you off at home on our way back up to Roxwood?"

"Okay," she said. No one mentioned the possibility of another night together.

"Great," Mom said. "Go get your stuff, you two."

I looked at Ava and she kept eye contact with my mom, always grateful for attention from Willa.

Imogen and I left them together at the table and gathered our things, stuffing pajamas and socks into our overnight bags.

"Do you think she's gonna be okay?" Imo whispered.

I peeked out the door and saw Mom holding Ava as she sobbed, her shoulders shaking, her head resting against Mom's chest.

Something pulled at my heart. Jealousy, maybe, at my mom giving Ava so much attention. But no, not quite. Rage, perhaps, at Ava's dad for inflicting this kind of pain. But that wasn't it either. When I turned back around to Imogen's hopeful face, I realized it was pity. For all the smoked fish and penthouses and queen-size beds with feather pillow toppers, she would never have the one thing she desperately wanted. Parents who cared.

"She will be," I said to Imo. "Okay, I mean. We'll help her get there."

CHAPTER 23

Now

Reveille blares long and loud over the speakers and I wake with a start. The sun is already so bright, even through the curtain, and I roll over, shoving my face into the pillow.

"You're hungover," Meg calls. It's more of a statement than a question and I groan a response. "Buck up, babe. It's K-day."

Fuck. The kids are arriving in the early afternoon and we both know there's still a shit ton to do to make the cabins look presentable. We shower and change quickly, and Meg grabs her clipboard before heading to the dining hall.

Breakfast is rushed, as everyone wolfs down eggs and pancakes, steaming bowls of oatmeal and fresh fruit, grumbling about the bratty campers whose parents asked for their kids' shit to be unpacked upon arrival.

"I'm not a fucking *maid*," Tommy says with a scoff, clearly not remembering that *he* definitely didn't fill his drawers by himself when he was a Rambler.

Ava and Imogen are swamped, taking orders from the senior counselors in their cabins. There's no time to ask Ava questions like *what the fuck is up with you?*

Meg drags me back to Bloodroot and pulls out a massive cardboard box filled with finishing touches for our cabin. She grabs a homemade chore wheel she made with her sloping, messy hand-writing. The inner ring is filled with campers' names and the outer ring is labeled with various cleaning tasks like SWEEP and TOILET. "Hang this by the door, yeah?" she asks.

I tack it to the bulletin board near the entrance, alongside the list of shower days, emergency exit strategies, and a rubric for Sunday inspection.

I glance up at the rafters and catch a glimpse of our plaque, the one that gave me such faith a week ago. *Sisters by choice*, we had written. I hope that's still true.

"What's next?" I ask Meg.

But before she can answer, the cabin door swings open and Meg scrambles to her feet. Mellie's standing in the doorway, holding a walkie-talkie. She and Meg are wearing matching striped Alpine Lake senior staff uniforms. She looks well-rested, more relaxed and at ease than she did yesterday when she told us Heller was dead.

"So glad to know I never have to worry about you two," she says, her voice light and excited. "These Ramblers will be lucky to have you, won't they?"

Meg laughs and smiles wide. "I hope they think so."

I examine Mellie's face for any sign of anxiety or concern. But there's nothing. Just the thrill of starting a new summer and greet-ing new campers. Yesterday's news is old and stale, a stain that could be scrubbed away.

She walks around the room, stopping at each bed to make sure all the dressers are stable, that each of our campers will have enough space for their towels and linens, and that there aren't any cobwebs hiding in the corners.

Meg's walkie crackles and comes alive. "Could you come down to special events? One of your kids has a birthday," someone says over the intercom.

"Ah yes, Fran Gertz from Philadelphia," Meg says. "She's turning nine. Christina made funfetti cookies."

"You really are so thoughtful," Mellie says, holding open the door for Meg. "I knew we made the right call promoting you." Meg blushes and waves her hand like it's no big deal but I know it is. Getting that kind of praise from the directors doesn't come often, especially if you're not a lifer.

When she leaves, Mellie and I are alone.

"Well," Mellie says, swiveling around. "How was the vigil?"

I swallow hard. "It was okay."

She cocks her head, the wrinkles on her forehead deepening. "Really?"

Shit. Mellie's always been able to read me like a book. She's been in my life so long, I don't even remember meeting her. Back when I was a toddler hanging out in the infirmary, she was always there, bouncing me on her knee as my dad counted Band-Aids and gauze pads. And when I was finally old enough to live in the cabins, she took one look at my worried face on my first day and knelt down beside me. "You're going to love it," she whispered in my ear. "You're home now."

I shake my head. "It was awful."

Mellie envelops me in a hug. "I've always tried to protect you, kiddo," she says, choking up. "I never wanted you to feel this kind of pain."

I nod into her chest. I wonder if this is how people with grandparents feel, that someone like Mellie would always be there to laugh at my jokes and clean up my messes. She might be around for homemade scones and jam, but none of the bad stuff—not the daily temper tantrums and screaming fights reserved for parents.

"I can't believe it," I say, pulling back from her. "I don't understand how this could have happened."

Mellie's mouth puckers. "He was drinking, sweetie. Did your dad tell you?"

I sniffle a yes. "The police aren't even going to investigate?"

Mellie shakes her head. "There's nothing to look into."

I perch on the side of the bed, tapping my foot against the floor. I know Mellie's right, but something doesn't sit well in my stomach. Something feels . . . off.

Jordan Adler's words wind their way through my brain.

That fucker got what he deserved.

But Jordan's full of shit. Has been since he was twelve years old, pelting water balloons at me as I rode by the dilapidated Adler family cider mill on my way to school. I push him out of my mind, try to forget what else he said to me at the vigil.

I know.

I clear my throat. "What happens now?"

Mellie sits down beside me and rests one hand on my back. "I wish I could say everything will be okay, but I can't," she says. "That would be a lie. And you, Goldie Easton, do not deserve to be lied to."

She presses a thumb to my cheek, wiping away a tear. "You may never know all the details of that boy's death. And you will have to live with that. But know that what you're feeling now is temporary. Soon, hopefully very soon, this will all feel like a bad dream. It will be part of your past and you will have moved on. Heller McConnell is not your story. *You* are your story."

Mellie looks around the cabin. She fixes her face into a smile. "But today, we have some campers to greet."

Right after lunch, the loudspeaker erupts overhead. "K-day! K-day! Ten-minute warning!" Stu calls out, a gleeful lilt in his voice. "I repeat, ten-minute warning! Guard your posts, Alpine Lakers!"

My heart feels light and a flutter fills my stomach. I love the first day of camp, always have. It's full of possibilities.

I pull on my stark white Alpine Lake counselor T-shirt and roll up the sleeves. I rush out the door, toward the gates where all the counselors are lining up, and head over to Meg, who's unrolling a big-ass banner with all our kids' names on it.

"Not bad, eh?" Meg says, marveling at her awful handwriting on the brown butcher paper.

"It's basically chicken scratch," Levin says, walking by. He winks at Meg, all flirtatious and sweet. His sad, hollow eyes from last night seem to be gone, and he jogs off toward the senior staff area.

"You guys officially back together?"

Meg's face reddens but she smiles, gives a quick nod.

I start to laugh as someone bumps me from behind. I turn to see Ava shimmying up toward me.

"Ready to scare all these little monsters?" she asks, like nothing weird happened yesterday. Like everything is fine.

She's holding her cabin's banner and her hair is piled high on top of her head with a bright red ribbon tied sloppily around her loose ponytail. She smiles wide, electric and excited.

I'm about to respond, but there's no time. The buses appear between the trees, and all of a sudden, the air is frenetic and dizzying as they come to a stop in front of the dining hall. Kids pour out of the buses. It's so easy to tell who's a new eight-year-old and needs hand-holding, and who's fifteen, ready to be reunited with friends they spent the whole school year missing. There are shrieks and tears and awkward stumbles over ginormous duffle bags.

Soon, Meg and I have gathered our girls, ten in total, and are ready to lead them back to the bunk. Ava's sisters, Jordie and Bianca, blend in with the others, even though they're both wearing sneakers that cost more than my laptop. I catch them glancing at Ava and whispering behind cupped palms. But they don't approach Ava and she doesn't look at them. No hugs or hellos. They keep to themselves, hanging in the back of the group.

"Let's go, Bloodroot!" Meg calls out, her voice joyful.

The girls scamper behind her and I bring up the rear, herding them all like little ducklings. Before we head down the hill, I look back over my shoulder to see Ava greeting her campers. She bends down to give them big hugs and welcomes them into her orbit.

CHAPTER 24

Then

We didn't know who else to call.

It was obvious from the moment we sat down at the breakfast table on New Year's Day. Dad cleared his throat. "I'm going to reach out."

Mom protested at first, but Dad wore her down. "We need help," he said. "They know how to handle crises."

I lifted my head from where it was pressed against the freezing window. I was a crisis. I wanted to say something, to get Dad to stop dialing. Stu and Mellie would never let me come back to camp if they knew what I had done—or what I *said* I had done. But when I opened my mouth to speak no words came out. My throat was raw and worn. I had lost before I had a chance to fight.

Plus, we all knew the truth.

Stu and Mellie had power in this town.

Even if everyone in Roxwood rolled their eyes when talking about Camp Alpine Lake and even when the campers tipped like shit on nights off, no one could deny that Stu and Mellie ran the biggest business in town. Some even said camp was the only reason Roxwood was still standing, that people still had jobs.

I moved to the couch, under a flannel blanket, listening as Dad made the call.

"Stu," he said, but then quickly shut his mouth. I could hear Stu on the other end speaking in that hushed, comforting tone he used with the homesick kids every summer.

"Uh-huh," Dad said. "So, you've heard." He glanced at me and then turned his back, walking toward the kitchen. "That's what we were thinking, too," he said. "Okay, see you soon."

Dad faced me, holding his phone in his hand like it was about to explode. "Why don't you get dressed and get in the car, sweets?" he said. "We're going to Stu and Mellie's." His mouth turned into something resembling a smile, but I could see the worry in his brow, the distress in his eyes. His baby had done something awful, something no one could undo. But he was damn well going to try.

Within twenty minutes, we were in the car with a box of brownies from Café Cloud, heading south. The drive to their house in Connecticut took four hours and we didn't stop once. Not even to pee. No one asked.

I had never been to their home before. Neither had Mom and Dad, and I don't know if any of us expected what we saw when we turned off the main roads and followed the directions down a dirt path. There was a gate and a security guard, a half-mile-long drive-way with statues dotting each side. It was a mansion. An estate. As I drove to the front door, I could spot a tennis court, a swimming pool, and a putting green. Grander than even Ava's weekend house in the Hamptons, than Imogen's home in New Jersey.

My stomach flipped as we walked to the door to ring the bell, but Mellie opened it before we even stepped foot on the welcome mat.

Mom thrust the box of brownies at her but Mellie ignored my parents and pulled me to her, pressing my head against her chunky white sweater. "Oh, sweetie," she said softly.

I followed her inside and looked around. There was a spiral staircase and art made of glass. The ceiling extended to the heavens and the foyer was bigger than our living room.

I always assumed Mellie and Stu were on *our* side of things at camp. Hired to make the wealthy feel special. But that's when I realized they had more in common with the families who sent their kids to Alpine Lake than people like my mom and dad or Christina, people who they employed.

Dad huddled with Stu in the kitchen and spoke in soft, hushed tones. I strained to hear them but gave up when Mellie led me to the living room and held me tighter, her sturdy grip keeping me upright.

"Come, dear, let's sit."

I followed her to the plush beige couch and watched Mom perch on the cushion's edge, careful not to leave an imprint.

Stu came to join us, sitting in a mid-century armchair, his hands clasped in front of him. Suddenly I felt very young, as if I were a Rambler, not a counselor. As if I was about to be spoon-fed a diluted version of the truth.

Stu spoke first. "What happened last night was a mistake, darling," he said tenderly, looking right at me with warm eyes. "An accident. You weren't drinking and you were driving an unfamiliar car. Isn't that right?"

A lie.

He cleared his throat and glanced at Mellie. "I hear you could be facing serious consequences," he said carefully. "But we think we have a solution to this problem. One that might make this all . . . go away."

A quizzical look passed between Mom and Dad, and I wondered if they were thinking what I was thinking.

Why would they help me?

But as he started talking, that thought was replaced by something else. A warm feeling bubbling up in my stomach, one that once you turned on was impossible to turn off. Hope.

CHAPTER 25

Now

The first week of camp is filled with so much *new*. New camper orientation, new kids to teach how to breaststroke, new girls who want their hair braided while they sit at my feet.

There are get-to-know-you games that feel stale by the second day, when most everyone has decided who their best friends will be, who they want to kiss. There are afternoon ice cream snacks, made-up chants perfect for dining room sing-alongs, and so many games of jacks to be played at rest hour. There are books of Mad Libs and thread for friendship bracelets, and motorboat rides with Ava and Imogen as we laugh at the girls bouncing behind us in the inflatable tube. There is nightly cookie patrol, where Levin picks a few lucky campers every evening to help him deliver bedtime snacks on his golf cart. There are leg-shaving parties on the lawn and secret tears, wept into the pillows of homesick girls. There are kids new to camp who are falling—*have* fallen—in love with this place and its power.

And yet, there is also me—trying to remember the way Heller smelled, the way he tasted. Trying to keep those memories lodged in my brain because now it has sunk in that the boy I loved, the boy who betrayed me, is dead.

By the time we get to Friday, I'm so beat, I can barely keep my eyes open long enough to marvel at the sunset, all purples and pinks and magical hues. My limbs are sore and my eyelids are heavy. But as I walk up from the waterfront, I try to remind myself there is no place I'd rather be.

My walkie comes alive at my hip and I hear Meg's voice boom through the speaker. "Goldie, can you get the mail? I'm dealing with a barf situation. Over."

"Copy," I say into the mic. I head to the office, which is right in the middle of camp, near the traffic circle and the gazebo. The wooden door is shut tightly, and when I push it open, I expect to be blasted with central air conditioning. It's one of the only buildings on campus to have it, and Pat, the receptionist who has sat behind the front desk for decades, usually keeps the place at a cool sixty-six degrees. But the room is stale and musty, with barely a breeze floating through.

"AC on the fritz?" I ask Pat. She's older, mid-sixties maybe, with cotton candy hair that's been dyed blonde. She always wears bright pink lipstick and high-waisted khaki shorts.

Pat looks at me like she's about to faint. "Hasn't been working all week," she says, nodding to the thermostat mounted on the wall behind her. "The electrician came by this morning and said it needs to be replaced."

I squish up my face. "When are they gonna fix it?"

Pat groans. "When an asshole parent complains!" She covers her mouth and laughs. "But you didn't hear that from me."

I smile at her and grab a stack of letters and envelopes from one of the bins at her feet.

"Thanks, Pat," I say, and head outside where it's ten degrees cooler.

- - -

After dinner, all the Ramblers gather in a circle in front of our cabins as Meg reads out the evening activity options from the highlighted papers attached to her clipboard. Ava's bunk is sent to go fishing with Levin on the barge. Imogen's cabin is off to a dance party in the studio. And Bloodroot is going on a starry night walk up to Creepy Cliff.

Jordie grabs at her sister Bianca's hand, and I wonder if the Cantor twins are nervous, scared of the dark or the woods. I watch Ava closely, but her face shows no signs of empathy. She ruffles the hair of one of her campers and sticks out her tongue, making the girl laugh. Soon Meg rallies our bunk to stand and follow her toward the trail. I fall in line, hanging in the back with Jordie and Bianca.

"Why is it called Creepy Cliff?" Jordie asks.

"Because some older kids once thought it was fun to scare campers like you," I say in my best *everything's going to be fine* voice. "There's really nothing creepy about it."

"Well, it seems scary," she says as we get closer to the mouth of the trail.

"That's why we have headlamps," I say, tapping the one strapped to my forehead. "And you have flashlights."

"Why can't we do this during the day?" Bianca says, fiddling with a small flashlight that I'm pretty sure is covered in Swarovski crystals.

I forgot how many questions kids have. Always wanting to know why the sky is blue and *is your red my red?* We asked a million, too, always deploying dumb thoughts to bug our counselors, to annoy them into submission. It worked on everyone except Meg, no surprise.

"It's the best time to see the stars. Bet you don't get skies like this back in Palm Beach."

The twins shrug and exchange a look. "Dad doesn't really let us out much at night," Bianca says.

Jordie nods. "He's totally *paranoid*," she says, putting a snotty accent on the final word. "That's what Mom always says."

"'Someone's always watching!'" Bianca laughs, clearly pretending to be her mom.

"Your dad thinks someone is watching you?"

Jordie shrugs. "Like I said. Paranoid."

"Why don't we catch up with the others?" I ask, realizing we're about twenty feet behind the rest of the cabin.

They sigh but speed up, following Meg up to the cliff. The terrain starts out flat and damp, getting colder as we duck under a canopy of trees. We're guided only by the beams of our flashlights. But soon the branches give way and the trail becomes an incline, so it feels like we're climbing a staircase to the sky. The moon is full and bright and the stars blink back at us. I click off my headlamp and whisper into Jordie's ear. "Turn off your light, pass it on." She looks at me with concerned eyes, but I nod eagerly, wanting to show them the magic of this place.

She whispers to the next girl in line, and soon all the flashlights are off and it's only us and the moon and the stars. The girls hush, enamored by the moment, and I sigh, letting my heartbeat steady.

"Wow," one girl whispers.

Meg keeps leading us forward, and soon the girls start talking again, their chatter dampened by the vastness, the awe. I'm comforted by the sounds of campers, by Kelly and her well-meaning probing, asking the new girls what sports they love and if they prefer Christina's chocolate chip or blueberry pancakes. By Fran, who everyone knows loves theater and wants to land a starring role in the camp musical even though those are reserved for older kids. I listen as they get to know each other and form inside jokes and point out how the stars look so much bigger and brighter here than they do at home in Philadelphia, in Boston, in Manhattan.

Ten minutes later, Meg stops and turns around, her face calm and smiling. "Here we are, girls. Creepy Cliff." She extends her hands above her head and motions toward the vista, a full blanket of stars just over the edge, falling into darkness. "And now . . . cookie patrol!"

Meg reaches into her backpack and pulls out an armful of personal bags of Oreos. The girls squeal and follow Meg to the campfire ring for a well-deserved snack break. I move to follow them, but then a branch snaps behind me. I swivel, expecting to find a rabbit or a raccoon. But there's nothing, silence.

I shake my head—it's probably an animal—and take a step toward Meg and the campers, but then I hear something else, a deep whimper, almost a sob. It lodges in my ears and makes me freeze. I spin around slowly, bracing for what I'll find. The brush is a few yards away so I can't make much out in the dark. I peer at it, waiting for something or *someone* to jump out. There are always older boys hiding in here, waiting to scare the little kids, initiate them into camp. But something about that noise. It wasn't playful or joyous. It sounded desperate. Like grief.

I stare at the brush and take a step closer. The branches shake again, rustling with deliberate movement. Right then, a pale arm emerges from the brush, a barbed wire tattoo circling a bicep.

Cal Drummond.

I stop. He shouldn't be here. He's not allowed. In one swift movement, he steps out from behind the brush and looks around, his eyes wild, on fire, almost like he's being chased. He doesn't see me, but after a split second he takes off in the opposite direction, running fast, his feet flying out beneath him. He's headed back to the forgotten horse trail Heller once showed me. The one that leads to Roxwood, away from Alpine Lake property.

My heart pounds hard. Cal's never even been to camp as far as I know. Why would he come here?

"Goldie!" Meg calls from the campfire. "Better come quick or Kelly's got dibs on your Oreos."

"Go for it, Kelly," I yell. "I have to pee!"

I hear the girls laugh, the crinkling of plastic packaging, and before I can think better, I tiptoe over to where Cal was hiding. I move the branches aside and step into the brush. I snap on my headlamp and shine it all around. There's nothing unusual, just sticks and leaves, the smell of pine and damp moss. The smell of nature, of life.

I squeeze my eyes shut, wondering if I imagined him here, if Heller's death is messing with me in strange ways. I will myself to go back to the group, to be a counselor, to do my job.

But when I swipe a branch aside, something hard crunches underfoot. Whatever I stepped on *isn't* nature. It's man-made. It doesn't belong here in the woods.

I step back and crouch low on my heels, pointing my headlamp down to see what's there.

When I do, I nearly lose my balance. Right in front of me is

Heller's face, set inside a piece of plastic. He's smiling and calm, his dark curly hair falling in a wave over his forehead. The photo must have been from the fall, before New Year's, before he cut his hair short like the other guys on the hockey team. He's looking out at me from a cracked ID badge, and even with the break line slashing through his face, he looks happy, beautiful. Alive.

I pick the thing up and hold it in my hands. I rub my thumb against it, wiping off some of the dirt, and shine the light against it again. There at the bottom of the badge it says ROXWOOD COUNTY CLERK'S OFFICE EMPLOYEE. I flip it over and there's a barcode and an electronic stripe. This must be what got him into work.

I stand up straight and clutch the badge. Heller died in the lake, nowhere near Creepy Cliff. But that means Cal dropped it here, right now. If he did that, why did he have it in the first place?

I turn the badge over in my palm, inspecting it against the glow of the night. My pulse pounds in my ears as I try to make sense of this.

Before I can decide what to do, I hear Meg's voice, cutting through the trees.

"What are you doing, taking a dump? We gotta get going!"

The girls giggle behind her and I shove the ID deep into the pocket of my sweatshirt.

"Coming!" I yell.

I push aside the leaves and make my way over to the girls, squeezing the plastic against my stomach.

"Everything okay?" Meg whispers, while the girls stuff Oreos in their faces.

"Yep," I say with a fake smile.

Meg ushers the cabin toward the clearing and I bring up the rear again, following the group out of the woods. I try to listen to their chatter, to follow along with their jokes. But I can't stop my mind from racing, from coming back to the obvious question:

Why was Cal here with Heller's ID?

CHAPTER 26

Then

Back when we were still friends, before puberty hit and our lives diverged, Cal always asked me to describe camp to him. Once, when we were nine, we were pumping our legs on the swings at the local park and he wanted to know why I liked swimming at camp rather than at the rocky town beach.

"There's sand over there," I said. "And lap lanes. And sailboats."

"And you can go in whenever you want?" he asked.

"Twice a day. Morning and afternoon."

Cal was quiet, thinking it over. "How come we can't use it?"

"I dunno. You gotta be a camper, I guess." It hadn't really occurred to me that I had access to something no one else in Roxwood really did.

"What are you doing this summer, anyway?" I asked.

"Connie usually figures something out by the time school ends." We didn't talk about his mom much, but it freaked me out that he called her by her first name, even at nine. He never said why. But he didn't tell me much about her at all.

"Maybe you can come to Alpine Lake," I said. "I can introduce you to Ava and Imogen and all my friends. You'd love it."

Cal perked up. "Really?"

"Ask your dad," I said.

I didn't think anything of the conversation that night, not after we jumped off the swing set and raced home. Not the whole next morning either. But when I saw Cal at recess the next day, he was sullen and quiet.

"What's wrong?" I asked.

"I can't believe you told me to ask my dad if I could go to camp." Cal toed the dirt, blinking fast.

"What do you mean?"

Cal stood up and turned his back. "It's for rich kids," he said. "Spoiled out-of-town brats who like to play country and leave their garbage on the trails. That's what my dad said."

"That's not true!" I yelled, curling my fists by my side. It couldn't be. That's not who my friends were.

"If it's so great, why do you think no one else from Roxwood goes there?" Cal asked. "Why are *you* the only one?"

I didn't have a response. All I knew was that I loved camp. I loved my friends.

"It's because you go for free," Cal said. "And no one else wants to spend time around people who make us feel like Roxwood trash."

That's when I lost it, pushing Cal into the dirt. He brushed himself off and lunged at me, but by that time a teacher stepped in the middle of us and sent us both to the principal's office.

We never spoke of it again, not after Cal gave me a peace offering—half of his turkey sandwich. But I never forgot the words he'd recited from his dad, *Roxwood trash.*

CHAPTER 27

Now

The sun bounces off the lake and I sway back and forth in my lifeguard seat on the dock. The air is breezy and I glance up. Clouds sail by, the sky a swath of blues and grays. I shiver and curse the fact that I didn't swim out here with a sweatshirt, like some of the other lifeguards did, fluttering their feet like kids with a kickboard as they held hoodies in the air so they wouldn't get wet.

I scan the waterfront and watch Levin in the head guard chair, his dark hair nearly blending into the lap lanes. Imogen's standing knee-deep in the shallow end wearing an oversize crew neck, focused intently on some of the younger kids scrambling on the rocks. Behind me, a boat whizzes by, dragging an inflatable tube, and I hear Ava's deep, gravelly laugh echoing across the lake. I straighten my shoulders and avoid the nagging feeling that I'm left behind, left out. How can that be true when I'm right here? I'm right in the middle of *everything*.

But I know I'm not. Because Ava and I have barely spoken since the kids arrived. It's easy to get swept up in the *camp* of it all. To not see someone for a day or two if your schedules aren't aligned, or if they're on homesick duty, taking care of weepy campers during rest hour. People forget being a counselor is a 24/7 job. It doesn't bend to your needs, or stop when you get tired. The only time we have "off" is sacred and bookmarked. It's all we look forward to—those two nights and one day a week where our time is ours again and we're free to collide and combust and explode in all different directions because we're finally given what we came here to find: freedom.

In a few hours, we'll have our first night off since the kids got here. It's all anyone could talk about at lunch, plans whispered in the dining room, shared on the soccer field or by Mom's wood-working shed. It's a thrill, the construction of it all. But those free periods, those exquisite hours of euphoria . . . that's also the time where you have to give yourself over to real life and remember that things outside this bubble exist. Things like *Heller McConnell is dead*. And *Cal was here—with Heller's ID badge*.

Maybe that's why I'm dreading a night off.

Levin blows his whistle three times, long and loud, a signal for everyone to get out of the lake, that the period is over. It's also our final swim session of the day, so I jump off the chair and shoo the kids away, back toward the beach. It only takes a few minutes before everyone is loaded onto yellow school buses, ready to be whisked back up to upper camp, a treat only the older kids get to enjoy. Smaller kids walk to build strength, Stu likes to say.

I climb on last and don't bother to take a seat for the quick ride. But as we go over the first speed bump, someone grabs my hand. I turn to see Ava in the seat behind me, her hair wet, hugging her skull. She pulls me down to sit on her lap. Imo's next to her and they both have devilish grins on their faces.

There's no hint that there's anything off between us, and something settles deep inside my core.

"Do we dare?" Imo asks.

Ava squeals and bounces me up and down. "We dare."

I hold my breath for a beat, waiting for what's to come. Imogen counts us down and on three we start singing the Camp Alpine Lake alma mater as loud as our voices can go.

> *Welcome all to Alpine Lake,*
> *Where our bonds shall never break!*
> *By the shore, the hills around,*
> *We make Stu and Mellie proud!*

Even Levin, who's standing at the front of the aisle, gets into it, busting out the next verse.

> *Climbing rocks and swimming laps,*
> *From reveille all the way to taps!*
> *Alpine Lake is full of friends,*
> *Who'll be with you till the end!*

Ava cracks up and hugs me closer to her. We pull into the traffic circle at upper camp but no one gets off. Howie, the ancient bus driver who's been here since the early 2000s, groans, but he knows how this works. We won't get off until he sings, too.

Finally, after we get to the last chorus, he clears his throat. Ava holds me tighter and laughs into my back.

> *Camp Alpine Lake!*
> *We love you oh so dear,*
> *And if you don't accept us,*
> *we'll kick you in the rear!*

He pauses for a second while the whole bus claps. Then the door opens with a loud hissing noise. "Now get out of here!"

Ava pushes me to stand and we rush off the bus and run to our cabins.

"That never gets old." Imogen tilts her face to the sun.

"I love us," Ava says.

"I do, too," I say, wondering how in the world I could ever think that anything was wrong.

Since it's Thursday, as per tradition, it's time to head to West Lake, the sake bomb spot outside town.

Meg senses my unease as I drag a dark pencil across my eyelid.

"Are you, Goldie Easton, in desperate need of a breather?" she asks, setting down a ratty old paperback.

The kids are changing for dinner, wringing out their towels from the clothesline and giggling at something that happened at rest hour. The prospect of staying here, with them and Meg, and the cuddles they dole out like candy . . . it's tempting. Mostly because I'm afraid of where my brain will go when they're not here to occupy it.

"I guess so," I say. "You know how these nights get." I glance at Meg and she's looking away, her usually cheerful face sallow. "You okay?" I ask. "Things still good with Levin?"

Meg turns to me and blinks a few times before smiling, wide and fake. "Oh yeah," she says. "Despite the whole *I found a dead body at my workplace* thing. Other than that, everything is great."

I flinch. The image of Heller, lifeless, soaked to the bone. It's too much. Too brutal.

"Sorry," she mumbles. "I know you two have history."

"That's okay," I say, a reflex. But I wonder how she knows that. The rumor mill must be working overtime.

"Has Levin said anything?" I can't help myself. I need to know. "About what it was like? Finding him?"

Meg shakes her head. "Nah," she says. "I keep telling him to call his therapist back home, but I think he wants to forget all about it."

I clear my throat. "Glad he has you to talk to."

"Mm-hmm." Meg leans her head against the wall and presses the palms of her hands into her eyes. She lets out a big, heavy sigh and her shoulders slump forward. I make a mental note to check in with her more, be a better co-counselor in the coming days. But then I hear Ava's call from outside the cabin.

"Oy oy oy!" she yells, her hand cupped around her mouth.

I lean out the window and return the call. "Ah-oooga!" Imogen does the same from her cabin and Ava dances in a circle, causing her campers to laugh with big, moony eyes.

"I wish I had those kinds of friendships," Meg says, coming back to herself. She stretches out in her bed.

"What kind?" I ask.

She looks at me like I'm dumb. "The kind that can't be broken," she says. "You three. The weirdest trio. If I saw you girls now, I'd never put you together as a unit. It's like you grew up and out, away from each other, but refused to let each other go. See that a lot here."

"Are you close with anyone from growing up?" I ask, realizing I barely know anything about Meg's life in the UK.

"Nope," she says. "I never want to go back there. That's why I came here."

I want to press her more, but Ava calls again and I know I need to leave. I give myself one last look in the mirror. If I squint hard enough, I can see who I was when I last lived in Bloodroot, when I was so young and when the most important thing in the world was being as close to Ava and Imogen as possible. Maybe that still *is* the most important thing.

"Gotta go," I say, giving Meg a wave.

"I have no interest in living here alone for the next seven weeks if you get fired, so please don't do anything stupid," she says.

"I'll try!"

When I get outside the cabin, Ava's standing with Imogen, teetering on sky-high heels. Both of them are wearing denim skirts, their thighs exposed like slabs of meat.

I tug at the bottom of my lacy tank top, suddenly self-conscious, until Imogen looks at me with those wide, sparkling eyes. "You look amazing. Come on."

She leads us to the bus, where Howie sits in the front seat doing a crossword puzzle. All the other underagers line up, waiting to climb on. The air smells of musky department store cologne and vanilla body wash, and there are murmurs of excitement, hope, and debauchery.

"I cannot believe we've been here two weeks and we haven't been to West Lake yet," Tommy says. He bounces on the soles of his flip-flops and I wonder for the millionth time what Imogen sees in him.

We board the bus, and I look out the window as we pull out of the traffic circle, away from camp. I push down the sinking feeling in my stomach and turn back to Ava, who's deep in thought and uncharacteristically quiet.

A frown is plastered on her face, and for a split second I think of seeing Cal the other night in the woods, the ID badge crunching underfoot.

Ava looks up at me then and her face brightens. A smile appears. "Sake bombs on me, okay?" she says.

I nod and rest my head on her shoulder, pushing Cal and Heller from my mind.

Soon we get to Main Street and the bus driver keeps going until he gets to the very edge of town. From here some of the group splits off and heads to the bowling alley, but the majority of us prance down the street for another ten minutes until we arrive at West Lake.

It's a dumpy, short building that used to be a souvlaki place. But West Lake became notorious among the Alpine Lake crowd soon after it opened. We heard stories about it when we were campers, when the counselors would come back drunk and silly, their tongues dyed blue from boozy tropical punches that were served with paper umbrellas. We would stay up late so we could listen to them barge through the cabin doors, giggling and hiccupping as they tried not to vomit. Ava, Imogen, and I would huddle close together, hoping they wouldn't notice we were all in the same bed— they never did—and cup our hands over our mouths so we could overhear what the counselors were up to.

It was a game we played, finding out who was hooking up with who, who was fighting, and who would remain friends come September. We studied the counselors, hoping they would give us clues about our futures. *Do things get easier when you grow up?*

But that's how I came to know the phrase *sake bomb* and that West Lake is owned by a white lady named Lisa and that one year, some volleyball counselor hooked up with a waiter in the bathroom. When I was eleven, once fall came around, I asked Mom if we could go there one night for dinner. I wanted to see what all the fuss was about.

She and Dad burst out laughing. When they saw my confused expression, they patiently explained that the food at West Lake was absolute trash and, honestly, an abomination to all Japanese food, a claim Imogen backed up when she tried their limp hand rolls last year.

I kept passing by West Lake during the winter months, waiting for it to turn into something magical. But it was always *there* with its dingy neon sign and a fogged-up window decorated with paper cutouts of stars.

And yet . . . it was still an oasis for Alpine Lake counselors on our nights off.

Tonight, walking into West Lake is like walking into prom. There's a sign on the door that says CLOSED FOR PRIVATE PARTY. The overhead bulbs are off, but string lights hang from the walls and a disco ball is suspended from the ceiling, reflecting light all over the room. Five round tables, each with ten banquet chairs, are set up throughout the space. The room smells like rubbing alcohol and beer.

I roll my shoulders back and feel a calm settle over me. It's just us. Just the counselors.

Ava grabs our hands and leads us to a table in the middle of the room with Aaron Jacobson and his two buddies Craig Rosen and James Wood. They're a year older than us, all known for being perfect gentleman in the middle of their Ivy League careers. Craig, the one with sandy hair and kind eyes, was my first kiss back when

I was twelve. It happened at the DJ social that year, and the day after, he sent me a Charleston Chew from his canteen haul. The next week, he told me he thought he was gay and asked me not to tell while he figured it out. He came out to everyone last year, though, right here at West Lake. Stood up on a chair and announced it to the whole room. Aaron and James, his best friends since forever, sprayed him down with champagne and carried him around the room like he was a prince.

"These seats taken?" Ava asks.

"Oh hell yeah, now the party's here!" James says, rubbing his hands together. Ava drops her purse into a chair, then walks right over to Lisa. She gives her a hug and hands her a shiny black credit card. "Those two over there," she says, pointing to Imogen and me. "Whatever they want, okay?"

"You got it, darling," Lisa says with a wink. Then she clinks a fork against her glass and clears her throat. "You know the drill," she says, loud and long. "Twenty bucks gets each of you four rolls, a side of tempura, edamame, and a round of sake bombs. Everything else you pay à la carte. Capisce?"

"Capisce!" we all yell. Imogen nearly bounces out of her seat.

I tried to tell Heller about this place once, back in the fall, but he didn't believe me. Lisa never let any of the kids in Roxwood come here. She thought it was too dangerous, that they would spill the beans and get her liquor license revoked. They never got to take advantage of the Alpine Lake special.

By the time Ava's back in her chair, we each have a shot of sake and a pint of cold beer in front of us. Craig clears his throat and climbs up onto his chair, one drink in each hand.

He's wearing a loose white T-shirt and crisp jeans, his face tan from working on the baseball field. I try not to ogle his biceps when he holds his arms up in the air.

"There are good ships and wood ships," he says loudly, his voice echoing throughout the room. "Ships that sail the sea . . ." Then he pauses and sticks his neck out like he's waiting for everyone else to join in.

James groans but stands on his chair, too.

"Isn't it time to drink?" Aaron shouts, which makes everyone laugh. But it's tradition. Soon we're all standing, either on our seats or on the floor, ready to scream the words as loud as we can.

"But the best ships are friendships, may they always be!"

"Bombs away!" Craig says.

I drop the shot into my beer and bring the glass to my lips, sipping and then chugging. I close my eyes and fight the burn in my throat. Imogen grips my arm and we both urge each other to keep going. Ava finishes first and wipes her arm across her mouth. "Another round?"

That's all it takes for the party to explode. Someone hooks their phone up to the stereo and presses play on an old Spice Girls song, and the back of the restaurant becomes a dance floor. Lisa brings us bright blue drinks with orange slices and winks as we grab them and head toward the music.

Ava shakes her hair out so it falls in waves, and I swing my hips a bit, sipping my punch through a neon straw. I look around, at these people I've known forever, and wonder how we all ended up here at this crappy restaurant on the outskirts of this crappy town. But there's no time to think too hard because soon we're surrounded, swallowed up by the yelps and the hooting and the glow sticks that seem to appear out of thin air.

Tommy pulls up behind Imogen and begins grinding on her like we're at a club. Imogen spins around and presses her mouth to his, all tongue. She balls his shirt in her fist and it takes all my willpower to not twist my face up in disgust.

Ava throws her head back and laughs, resting one manicured hand on my shoulder. "This girl, I cannot," she says, waving in Imogen's direction. Imo holds one middle finger up at us while still sucking face.

I crack up and hold on to Ava's wrist, trying to stay upright. She leans into me and laughs, too. I try to look at her clearly then, and when the light hits her she's an angel, a mermaid, a goddess. Affection bubbles up in my throat, and Ava must sense it because she pulls me to her.

"I love you, Goldie girl," she says. "No matter what, I love you. I love you. I love you."

"I love you, too," I whisper, meaning it more than I've ever meant anything in my whole life.

I spend the next hour alternating between dancing in the middle of the dark room and wolfing down terrible avocado cucumber rolls—no one dares eat the fish—and laughing as Imogen yells at us to "line your stomachs, ladies!" At some point the front windows begin to fog up from all the fun, the sweat, the *belonging* that is happening in here and I start to think we're not in Roxwood anymore. We're in New York or California or Aruba. Anywhere but here.

Craig lifts me up from my middle and spins me around. "I'm gonna get some air," he shouts. "Come with?"

I follow him out into the night and am greeted with a breeze, cool against my neck, damp with sweat. Craig motions for me to follow him to the alley and he pulls out a vape, inhaling from it and then coughing.

He passes it to me and I do the same.

Craig looks at me and starts laughing. "Man, I can't believe we're here," he says, shaking his head. "It's like you wait ten months to get back to this place and then once you're here you spend the whole time trying to remember every second, make time slow down. You know?"

I nod. "Your friends at home must get it, right?" Craig's from the North Shore of Long Island, where it's basically law that you attend some sort of sleepaway camp. I imagine his friends at Yale are the same way.

Craig shrugs. "Yeah, but I'm the only one who *still* goes."

"What does everyone else do?"

"I don't know, get fancy internships or some shit. Seems like half my dorm got gigs on Capitol Hill."

"Huh," I say, trying to picture what that would be like. "But you'll come back next year, right?"

Craig flashes me a small smile and takes another hit of his vape. "I wish," he says. "My parents said this has to be my last summer here. Tryna make the most of it."

"The pay too shitty?" Even with room, board, and meals covered, we barely make minimum wage at Alpine Lake, though none of the lifers seem to mind.

Craig shrugs. "Gotta move on. Do something real. Flesh out that résumé."

A lump forms in my throat. I've watched so many older kids graduate out of here, finish their eight summers as campers, work through their junior counselor year, become a regular counselor and then . . . yeah, I guess not many stick around after they get to college. After life becomes more complicated than midnight raids, ice cream sundae bars, and skinny-dipping in the lake. When climbing a corporate ladder seems appealing. Necessary.

Suddenly it dawns on me: I am going to be the only one left.

As if Craig reads my mind, he cups my chin with his warm hand. "Hey," he says. "Don't think about that right now, okay? Days here last weeks. Weeks last months. Right? That's what we say."

He starts to go on about how we need to live in the now, but all of a sudden, I can't focus because something taped to the corkboard on the side of the building catches my eye.

"Let's get back in there, yeah?" Craig says.

"You go ahead," I say, trying to find my breath. "I need a little more air."

Craig ruffles my hair and throws back the door. When it swings shut, I reach out and touch Heller.

A picture of him. Printed in black and white. It's his school photo. The one where his hair falls over his left eye and his smile is a bit crooked. It's tacked right next to some other flyers advertising babysitters and guitar lessons.

But when I look closer, I see the photo is a clipping from the local paper, the *Roxwood Read*, which is mostly known for writing about whatever news is coming out of Town Hall and how to renew your fishing license.

And there, on the front page, is Heller McConnell's face.

I pull the clipping down and try to read it, but the letters dance in my head, foggy from the booze. I squeeze my eyes shut, and when I open them, I can finally make out the headline.

SUSPICION LINGERS IN
HELLER MCCONNELL'S DEATH
AS FAMILY TRIES TO MOVE ON

The air starts to spin around me.

I want to read the whole thing but Imogen calls my name from the door. "Come on, Goldie!" she says. "Ava's threatening to do a stage dive from the table if you don't get back in here."

I rip the article from the board and stuff it in my pocket, vowing to read the whole thing later, when I'm alone.

But as I head back inside, all the air wooshes out of my lungs.

Heller's death wasn't an accident.

CHAPTER 28

Then

I found out Heller was cheating on me right around Thanksgiving. The Wednesday before.

We had a half day at school and a group of Heller's friends had gathered at his hut in the woods before heading to Truly's to see all the kids who had graduated the year before.

I was sitting in between Ruthie Dollinger and Trina Smith, two basketball players who had been orbiting Heller and his friends since middle school. They had gone through periods of being mean to me, tripping me in gym and pointing out whenever I bled through my jeans. But since I was with Heller, they wanted to hang out, as if I had always been one of them.

Ruthie passed me a warm beer from the cardboard box in front of her and pushed her short dark hair away from her eyes. "Scale from one to ten, what are my odds with Peter Spiers tonight?"

Trina covered her face with her hand. "Didn't he get fired from Frank's Auto for being hungover? You really want to hit that?"

Ruthie shrugged and motioned to Heller, Cal, and the rest of the boys huddled around the TV, playing video games. "Better than this shit."

Trina nodded. "Fair."

I wanted to nod, too, but I couldn't. My allegiance to those boys was the only reason I was there, quietly listening to all the ways Ruthie wanted to fuck a washed-up football player whose claim to fame was setting off the sprinklers on his last day of school.

"Heller's the only good one," Ruthie said, lolling her head back before turning to me. "But if I were you, I'd probably confront him about the whole Sally Burke thing."

My throat went sandy and I glanced over at Heller, oblivious in his gamed-out bliss. I knew I could either play along and act like I knew what she was talking about, or make a fool of myself by not knowing. But it wasn't my choice to make. My face gave me away.

"Oh shit. You don't know?" Ruthie asked, leaning forward. She looked pleased.

Trina whistled and wiggled her eyebrows. "You gotta tell her now," she said. "Literally everyone knows."

But Ruthie didn't need convincing. "Going out for a smoke!" she called, and motioned for Trina and me to follow her outside.

She sat on a stump a few feet away from the hut and started talking. "Sorry to burst your bubble, Goldie, but your man is a lying cheat, just like every other dude."

I didn't know what to say so I dragged my foot against the ground. There was no way this could be true.

"You know how he has that gig at the County Clerk's Office?" Ruthie said. "Well, he stays there late all the time, which I'm sure you're aware of since you guys are, like, *dating*."

The word was dipped in acid but she was right. Heller spent *so* much time there, padding his résumé and helping out. He said he liked how it smelled like a library and that the papers were always yellowed around the edges. It made him feel like he was a part of something bigger than himself. He loved that Roxwood had history and he wanted to know it all.

"Well, *apparently* there's a secretary named Sally Burke who's like twenty-three and I heard she's been trying to *seduce* him after hours. That's why he stays there so late."

I looked back into the cabin through the window at Heller, his eyes small and crinkled as he threw his head back laughing. My face flushed but I tried to tilt my chin up to make it seem like I didn't care.

Trina clucked her tongue and shook her head. "We all get fucked sometimes, Goldie," she said. "Make sure you get tested for STIs." She shivered. "Who *knows* what that woman has."

I should have confronted Heller right then and asked him if it was true. I should have done so many things. But instead, I stayed silent. I went to Truly's with them. I sat perched on a barstool sipping whiskey Diet Cokes and laughed at their awful jokes and smiled when Heller slipped his arm around me.

I let Ruthie and Trina think I was weak and spineless for not standing up for myself. But in the end, that's exactly what I was.

CHAPTER 29

Now

Bloodroot is alive with the sounds of excited girls, the smell of burnt hair sliding through flat irons, and the promise of possibilities. The first DJ social of the year puts everyone in camp on edge. Back when we were campers, we would bring outfits specifically to wear on these nights. Short skirts and tank tops. Cotton minidresses and palettes of glittery eyeshadow we only brought out for the two dances and banquet—the most special of them all.

I usually discarded what I had brought and opted to wear something from Ava's or Imogen's closets. Something that fit a bit better and was pressed clean. Something that sparkled under the neon lights and made heads turn when I walked into the Lodge.

As a counselor, though, you don't dress up. You put on shapeless sweatpants and oversize T-shirts and act as chaperones, egging on the campers and their innocent fun.

Still, I can't help looking at these girls getting ready in the cabin and feeling like my heart's going to beat out of my chest. The anticipation, it's contagious. And it's distracting me from thinking about Heller.

"Goldie, will you give me a braid crown?" Jordie asks.

"You know it," I say from inside the counselor room. I flip open my box of hair ties, but before I can shut it, I see the newspaper clipping I pulled down from West Lake. The one that speculated about Heller. I've been avoiding reading it, as if knowing more about his death will make it even more real. But now I open the paper gently, laying it flat on my dresser. I hold my breath and start to read.

SUSPICION LINGERS IN
HELLER MCCONNELL'S DEATH
AS FAMILY TRIES TO MOVE ON

While Heller McConnell's official cause of death was "accidental drowning," according to the medical examiner's office, some of his friends have expressed doubt about the circumstances surrounding the beloved young hockey star's passing.

"Heller was as strong as they come in the water," said Cal Drummond, the deceased's longtime friend. "He was practically born on the lake. It doesn't add up."

A toxicology report confirmed that the eighteen-year-old was drinking before his death, but his blood alcohol level was below the legal limit. "Even if he was under the influence, that boy could swim faster than anyone in this town," said Ruthie Dollinger, a classmate since preschool. "Hell, I've seen him swim a mile piss-drunk in the winter."

Other folks are skeptical about the cause of death because of where he was found—inside the bounds of Camp Alpine Lake's waterfront, according to Ray Levin, 24, the head lifeguard at the nearby sleepaway camp. Levin told police, "He was lying in the water facedown, his clothes tangled in the lap lanes. I found him at 5:30 a.m. with no pulse. It was the worst thing I've ever seen."

Camp Alpine Lake has had a complicated history with Roxwood over the past decade. A driver to the town's economy, the camp has become something of a lightning rod in recent years.

"All the folks associated with that place act like they're better than us," said Rick Drummond, a cook at Keene's Diner. "The directors don't even tip when they come in."

But the McConnell family insists that their son's death was an accident and that Camp Alpine Lake has been extremely cooperative, even offering to pay for his funeral and burial. "Roxwood's a safe town," his father, Judah McConnell, said. "This is devastating. But there's no foul play here."

"It's a tragedy," said Dylan Adler, 18, the former captain of the Roxwood High School hockey team. Adler sustained serious injuries after a car accident where McConnell was in the passenger seat but said McConnell was "a real support" throughout the year. "He always said I'd play hockey again," Adler said. "I'll spend the rest of my life trying, like he tried to help me through my recovery."

I turn the clipping over, unable to read any more.

"Goldie?" Jordie calls.

"One second." I press the heels of my palms against my eyes, trying to regain my composure. How could Heller's family not want to investigate his death? I'll never understand it. But I hate what Cal's insinuating—that something messed up is going on *here* at Alpine Lake. Is that why he was here with Heller's ID? I brush back my hair and shake my head, knowing nothing I can think or say right now will solve this.

I make my way into the camper room, over to Jordie's bed. "Finally," she mumbles as she sits between my legs. She leans back so her honey-blonde hair falls into my lap. It's thick and shiny like Ava's. *Focus on the girls, not on Heller.*

I separate Jordie's hair into a few sections and start to twist it into ropes and weave it over her scalp. Bianca sits cross-legged on her bed next to us, a book in her lap.

"You want one, too?" I ask, but she shakes her head without looking up.

"Where'd you learn how to do this?" Jordie asks.

"Ava taught me one summer," I say.

Jordie's quiet and I wonder if that was a mistake, if I should never have brought Ava up at all. But then she speaks. "Ava's good at hair."

"She's the best at it," I say, but I wonder how she knows that.

Bianca picks at her nails next to us and taps her foot in front of her, unable to sit still. None of the other girls come over to ask the twins what they're going to wear or if they can borrow eyeshadow. The two of them are alone in this corner of the cabin, a bag of Twizzlers between them. I peek around at their area and spot a photo of them with their parents, a perfect-looking family. I flinch looking at Ava's dad, Mark. Sucks how one guy can be a scumbag to one kid and a great dad to two others.

You're not supposed to bring up the kids' parents. Mellie says it makes them homesick and it's better to let them mention them first. But I can't help myself.

"Have you gotten lots of letters from your mom and dad?" I ask.

Bianca looks up. "Yes!" she says. She reaches down to the plastic box beneath her bed and retrieves a stack of envelopes.

"Mom sends us so many boring letters," Jordie says. "All about her golf games." She rolls her eyes.

"Dad's are way better," Bianca says. "Like this one." She opens a card and begins to read. "Dearest daughters, How I miss you! I wish I could have taken you with me on my most recent trip to New York. I ate all those macarons you love from that bakery in SoHo and will send some to you soon. We'll go together after camp."

Bianca closes the card and smiles, dragging a finger over the pretty flowers on its front. "Dad's the best."

I nod in agreement but something gnaws at my insides. *My most recent trip to New York.*

According to Ava, her dad's *never* in New York. Not even for her graduation.

"Hellooo," Jordie says. "Earth to Goldie! Are you done yet?"

"Sorry," I say, taking stock of my work on her head. "There. Perfect."

As soon as we enter the Lodge, I'm greeted by a wave of drugstore body spray and the sounds of bad electronic music pounding from the speakers set up at the front of the stage. All the sofas that are usually in here for movie nights and camp plays are pushed toward the back, where the counselors drape their bodies over them like scarves.

"Goldie!" Imogen calls from the couches.

I head over to her and flop down in the empty seat, our legs intertwined.

"Man, remember how obsessed we were with these things?" she asks, surveying the kids as they gear up for a round of freeze dance.

Imogen giggles so hard she snorts and I swivel my head.

"Oh my god, Imo, you didn't."

She starts laughing again, until she has to put her head between her knees to stop. "It's . . ." She laughs. "Your head is enormous."

I tilt my head back toward Tommy, who's sitting a row behind us. "Gummies?" I ask.

He nods, having his own laughing fit. "James picked them up at the dispensary. Want in?" Tommy opens his palm to reveal a piece of candy that looks like a watermelon slice. "It's a baby one, you should be fine."

Why not? Another distraction from the *Roxwood Read* article can't hurt. I take it and stuff it in my mouth in time for Imo to nuzzle her head toward me. "Oh man, your sweatshirt is so soft."

I swat at her cheek and turn to Ava. "You, too?" I ask, nudging her shoulder.

Ava wrinkles her nose and shakes her head. "You know THC messes with my stomach. I prefer my own form of recreational medication." She shoves her water bottle under my nose and I'm assaulted by the smell of vodka.

"Geezus, at least cut it with something."

Ava laughs and takes a sip before wincing. "Definitely would have been a good idea."

We spend the next hour laughing at the kids who are either on one of two levels: grinding like there's no tomorrow or glued to the wall, looking bored or terrified.

Tommy bounds over to the DJ stand and grabs a bunch of glow sticks that are definitely reserved for the kids, and we all start to assemble them into bracelets and crowns, until we look like motivators at a tristate bar mitzvah. It takes a little while for the gummy to kick in but pretty soon I'm lost in my own giggle fit, blowing raspberries on Imo's back and trying to remember if my mouth was this dry an hour before.

The social winds down and Meg comes up to us, shouldering her backpack. "Ready?" she asks. But as soon as I break into giggles, her face falls, a frown forming on her lips. "Oh no. Not you, too?"

I nod. "Oops." Imogen cracks up next to me.

"It's like a freaking circus in here these days."

"I'm sorry!" But I hinge at my waist, laughing between my legs.

Meg sighs like she doesn't have time to deal with this mess and then she points to Imo and me. "You two, get your shit together and come back in a few, okay?"

We both nod, grasping each other in a fit.

"You owe me," she says. "Levin's taking me to dinner on our night off and I'm totally leaving you with the kids until sunrise!"

"Anything for you, Meg!" I say.

She shakes her head and mutters under her breath, "Dummies." Meg starts herding the girls, hyper with that after-social glow, out the door and back to the cabins.

"Ooh, let's go raid the cookie patrol shed," Imogen says, holding both my wrists.

Suddenly I'm famished and that sounds like the best idea

in the world. We grab Ava and stumble up the hill toward the small red building, which is used to house industrial-size boxes of individually wrapped bags of snacks like Kit Kats and Goldfish. Lorna Doones, too, but everyone knows those are the worst.

When we reach the shed Ava twirls around, tossing her water bottle high over her head, trying to reach the stars. She's singing something but I can't make out the words.

"Ava, you keep watch, okay?" Imo says, even though we both know we'd never get in trouble for taking from cookie patrol. The special events team gives the code to lifeguards on an honor system, but when you're a camper, coming into this shed was like being given a golden key.

Ava nods and continues sipping her water bottle. "Grab me some Swedish Fish, okay?"

Imogen keys in the code, pushes the door open gently, and steps inside. She turns around and presses a finger to her lips in a shushing motion before breaking into another fit of giggles.

My stomach hurts from laughing but I double over, too, steadying myself against a stack of cardboard boxes stuffed with bags of salt and vinegar chips.

"Okay, what do you want?" Imogen asks. We're both staring at mountains of snacks and every single one looks inviting. I weigh my options, sweet versus salty, crunchy versus chewy, and Imogen starts jumping up and down. "Come on, already!"

"Fine, fine. Wheat Thins," I finally say.

"Excellent choice." She grabs a handful of baggies.

"And a Nutella packet," I say. "Lethal combo."

"Ooh, I like your style," Imo says. She scans the rows. "Alas.

No Swedish Fish. Wanna ask her what else she wants? Sour Patch Kids or Haribo or something?"

I tiptoe back toward the door and peek outside, but Ava's gone. I push it all the way open and stand on the grass, the warm night enveloping me like a blanket.

I look around, searching for Ava and her shock of blonde hair stark against the night. But she's nowhere.

Until I turn toward the office, where I see a splash of hair peeking out from under her hoodie. She's hunched over, sitting on the bench, and she's not alone.

She's talking to someone, a short man with a baseball cap and a striped senior staff shirt. Obviously Stu. He's fiddling with the buckle on his fanny pack, where he keeps his extra diabetes stuff, which is odd. He only plays with it when he's nervous.

I'm about to call out to them, but something stops me. It's the weird look on Stu's face. I've only seen it once before. And it tells me everything I need to know.

Stu is stretching his neck upward like he's frustrated and Ava's starting to curl in on herself, meek and small.

For a second, I wonder if they caught her drinking. But even though that's a major no-no, Stu and Mellie are keen to overlook it. *Kids being kids.* Especially if your dad gives as much money to the camp as Mark Cantor does.

I take a step forward, trying not to make any sounds. I want to hear what they're saying.

Ava's voice floats above the trees. "What do you mean?" she asks.

Stu's voice is muffled but I can make out a few words. "Your father . . ."

He stops and rubs his forehead with his thumb and forefinger. "You know how important this is."

Ava's quiet, but even from here I can see the weird, pained look on her face. But before either one of them can say anything else, a loud tumbling sound comes from behind me. I turn around to find Imogen on the floor of the shed buried under a mountain of mini-M&M's packages.

"Help," she squeaks before laughing again. I grab her hand and pull her to stand, plucking a Starburst out of her hair.

Ava glances our way and starts up the hill. She doesn't say anything when she reaches us, and when Imogen hands her a package of Sour Patch Kids, she tucks it into her pocket. "Thanks."

CHAPTER 30

Then

My punishment was simple: Since I was already eighteen, I would be placed on probation, ordered to pay a fine of $1,500, which I dug out of my haunted house savings, and would participate in weekly community service under Stu and Mellie's supervision. Mellie said I avoided three years of jail time, the maximum sentence for grossly negligent operation of a vehicle, because the police chief owed them a favor after camp helped fund their new fleet of trainees with lucrative security contracts.

After all the paperwork was signed, Stu gave me the code to the all-year cabin at camp. They said I could spend my afternoons there, doing odd jobs.

My little office was in the small off-limits building on the border of camp property. It was short and made of logs, with only one bedroom. But it was an oasis where Mellie and Stu stayed when they visited camp in the winter and where special VIP guests lived in the summer since it had central heating and air conditioning. It was decorated with chunky knit blankets and professional photographs of European cities where Mellie and Stu liked to vacation.

I'd been there before when they invited us over for brunches and dinners during the school year, which made me feel special. It was one part of Alpine Lake I knew better than any other lifer.

Being invited into the cabin meant I had a place to go that *wasn't* Roxwood High. Instead of subjecting myself to eight hours a day of torture, I spent lazy afternoons grading would-be campers' admissions tests and answering emails from uptight parents while snuggled up on the overstuffed couch, hiding beneath the fancy blankets embroidered with the Alpine Lake logo. When I had spare time, which was often, I dusted their bookshelves, swept the hardwood floors, and took long, lonely walks around camp, down to the waterfront, over to the soccer field, up and around the empty horse stables. I reacquainted myself with the place that made me feel most at home.

But I also stopped going to school, stopped studying, stopped practicing for my lifeguarding test. I failed three classes, and even though I had been accepted to University of Vermont, they rescinded their offer when they found out about the accident and my "change in behavior," as they called it.

I had buried myself in an alternative reality, turning daytime cable up on high, imagining in the darkest moments what it would be like to live like Stu and Mellie, near Roxwood but never in it.

I had made peace with the fact that I was tossed out of a world I never really wanted to be in in the first place.

CHAPTER 31

Now

The kids are decked out in their brightest reds, whites, and blues, and the special events counselors must have spent all night hanging the Fourth of July–themed pennants from every building at camp. Everything is festive, shouting out *don't you love America?!*

"Fourth of July is fucking weird," Imogen says. Afternoon swim is canceled today to make room for the annual relay races and hot dog eating contests, so we're sitting in lawn chairs sucking on watermelon slices, watching our girls tie themselves to each other with bandanas and hobble down the field for a three-legged race.

"It's like, why are we celebrating the fact that our country was built on racism, elitism, and colonialism?" Imogen shakes her head and tosses her rind in the garbage next to her.

"God bless this bullshit," I mutter.

Even with all the bizarre patriotic crap, I always love this time of year. It's a few weeks into session, when everyone has fallen into a rhythm. Friendships have solidified. The competitive kids have found their tennis partners. The dorky kids have figured out that Mom's woodworking shed will accept them no matter what. And the counselors who are desperate for a fling have paired off, zeroing in on the places around camp where muffled moans can't be heard.

Imogen leans back in her Adirondack chair so her face is next to mine. "Tommy and I were thinking about heading behind the stables after fireworks tonight. Can you cover with Meg for me?"

I snort. "Obviously."

She smiles. "I'm pretty sure we're gonna have sex this time." Some kid at the lemonade cooler turns around, her eyes narrowed with curiosity.

I smack Imo on the shoulder. "Shh!"

She holds a hand over her mouth. "Sorry." Then we both break out in laughter.

"What's so funny?" the kid asks.

"Imogen farted."

Imogen smacks *me* this time but the kid giggles. "That is funny."

I throw Imo a side look like *see*. She laughs even harder. Tommy glances at Imo from across the relay race and sticks out his tongue, wiggling it like a snake.

"Oh my god, I'm gonna barf." I pretend to heave over the side of a chair, and the motion makes Heller's ID badge press into my stomach. I never took it out of my sweatshirt pocket.

Imogen covers her face with her hands and starts kicking her legs out in front of her. "Stop, I'm dying!" she says through laughter.

Ava plunks down in her seat and lets out a sigh. "Were we this awful when we were Ramblers?" she asks, wiping sweat from her forehead. "Because if I have to comfort one more kid who's worried—not about missing her parents, mind you!—about the stupid friendship dynamics of being nine years old, I'm seriously going to scream." She reaches for my lemonade and takes a sip. "I seem to have missed the memo that we'd actually have to take care of kids this year. These little brats . . ."

But Ava trails off as Mellie walks by, smiling wide at the three of us. Like nothing happened last night. Like Stu *didn't* say something weird about Ava's dad. But something must pass between them because for once, Ava looks a bit unnerved.

"'These little brats' what?" Imogen asks.

"What?" Ava says.

"You said . . ."

Ava waves her hand. "Whatever, all I know is we definitely didn't fight about silly shit like they do. Can't they be grateful they're here at all?"

I want to remind her that we *did* fight. Viciously. With words that singed our skin and left scars so permanent I feel them in my sleep. But Imogen shrugs and smiles wide at Tommy, who's still making googly eyes at her from across the race.

Ava's twin sisters walk by wearing matching jean shorts and white shirts with red stars on them. They both have red bandanas tied around their ponytails, red laces in their white sneakers. They look happy, skipping and holding slices of watermelon. I'd love to see them branch out and make friends with the other girls in the cabin. Caroline maybe, who thinks it's cool they live in Florida because her grandpa is in Boca Raton. But I know there's no use forcing friendships here. The girls will revolt and end up hating each other instead.

I smile at them but Ava practically snarls in their direction. I say a silent prayer that they don't notice. They know to keep their distance from their older half sister.

Ava shudders. "Don't they know wearing matching outfits is for *babies*?"

I want to remind her that they *are* babies, and plus, we were obsessed with matching when we were that age. We always had three-way phone calls before camp to make sure we would be in sync when it came to things like the annual Hoedown Fourth of July. Red tees and denim shorts. Matching glitter to press onto the apples of our cheeks. But when I open my mouth, Imogen throws me a look and I give up, knowing when the twins are involved it's best not to say anything at all.

The whole camp gathers for the Fourth of July barbecue on the main lawn, and the air smells of charcoal and grill smoke. Big long tables are lined with burgers, hot dogs, and vats of slaw. Over by the dining hall, Christina sets up an ice cream sundae bar that seemed to stretch a mile long when I was little. Soon, when the kids are stuffed and sleepy, we'll lead them to the massive soccer field, the farthest, most remote area of camp, for a fireworks display. Heller told me once that the Alpine Lake show is *way* more impressive than the one put on by the Town Council, so everyone in Roxwood would drive their trucks to the Applebee Grocer parking lot, which is on a hill and has a great view of camp. There, they spread out blankets and lawn chairs on the gravel so they can watch the fireworks explode into the sky.

But when you're here at Alpine Lake you're not thinking about things like grocery stores and parking lots. You're thinking about how Fourth of July is one of the most important nights of the summer. It's one of the only all-camp events where you don't have to sit by cabin or by group. You can choose where you sit and more importantly—who you sit with. You understand deeply that if someone's arm slinks around yours, the rest of your summer might be completely and totally altered.

"Time to round up the troops," Meg says.

We make no movement to get up.

"Oi," Meg says, crossing her arms. "Gonna make me say it twice?"

There's an edge in her voice that causes me to wince.

"You okay?" I ask.

Meg blinks twice like she's trying to make out what I said. Then her smile's back, her eyes sunny. "Of course," she says before making shooing motions at Ava, Imogen, and me. "Just get 'em loaded up with ice cream and then send them to the soccer fields."

We heave ourselves out of the chairs as Meg walks away.

"Geez, what's up with her?" Imogen asks.

"No idea," I say. I brush off her weird vibes and head over to the Bloodroot girls, huddled around a picnic table covered in paper plates, cherry pie stains, and half-eaten hot dogs. They hold hands and skip their way to the ice cream line, jumping and overjoyed with the possibility of something *new*, something *exciting*. I smile when I see Jordie and Bianca nestled in the middle of the group, their matching bandanas visible from my spot behind them.

But then I hear a rumble coming from the driveway near the gazebo. I turn to see a big white truck with the words GUS'S FIRE-WORKS printed on the side. It comes to a stop and a bunch of people pile out of the side door. I peer at the group and try to make out familiar faces, to see who got summer jobs playing with explosives. It was a popular gig for stoners and athletes, kids who carried around Zippo lighters.

The front door of the van opens and Cal Drummond steps down, turning to face camp. His eyes are narrowed and a scowl is pasted on his face. I grip Heller's ID badge in my pocket, feeling the plastic dig into my skin.

"Boo," Imogen says, coming up behind me and wiggling her fingers around my ear.

I jump, nearly hitting her in the face.

"Oh my god, did that actually scare you? You *have* to start watching horror movies. What if I become a final girl when I get to Hollywood?"

I laugh nervously but keep my gaze on the Cal, who is now unloading all the gear onto a golf cart to take down to the soccer fields.

The girls in my cabin fill their bowls with various flavors and toppings. Right behind them, Cal hops on the back of the golf cart and whizzes down to the field, but not before looking over his shoulder, right at me. He lifts one eyebrow in acknowledgment but then turns away.

Suddenly I want to rush to him and push him off the golf cart. I want to throw him to the ground and scream. I want to ask him, *Why were you here the other night? Why did you have Heller's ID?*

Ava nudges me with her elbow. "Want some?" she asks, biting right into a scoop of java chip ice cream with her front teeth. I shudder.

"How can you do that? Don't your nerves freak out?" I ask.

She smiles wickedly and does it again.

"Bahh, stop!"

I pull my lifeguarding hoodie tight around my middle, feeling the badge outline against my stomach, and lead all the girls over to the soccer field. When we get there, I start laying out blankets and pillows. Imogen spreads out a sheet and a bunch of campers scramble to grab seats on top of it. Ava starts belting out some Faith Hill song and all the girls join in, staring up at her adoringly.

Ava motions for me to sing, too, but I'm distracted. Cal is over by the fireworks station setting up like this is any other year, any other Fourth of July display. I watch him closely as he heaves equipment over his shoulder and wipes his brow with a rag from one of the pockets in his cargo shorts. He looks around, drinking in camp, and I wonder how it looks from his perspective—if he's judging all the "richies," if he's thinking of himself as Roxwood trash.

Ava comes up next to me and throws an arm around my shoulder. She nods over to Cal. "This town keeps getting smaller."

"Yup," I say, not taking my eyes off Cal. "Hard to avoid people."

"At least you're getting out of here. Wait—did you ever decide where you're going next year?" Imogen asks.

I take a deep breath but my tongue feels heavy in my mouth. *Now.* Now's the time to tell them everything, to explain that I was lying all those months ago. I wasn't "waiting to decide" between a few colleges. I still have a semester of high school to retake.

But a bang breaks out high into the sky, and a hush falls over the field. I look upward to see the first set of explosives tear through the night. Ava gasps next to me and takes my hand. Imogen steps back and follows Tommy over to the stables. I glance at Ava, at our fingers intertwined.

For the millionth time this summer, I wonder how big the

chasm is between us and think of all the moments we still haven't shared. Like where she was the night Heller died and what's going on with her dad. Or what's going on with *me*.

"I'm gonna get a soda," I whisper. "Want anything?" Ava shakes her head and leans back, watching the fireworks ascend into the dark night sky.

I wrap my arms around my middle, holding my hoodie close to my stomach, and walk over to the cooler in the back of the crowd near the soccer shed. But instead of lifting it open, I tiptoe to the soccer equipment shed where Cal is leaning up against the wall, his arms crossed over his chest. When I approach he doesn't look up.

My hands shake and I shove them deep in my sweatshirt pocket before I start talking. "I saw you the other night. Up by Creepy Cliff."

Cal meets my gaze. I can see his eyes are rimmed with red. He looks up, his handiwork exploding in the sky.

"Why?" I ask. "Why were you here?"

Cal starts fidgeting with his hands, like he used to do when the teachers would call on him in class. "I took a walk."

"Bullshit. This place is miles from your house. You can't stroll on over here."

Cal leans back against the shed. "What do you want me to say, Goldie?"

Something inside me snaps and it dawns on me for the first time since Heller died that I'm furious. The rage and grief, all-consuming and hot, begins to boil in my stomach and I need to get it out. I need to scream at Heller and pound my fists against his chest and demand he explain why he left me here with this mess, these lies, this burden. But he's not here. So I explode.

"I want you to explain this." I hold Heller's ID up so Cal can see it. His face pales and his jaw drops open.

"Where did you get that?" he asks, taking a step toward me. I instinctively back up, until I realize I'm out of sight of anyone from Alpine Lake. Now it's just Cal and me behind the soccer shed.

"You dropped it," I say. But as soon as the words leave my mouth, I wonder . . . what if Cal had something to do with Heller's death?

Sure, he gave a comment to the *Roxwood Read*, but that could have been a decoy move. If that's true, I don't even want to think about what he could do to me. But I need to keep pressing. I need answers. "Why did you have this?"

Cal keeps coming toward me. I forgot how big he is. How wide his shoulders got over the years. So many seasons playing hockey made him hard and mean. He cracks his knuckles and reaches for me. For a second, I think he's going to wrap that hand around my neck, but before I can scream, he snatches the ID out of my hand.

The anger leaves his face and his eyes are sad and somber, full of pain. "Heller gave this to me the day he died," he says. "He told me to hold on to it in case anything happened to him."

"Bullshit."

"He told me he was coming here to get answers."

"Answers to what?"

Cal shrugs. "I don't know. But he said if he didn't make it back home, to use the ID."

"Wait." Suddenly my brain is moving too fast and I'm trying to figure out what all of this means. "Heller came here knowing he might . . ."

"Die," Cal says. "That's what it seems."

"What? Why?"

Cal shrugs. "I dunno."

"Who would do something like this?"

Cal looks at me hard but his mouth is a thin straight line. He has no answers. No theories. That's why he came to Alpine Lake.

I press my fingers to my temples, racking my brain for anything. Something. But then I remember the vigil.

"Jordan knew."

"What?" Cal asks.

"Jordan Adler knew I wasn't driving."

"No way."

"He told me at the memorial." I squeeze my eyes shut and whisper Jordan's words. "'That fucker got what he deserved.' That's what he said."

Cal eyes go wide and he drops his arms by his sides.

"What if Jordan was confronting Heller?" I ask. "What if he wanted revenge on Heller for what he *actually* did to Dylan?"

You don't say those kinds of things. Not about the golden boy of Roxwood.

Cal shakes his head. "No way. Jordan's my boy. That guy loved Heller like a brother."

"Except Heller hurt his *actual* brother."

We're both quiet as the fireworks explode above. My gut is telling me something wasn't right about the way Jordan Adler spoke of Heller, but my gut has been wrong about so much. I once thought Heller would come clean. Cal, too. But neither of them did. So why would I trust myself in this instance?

After another firework, Cal speaks. "How does he know?"

I shake my head. "Didn't say."

"And he never once said anything?"

"Neither did you."

Cal steps back like I've slapped him. The silence between us stretches on. Until I realize he didn't answer my first question.

"Why were *you* here that night?"

Cal sighs. "I was looking for answers." His voice is small and he looks up again at the fireworks. "I know you are, too. Maybe . . . maybe we can help each other?"

"The last time I thought you'd help me, I was sorely disappointed."

"You don't know anything." Cal's jaw tightens.

"I know Jordan's not the only one who knew Heller was driving. *You* saw him behind the wheel. *You* could have come forward and told the truth. *You* could have stopped everyone from making my life hell."

Cal narrows his eyes and leans over. For a second, I think he's going to puke, but then he looks right at me, like he's going to say something important. But he doesn't. He toes the ground with his shoe.

I throw my hands up. "Great. Stay silent like you always do."

Cal's fury bubbles to the surface and he stares at me, his gaze sharp. "I know you're mad. You should be. Grief is fucked up. When my mom died . . ." He shakes his head. "All I felt was rage. But right now, I want to find out the truth about Heller."

He looks down at the ID badge in his hand. "Whether Jordan had anything to do with this or not, I need to find out what happened." His back straightens and he looks right at me. "He died here. You're the only person from Roxwood who has access to Camp Alpine Lake."

"You need my help."

Cal nods begrudgingly.

I squeeze my eyes shut and picture Heller. The curves along his biceps. The way his chest rose and fell when he slept peacefully beside me. I think about his plans, all the things he still had left to do in this world. I recall the horror in his eyes when he saw Dylan lying in the road, his legs contorted. I think about what I sacrificed to help him achieve his dreams.

I don't owe Heller anything. But I know if I say no to Cal now, I'll spend the rest of my life wondering what happened to the boy whose future I put before my own.

"Okay," I say.

"Okay?"

"I'll help you find out what happened."

Cal's face breaks out in relief. "Thank you, Goldie, seriously. I—"

"On one condition," I say. "After we figure this out, I'm going to tell the truth. I'm going to come clean about what happened and I want you to back me up. Everyone needs to know the truth."

Cal's face falls.

"Heller's dead, Goldie. You want me to ruin his reputation?"

I know it's my only shot so I have to keep my cool. "You think on it, Cal. And until then . . ." I snatch the ID out of his hand. "I'll hang on to this."

Cal looks up, bewildered. He's not used to this version of me. The girl who sticks up for herself. The girl who decides to fuck all the paperwork, all the backdoor deals, the cash she'd been handed in one lump sum. I've missed this part of me. But she's back. Finally.

A firework explodes in the sky and I walk back to my girls, leaving Cal and his questions behind. I take one final look at the ID badge in my hand, and though I feel bold, I can't shake the lingering fear gnawing at my chest.

If Heller was murdered, who wanted him dead?

CHAPTER 32

Then

I officially lost myself on the last Monday in January.

It was frigid and snowing, one of those days where you know you'll barely see sunlight, where getting out of bed, putting on your snow boots, and stepping out the door is an accomplishment. It was also the day my dad woke up to find urine freezing into droplets on our garage door, a pickup truck full of hockey boys speeding away.

When I got to school, I headed to the library for Monday assembly. I should have known something would happen. Dylan had done an interview on the local news channel over the weekend, breaking down into tears about how he'd never play hockey again, about how his family was drowning in medical bills and they were launching a crowdfunding campaign to get him the best physical therapy in New England. His brother, Jordan, sat beside him, clenching his fists, stewing with rage.

I hoped I could blend into the background that week. That I could revert to who I was before Heller came into my life.

But I was so naive.

Because as soon as I stepped into the library, the room got quiet. All eighty-six of my classmates turned to look at me. Teachers were running about, frantically tapping at keyboards and shooting me nervous glances. My cheeks burned as I scanned the room.

It didn't take long to see what was up.

On every single computer, my face stared back at me. Sunken eyes with liner drawn around my lids. A blank stare. Disbelief. My hair was matted and wet from snowflakes. I was still wearing my winter coat, stark against the white backdrop.

Someone had pulled up my mug shot from the accident and made it the background photo on all the desktops in school. It was the screensaver, too, I learned as some of the computers went idle.

I looked around the room for Heller, to see where he was, if he had been part of this. He was sitting at a big rectangular table in the back with Cal, an open book in front of him. His gaze met mine and his lips parted slightly. I wondered if he would stand up and say sorry right then and there. His eyes told me he wanted to, that there was a mixture of pity and shame swirling within him. But Heller did nothing. He said nothing.

It dawned on me in that moment that I hadn't really known Heller. I thought I did, since I knew his middle name and how he liked his coffee, how his laugh was a giggle a few octaves higher than his announcement voice, and how he liked to smell my hair after he thought I went to sleep. I knew he was ambitious in a way that only comes from being the biggest fish in the smallest pond, and that all he wanted to do with his life was make Roxwood *better*. I knew he was lactose intolerant but loved ice cream enough to withstand the stomachache, and that his skin was a bit rough, bumpy in some hidden spots.

But that wasn't much, was it? Because in the end, all I really needed to know was that when he *could* have saved me from this—from humiliation and heartbreak and devastation beyond repair—he chose not to.

The library was silent. I guess everyone was waiting to see how I would react, if I would scream or laugh or burst into tears.

I didn't do any of those things. It didn't occur to me.

Instead, I turned on my heel and walked right out the door.

CHAPTER 33

Now

The rain starts softly at first, landing on the white wooden dock in quiet plunks. A group of thirteen-year-old boys are treading water in front of me as the lake begins to ripple, little pools spreading outward.

I turn my head to the sky and see the pale blue that was there at breakfast has become a cloudy gray, and over by town an obvious storm is beginning to swirl.

"Ooh, it's gonna pour," some boy yells.

"Shut it, Shapiro," Levin says. But worry lines form on his forehead and I know he's debating about whether or not to call off instructional morning swim.

Levin blows his whistle. "Breaststroke to the far dock and back, then tread for another sixty seconds. Ready, set, go."

The kids make a fuss but take off, cutting through the icy lake with their flimsy strokes, heads bobbing up and down for air.

Levin is quiet and I wonder what the waterfront means to him now that he found a dead body here. All I want to do is ask him if he saw someone fight with Heller. Someone full of rage and ire, someone with a motive. Someone like Jordan Adler.

"Are you thinking about him?"

My head snaps up and I find Levin looking at me like he's reading my mind.

"I am, too," he says. "Hard not to."

"Can I ask you something?" My voice is almost a whisper.

"I guess."

"People in Roxwood . . . they think something bad happened to Heller. That it wasn't an accident."

Levin's eyes stay straight ahead, watching the kids shiver in the water. "That's not a question."

"You found him," I say. "Was he . . . Was there anyone else . . ."

"Are you asking me if I think that boy drowned by accident?"

Before I can answer, a bolt of lightning slices through the sky, striking down somewhere far, but not far enough, away. I yelp and Levin blows his whistle three times, long and loud, the signal for everyone to get out of the water as fast as they can.

"You heard him!" I yell. "Everybody out!"

The boys hoot and holler, thrilled that morning swim is canceled, and soon everyone is on the sand, bundled in towels and sweatshirts, making a mad dash for the trail that will lead them back to their cabins before the rain starts.

"Goldie," Levin yells. "Tie up the kayaks?"

I rush over to the wooden stand, ducking under the canopy of trees. The sky erupts and sheets of rain drop from the sky.

Everything's wet within seconds, but I flip a few boats upside down on elevated wooden racks and tie knots around the ends to keep them from getting swept away by the wind.

Pleased with my effort, I swivel on my heel and prepare to run back to the beach.

"Ow!" Levin's always saying to wear sandals over here, even though it's mostly grass and woodchips. But something's bound to prick you once in a while. I steady myself against a tree and lift my foot up to see the damage. It's a little red in the soft fleshy area of my heel where something poked it, but there's no blood.

I set my foot back down on the muddy ground but then something shiny catches my eye. I bend down to see a flash of silver nestled in between twigs. It has a sharp edge, like one of those fancy silver bracelets the girls are always wearing after their bat mitzvahs.

It's camp policy to leave all valuables in the cabin while swimming. They instituted that after Ava lost a diamond earring in the lake when we were ten. Mrs. Cantor left a furious message for Stu, telling him not to let her bring those things down to the water.

Not that anyone could have told Ava *no*. Not really.

I grasp the charm and pull the piece of jewelry up from the ground, ready to hand it off to one of the group leaders who can give it back to whichever kid lost it.

But when I feel the weight of it in my hand, I stop.

No.

It can't be.

It is, though. I squeeze the object tighter, feeling its sharp edges and hard lines, the tiny chain running through the charm. I know what I'm going to find when I open my fist. But when I do, it doesn't make it any easier.

There in my palm is a silver lightning bolt. It's hanging from a thin chain with a small clasp, dainty and elegant, which is broken in my hand, as if someone ripped it from its owner. It's Heller's lightning bolt.

I lean back against the tree and slide down so I'm sitting on my heels as rain falls around me. I hold the chain up, letting the charm dangle back and forth.

I close my fist around the necklace and start to stand. But something stops me. There's no reason for any piece of Heller to be *on* camp property at all—not if he died like everyone said he did, by drowning in the lake. If that were true, then he never would have set foot on the waterfront.

My limbs feel shaky as I push myself up. I curl up the necklace so it's completely hidden and hold it tight within my fist.

The skeptics in Roxwood have to be right.

I put one foot in front of the other and make my way back to the sand.

My brain can't make sense of anything, and I watch the lifeguards race around the waterfront, tying up sailboats and throwing kickboards in the shed. I look around for Ava and Imogen but they must already be heading up the trail.

"Get in," Levin says. He's sitting in the driver's seat of a golf cart, his striped senior staff shirt growing damp in some spots. His bare foot is on the pedal, ready to take the road to upper camp.

I look down and see I'm already drenched and my towel is starting to drip. I shuffle in beside him and look around to see if anyone else needs a lift, but all the lifeguards are gone. It's only Levin and me.

"Bloodroot, right?" he asks, when we get on the gravel.

I nod and turn my head back toward the waterfront. Wind blows the flags every which way and the water looks choppy and rough, like a whirlpool is spinning beneath the surface. If only the weather was the most dangerous thing about this place. I hold Heller's necklace tighter in my palm.

Levin's knuckles are white, grasping onto the wheel tightly. His face is full of worry, cloudy and far away. If he's telling the truth about how he found Heller, maybe he would know why the necklace was here. Maybe he pulled him up on the sand.

"You found him in the water?" I ask, my voice barely audible above the storm.

Levin keeps looking forward.

"Did you touch him? Bring him up on dry land?"

"Not supposed to touch a dead body. You learned that in first aid class, too."

Rain plunks down all around us and my vision goes blurry, realizing Heller *was* on camp property. Maybe, just maybe, Jordan Adler was here, too.

"Did you see anyone else here that night?" I ask. "A boy around my age? Greasy hair? Built like a linebacker?"

Levin looks at me out of the corner of his eye and grunts.

"What's that supposed to mean? Is that a yes?"

"It means I shouldn't be talking to you about this."

"Why?"

"Because I said I wouldn't."

"To who?"

Levin's quiet. I look at him then. There's only six years between us. In that time, he's lived whole lives, gone to college, learned how to command a classroom full of freshmen. And yet he chooses to come back. To spend his time here, caring about campers and staff. Even after all his Alpine Lake friends went off and got jobs in finance or consulting or big law, Levin is . . . here.

"Who did you promise you wouldn't talk about this?"

Levin pulls up onto the grassy knoll outside Bloodroot, which is now slick with mud. "Meg, okay?" He shakes his head. "She's worried about you, says this is hitting you really hard. I'm doing what she asked."

"But—"

"Drop it, Goldie," he says. "Do you know what this kind of questioning could do to a camp like this? It's a scandal. The fact that his death was deemed an accident so quickly is a gift. Don't you see that? So don't ask me about Heller again, okay?"

The rain is coming down hard and a few kids are spinning in circles on the lawns, laughing like their faces are about to fall off even though their clothes are soaked right through. But I can only look at Levin, the coolness in his face, the stoic expression. There's nothing to do but get out of the golf cart.

He takes off without saying goodbye.

"That Levin?" Meg rushes outside, holding her poncho close to her stomach. "That arse didn't even say hello." She looks at me, soaked, and points to the door. "Get inside, you nut!"

Reluctantly, I dash into Bloodroot and leave my towel on the porch. The girls are electric, rushing around the cabin, preparing themselves for the best rain day ever. There are decks of cards, pillow forts, jacks, coloring books, and markers strewn about the floor. A group of girls in matching tie-dyed sweatshirts have taken over the back corner playing MASH, while Bianca and Jordie are sitting with Caroline, their heads bent over a plastic box of beads and string.

But all I can think about are Levin's cryptic words and how

Meg, of all people, told him to keep things from me. Plus, his insistence to *drop it*, that an investigation might bring more attention to Camp Alpine Lake. But I can't imagine that would actually *hurt* the camp. Mellie and Stu would definitely want to find out the truth, too, especially if someone like Jordan Adler was involved. They're always looking for reasons to beef up security. A *townie* murdering another *townie* would certainly give them reason to keep camp secluded from the rest of Roxwood.

But it's now officially a rain day, which means we're stuck inside where there are no answers about Heller's death and where Jordan Adler was that night.

I head to the counselor room, careful not to interrupt the little groups of girls making their own magic. I want to ask Meg about why she'd demand Levin keep me in the dark, but there's a walkie talkie pressed to her ear. She nods in my direction as the boys' group leader says something garbled over the speaker.

"We're getting the Lodge," she mouths to me.

We both know that's the most coveted rainy-day activity, given to whoever is on Stu and Mellie's good side that day. There's a big pull-down projector and dozens of movies to choose from.

"*The Princess Bride?*" Meg asks.

"Fine," the boys' group leader says. "See you soon."

"Over and out," Meg says. "Dick."

I wring out my ponytail, lake water dropping on the floor. "Hope that was turned off."

"Who cares. Shower up?"

I make a show of sniffing my armpit. "I stink or what?"

"Like a wet pup." She throws a towel at me.

I begin to change, searching for the words to ask her what I need protecting from anyway, but then something crackles over the walkie. "Hey, Meg?" the boys' group leader says. "Can you guys bring some hot cocoa packets from the dining hall? You're closer."

Meg groans and looks out the window. It's pouring now.

"I'll do it," I say.

"For real?"

"Sure," I say. "Payback for getting stoned at the social." Plus, it'll give me more time to figure out how to ask her *not* to protect me from information about Heller's death.

She rolls her eyes but I can sense her gratitude. I turn my back to her and tuck Heller's necklace into my underwear drawer, before grabbing a sweatshirt from my dirty clothes pile. I pull a poncho over it and make a break for the dining hall. But as I run, I can feel Heller's badge moving around in the pocket by my stomach. I press my hand to it to make it stop.

When I get to the dining hall it's empty except for Christina, who I can hear humming from all the way in the back of the kitchen. Based on the smell, we're having her famous turkey chili tonight.

"Who's there?" she yells.

I poke my head into the kitchen and wave. "Here for hot cocoa. Got a spare box?"

"Ramblers must have the Lodge today, huh?"

"You know it."

She nods to one of the big crates stacked against the wall. I grab a few packets and head for the door.

"Oh, wait a sec, darling. Can I ask you a favor?" Christina wipes her hands on her white apron, stained with tomato and chocolate and who knows what else. "I'm out of cumin. Can you run to the store and get me one of those big plastic containers? Can't make chili without it."

I stare at Christina, sort of shocked.

She must read the surprise on my face because she shakes her head and throws up her hands.

"I know," she says. "I've been waiting on a spice delivery for over a week now. Pretty soon we're gonna be having salt and pepper meals." She scrunches up her face in disgust.

"Mail carriers on strike or something?"

Christina shrugs. "No idea. Every time I ask Stu about it, he says the delivery is on its way."

"Weird," I say.

Christina shrugs and reaches into her back pocket, pulling out a ten-dollar bill. "Cumin, though? Would you mind?"

If I say yes then I'll have to leave camp, and that means going into town where there are so many people who hate me, who wish *I* died instead of Heller. But when I take a step toward Christina, I feel Heller's badge move inside my sweatshirt pocket. If I'm able to get out of camp for a little while without anyone knowing, maybe I can make a pit stop at the clerk's office and figure out whatever Heller was trying to tell Cal or see if there was anything tying him to Jordan.

"No problem," I say. "But only if you run these hot cocoa packets down to the Lodge to Meg."

Christina hands me the bill and the keys to the kitchen van. "Deal."

CHAPTER 34

Then

There was one unseasonably warm day in early November when the temperature jumped above sixty and Heller skipped practice to take his dinghy out and see the sunset. It only had room for the two of us and a cooler full of snacks.

Together we sat in the middle of the lake and watched the sky change from blue to purple as we sipped hot apple cider spiked with rum.

The mountains surrounded us, creating a canyon, and Heller looked around, in awe of the quiet, the majesty.

"I wonder what this place looks like to your camp friends," Heller said.

I paused, surprised by his words. "They think it's beautiful."

"How come you haven't introduced me to Ava and Imogen?" he asked, his voice soft, almost hurt. "You always leave the room when they call you."

My cheeks burned. Was that true? It must have been because they *still* didn't know about him.

"Are you embarrassed of me or something?"

I reached for Heller. "You can't be serious."

But his mouth was a frown. "There are photos of them all over your room but you never talk about having us meet."

I sighed. "It's complicated."

"I don't see how."

I chewed on the inside of my cheek, wondering how to explain everything—that Ava and Imogen wouldn't understand Heller, they wouldn't *get* him or why I loved him. So, I found another truth. "I don't think you'd like them," I said. "They can be spoiled and bratty. They're status-obsessed, always eating fancy sushi and talking about their trips to Europe. They're not self-aware." The words began tumbling out. Things I'd only thought in private but never said aloud. But once I started . . . I couldn't stop. It was if I needed to hear them in my voice to admit to myself that they were true. "We've been close since we were eight but I don't even know if we'd be friends if we met today. They . . . they can be hard to love."

"They can't be so bad if they're your friends."

"They love me. They're loyal."

"That's not nothing."

"It's everything."

"Maybe we can go down there over spring break or something. See the city? Spend some time with them? Maybe you'll be ready to introduce me then."

I looked at Heller, hopeful and open, and decided to believed him. "Yeah," I said. "Maybe."

Heller looked at his watch and then back toward town. "We should be getting back."

"But then we'll miss the best part of the sunset."

Heller tapped his foot against the bottom of the boat. "I want to get to the clerk's office before dinner. I gotta talk to Sally about something."

"About what?"

Heller's face grew cloudy if only for a second, a tiny space replacing the intimacy between us. But as soon as I noticed it, his mouth turned into a smile.

"One more lap." he said. "She can wait a little while longer."

Heller kissed me softly and started the engine.

CHAPTER 35

Now

I try to ignore the butterflies in my stomach as I pull into the Applebee Grocer parking lot. No doubt in the middle of a rainstorm it'll be packed with folks loading up on provisions. But I keep my head down and push open the front door. Sure enough, the place is swamped. I make a beeline for the spice aisle and try to find the cumin as fast as I can.

I dodge my kindergarten teacher and one of the assistant hockey coaches, and grab a thirty-two-ounce plastic container of the cheap stuff, tucking it under my arm as I practically run to the checkout line. I plunk it down on the conveyer belt, hand the cashier Christina's rumpled bill, and rush out of the store without looking behind me.

I'm fumbling for the keys to the van when I see someone lurking around the side of the store, under an awning, smoking a cigarette. I pause, the keys sandwiched between my knuckles. When I see who it is, his name forms on my lips.

"Jordan Adler." Before I can stop myself, before I can think about what he might be capable of, I'm stomping over to him. When I approach, Dylan's brother is looking at me with a smirk, like he can't believe I'm standing there. He's wearing a sweatshirt and a baseball cap, covering his greasy hair. Rain falls in sheets around us but he doesn't seem to mind.

"Can't get the organic shit over at Alpine Lake?" he asks.

I try to keep my focus. "Where were you that night?"

Jordan's eyes grow stormy and he tenses, his whole body stiff. "Excuse me?"

"The night Heller died. Where were you?"

"What the fuck are you asking me for?"

My eyes narrow and I take a step toward him, summoning all the strength in my body. "You knew. You knew about the accident. How Heller hurt Dylan, ruined his chances of getting out of this place." I drop my voice so I sound like him. *"That fucker got what he deserved."*

Jordan shakes his head and his bottom lip quivers. He sucks on a cigarette and blows out a puff of smoke. "I did say that, didn't I?"

I nod, furious, confused.

"I say fucked-up shit when I'm drunk."

"Excuse me?"

"I was out of my mind at the vigil. Had to be to get through that. I was fucking furious at Heller. Still am. The kid was one of my best friends. Then he goes and does that shit to Dylan? Then he *dies*?" Jordan shakes his head. "Sure, he's gone, but I'm not gonna stop being mad at him. Not yet."

"Answer me," I say, forceful. "Where were you?"

Jordan stubs out his cigarette against the wall and reaches behind his back. He pulls out his phone and starts thumbing through his camera roll. When he gets to an image of a bonfire and a tent, he stops.

"I was camping in Maine that night with a dozen buddies. Check the location and timestamp."

I grab his phone and do exactly that, my heart rate slowing as his story becomes truth.

He yanks it back and shoves it back into his pocket. "You better watch yourself, going around making accusations like that."

"But . . . you knew. How?"

Jordan taps his foot, nervous. "One night when Heller got wasted. The guilt ate at him, I guess. He was mumbling over and over how he ruined your life."

I shake my head. That's impossible. When Heller got drunk, he became funny and gregarious, a king. Not sad and bumbling. But I was never with him at a party after the accident. Maybe he changed.

"I asked him what he meant and he told me. Broke down."

"What did you say?"

"I smacked him upside the head and said he was a fucking ass-hole." Jordan sucks on his cheek.

"Have you told anyone?" I ask, not sure what I want his answer to be.

Jordan shakes his head. "I tried to tell Dylan once but he wouldn't listen. He said Heller'd never do that to him. So, I kept it to myself after that. Figured no one would believe me." He looks up again. "No offense."

"None taken."

"Kid was the best, but he was also a piece of shit. Never could really forgive him after that. Bet you're glad he's dead. You should thank whoever did this, you really should."

My blood runs cold looking at Jordan's pleased expression, at how relaxed he seems.

"How can you say that?" Anger rises in my voice.

Jordan looks me up and down. "You know, you'd be the one with the motive if people found out you took the blame and now regret that decision. I don't know if I'd want that information coming out . . . people accusing you and all."

"I'd never hurt Heller," I say, tears pricking my eyes.

"Like he'd never hurt Dylan? Like he'd never hurt you?" Jordan reaches for another cigarette and we stand there as the rain pummels the cement around us. "I don't think you did anything to Heller, but other people in this town might. I'm telling you to watch your back, that's all. Don't go asking your questions too loudly, you know?"

"Fuck you." I fumble for the keys to the van.

"Good luck, though."

"With what?"

"Finding out who did this."

My hands shake on the steering wheel as I pull up to the County Clerk's Office, trying to push Jordan from my mind. If he didn't kill Heller, maybe his death really *was* an accident? All I know is that Heller's office better have some answers.

I throw the van in park and peek through the windshield at the tall brick building. Since it's a Saturday, all the lights are off and there are no cars in the parking lot. I hold Heller's badge tight in my grip as I dart to the side door where the ID scanner is tacked up against the wall. My plastic poncho sticks to my skin as I fumble with Heller's badge. I hold my breath but it works immediately, buzzing the door open.

I've never been inside the clerk's office. Never had any interest.

But it's like Heller described it. One big room with lots of desks and floor-to-ceiling bookcases lining the walls. They're all filled with bound books, newspaper clippings, and cardboard boxes. Heller said the good stuff—the *old* stuff—was in the basement, with some super complicated filing system he was always trying to learn. He often said he was worried a big storm or a flood would take the whole thing out, destroying every piece of evidence that Roxwood existed at all, since they could never afford proper barriers or insurance.

The room smells old, like a musty library that hasn't been cleaned in a while. I scan the corners of the ceiling for security cameras and don't see any. My shoulders relax a bit and I shimmy out of my poncho and shoes, discarding all my wet stuff in the hallway.

When I glance at the clock, I see I've already been gone from camp for half an hour. I have to make this fast.

I weave through the desks looking for Heller's, any indication that he had claimed a certain space. It takes me a few minutes, stepping over piles of notebooks and bins filled with shredded paper, until I find his desk, tucked away in the third row closest to the wall.

No surprise, the desk next to him has a nameplate saying SALLY BURKE. But I can't worry about that right now.

My stomach flips when I see the way he kept it, neat and tidy, like his bedroom. A few paperback books are lined up against the back of it, all nonfiction titles about the history of New England. A Roxwood hockey mug sits next to the clunky desktop computer.

But then I see what's tacked to the corkboard and my heart almost bursts from my chest. A photo of us. It was taken without either one of us knowing at a random party in the fall. We're facing each other, keeled over in laughter, in love. Heller's eyes are on me and I'm holding myself up with one hand on his chest, the other on my heart. We look so happy.

I can't believe he kept this.

My legs begin to shake and I drop to the office chair, sinking into the seat. I unpin the photo and hold it in my hands. I don't know whether to crumple it up and toss it in the garbage or hold on to it forever.

This kind of grief is strange because it feels unearned. I'm not quite sure it belongs to me at all since I hadn't known Heller in his final days or weeks or months. Certainly not enough to warrant the pit in my stomach, the raw scratching at my throat, the tears that sting and vanish before they can fall. I'm not worthy of this grief. It only makes me feel guilty.

I force myself to open my eyes and *do* something. I have to do what I came here for. Find whatever he wanted Cal to know. There must be something on the computer. I toggle Heller's mouse, but when the screen appears, I have to enter a password.

Obviously.

Heller was so private about his tech, there's no way I'd know it. I push the chair back and pull out the drawers in the metal filing cabinet by my side. The first one is empty, save for some pens and Scotch tape, but the bottom one is stuffed with folders, all labeled in alphabetical order. I can't search through all of this in time—or bring it back to Camp Alpine Lake without anyone seeing. But I thumb through them, trying to see if anything pops out.

They all seem to be names of businesses in town, full of forms requesting liquor licenses and tax credits. In the back of the drawer is the thickest one and when I pull it out, I cock my head to one side. Written on the tab in Heller's loopy cursive it says *Camp Alpine Lake*.

I flip through some of the papers, but I can't tell what they mean. Not yet. I grab my phone and snap a few photos, figuring I can look at them at some point when I'm back to safety. But when I try to stuff my phone back in my pocket, I accidentally elbow the photo of the two of us off the desk, so it lands facedown. When I lean over to pick it up, Heller's handwriting jumps out at me. He'd written something here in dark blue ink.

GE 1115HM0307

It only takes a second for me to realize what the marks mean. Our initials and our birthdays lined up together. It must be his password.

My heart races as I try to type the letters and numbers into the computer. After all this, he used my info to guard his secrets. *Why?*

Sure enough, the password works.

His computer is as organized as his workspace, but I don't even know what the hell I'm looking for. It's not like there's going to be a document labeled IF I DIE AT CAMP ALPINE LAKE, PLEASE READ ME but I start opening folders anyway.

Nothing seems that interesting, so I click over to his email, which he's thankfully still logged into. It takes a few moments for all his messages to load and when they do, I start scrolling.

As I move the mouse down, I try to picture him sitting in this exact seat on the day he died, wearing the round glasses he only put on while looking at a screen. He was probably eating an apple, pecking away at the keyboard, trying to figure out whatever the hell he was working on. He had no idea that in a few hours, he'd be dead. He loved this town so much. He wanted to give back to it in so many ways, to change it. To make it better. But why would any of that have led to his death?

I jump to the date he died and look at the emails that came in the morning, before he showed up at camp in the dinghy and spoke to Ava on the dock. None look particularly interesting so I move over to his sent folder to see what he was up to that day. It's all mundane, messages to coworkers and business owners, until I get to a series of emails that make me pause.

I hover over the first one, addressed to tips@nytimes.com and the subject line says simply, "Cantor Assets."

With shaking fingers, I open the email and start reading.

> To whom it may concern,
>
> I doubt you'll actually read this but I don't know what else to do. I'm an employee at the clerk's office in Roxwood, Vermont. I have uncovered evidence of a massive financial scandal involving Cantor Assets, run by famed financier Mark Cantor. I have proof. I'd like to share it with you.
>
> Sincerely, Heller McConnell

My heart beats fast as I look through the rest of his sent emails from that day. There are dozens of other identical, desperate messages sent out to various news outlets—*The Boston Globe, The Wall Street Journal, Bloomberg, HuffPost, Reuters, New York Post.* And it seems like no one wrote him back.

As the wheels in my brain start to turn, I hear the scratching of metal and a door swing open somewhere on the other side of the building. Someone's here.

I quickly take a photo of the screen and stuff the picture of Heller and me in my pocket. I set the computer to standby and rush toward the door, my heart beating fast.

"Hello?" someone calls. "Office is closed today."

The side door is only a few steps away and I can hear footsteps coming closer. I know I only have seconds before I can get out of the door without being seen.

The footsteps get louder but I make a break for the exit, stepping into my boots and grabbing my poncho as fast as I can. I swing the door wide open and sprint toward the van. When I get to the van, I throw it into drive, not even bothering to look at the clerk's office, to see if anyone saw me.

Go go go go. That's all I can think.

Until I get on the main road, only a few miles from camp. That's when everything hits me. If Heller actually *did* figure out that Cantor Assets was doing something illegal, something that was *harming* Roxwood, then he must have been trying to talk to Ava about it when he came to camp on his dinghy. And if he came to camp later that night to confront her again . . .

But no. That's impossible. I make a left into the Camp Alpine Lake driveway and go slow up the hill, through the rain, trying to ignore the obvious truth—that if Ava knew Heller had dirt on her dad, she would probably do anything to shut him up.

CHAPTER 36

Then

The night before visiting day our first year as campers, Ava was the only girl in our cabin who seemed nervous to see her parents. After flashlight time, she climbed into my bed and curled herself around me, shallow breaths seeping out into the night.

When I turned to face her, I saw she was crying. "I don't want them to come," she whispered. "They're going to fight."

I wrapped her in my arms but we were both so little then. All I knew about her family was they were rich. And her dad was mean.

It wasn't until I met them the next day that I realized how different our lives were. Her dad barely said anything and wore a shiny watch that he kept looking at while Ava's mom unpacked a Louis Vuitton suitcase full of presents. He looked at my bedding like it had germs, like he was afraid he might catch something.

That was when I learned what visiting day was really about—all the *stuff*. The onslaught of *stuff* that arrives with the parents. The *stuff* that's supposed to say *I love you*. Ava's mom came armed with all of Ava's favorite things from Manhattan—a box of black-and-white cookies from Zabar's, a big tub of banana pudding from Magnolia Bakery, and a tote bag of shiny new hardcover books from the Strand, some of them signed by authors. Ava opened each item with delight, sneaking peeks at her dad, who was standing in the corner of the cabin, uncomfortable.

Ava grabbed my hand and motioned for me to sit on the bed beside her. "I can't wait to share this with you," she said.

Her mom smiled politely as Imogen brought her parents over, too.

"What did you get?" Ava asked.

Imogen started listing items—her mom's onigiri, hand-wrapped and seasoned to perfection, slices of her dad's zucchini bread, cinnamon rolls, lemon bars, and dozens of handwritten letters from her cousins back home she couldn't wait to read.

As Imogen spoke, I saw Ava's parents exit the cabin and walk quickly to the side of the building, trying to stay out of sight.

Ava spotted them, too, but she didn't look. She kept her focus on Imogen and the Wexlers.

But I watched the Cantors, how their faces grew red as they became more animated, more furious, yelling with their hands, throwing their heads back in annoyance. I watched as Mark stomped off, toward the car, and as Ava's mom rubbed her temples with her fingers. I watched as she closed her eyes and sighed and walked right back into the cabin as if nothing strange had happened.

Mark never came again, and I grew to hate visiting day, how all the well-meaning parents only spoke to me to ask what Roxwood was *really* like.

Mom and Dad would often pop by, wearing their striped Alpine Lake senior staff shirts to say hello and remind the other parents

I wasn't some weird charity case. They'd hug Imogen's parents warmly and shake Ava's mom's hand with limp fingers. Then they'd head back to their stations to put on their own tour guide faces. The ones that said *we'll make sure nothing bad happens to your precious children.*

CHAPTER 37

Now

Christina's chili grows cold in front of me. It's dinnertime, only a few hours after I got back from the clerk's office, and all I want to do is talk to Ava, to get some answers. But I can't figure out what I even want to ask her.

Hey, is your dad involved in something sketchy? seems kind of messed up. So does *Did you kill Heller and then come into my bed and cry about it?*

Someone wraps their arms around my neck from behind and I almost leap straight out of my seat.

"Jumpy, are we!"

I turn around to find Ava crouching down, her face so close to mine. She smells like that blueberry shampoo and her smile is wide as she nuzzles into my hair.

"Sorry, tired." I don't know why my first instinct is to lie, but something inside me tells me there's no way I can confront Ava now, here in the dining hall.

"Well, whatever it is, please snap out of it because tomorrow is *visiting day*." She rolls her eyes. "I cannot believe I have to see the evil stepbitch here of all places."

I thought I would be rid of the horrors of visiting day by the time I was a counselor, when we were all on the other side of things, plastering on fake smiles and schmoozing with parents. But it gets worse when you're on the staff side.

"Oi!" Meg says. She pushes back from the table and starts leading our girls out of the dining hall toward evening activity. "You two and Imogen are staying for the all-staff meeting, yeah?"

"Reluctantly," Ava says, rolling her eyes.

"Ah, shut it," Meg says. "Report back if there's anything interesting, right?"

"You got it, boss." Ava smiles that big toothy grin of hers but drops it when Meg leaves. "These meetings always suck. They want to tell us how to impress the parents and convince them that this place is worth the bajillion-dollar price tag."

"Let's make fudge," I say, desperate to change the subject.

Ava follows me to the coffee bar, where I tear the tops off two packets of hot chocolate and hand her one. She tosses me a single-serve half-and-half and I dump it into the cocoa, mixing the two together to create a dark brown substance sort of resembling fudge. Discovered that trick when we were thirteen. We carry our paper cups filled with the sweet sludge over to the benches and plop down. Ava rests her head on the table and groans.

"Oh my god, it's going to be *fine*." Imogen sits down next to me and eyes my fudge. I hand it to her to taste. "The stepbitch won't even acknowledge you, relax."

"That might be worse," Ava mumbles.

Stu clears his throat at the front of the room and everyone shushes. I pull my sweatshirt up over my chin. He launches into a monologue about how we have to be on our best behavior during visiting day, how whatever we put forward will be what these parents take with them for the rest of the summer, how we should politely suggest they register their children for *next* summer ASAP to take advantage of the early bird discount.

"As you know, many parents choose to have their children re-apply after visiting day. There are incentives for families who book next summer now. Easier to pass the admissions exam. And if we want these kids to come back next year, we better make sure their parents know how much this place means to their children," he says. I perk up then. There's an underlying sense of urgency in his voice, one I haven't heard before.

"Some of you may remember that we started this summer with a tragedy," Mellie says, her voice gentle. "I want to remind you that this is *not* something we have publicized. Your discretion is appreciated." Heads nod around the room and there's a murmur of agreement. I glance at Ava and she stiffens beside me, her head jolted upright.

"As always, please put on your best faces, your cleanest staff shirts, and your biggest smiles," Mellie continues. "All good?"

Counselors around me reply, "All good!"

But my throat is like chalk. I look over to Mellie, who's standing in the corner of the room, clutching a clipboard to her chest. Stu and Mellie do their best to protect this camp from the outside world. They work tirelessly to create a bubble, impenetrable and sturdy, but what if Levin was right? What if Heller's death has made us vulnerable and open?

What if Ava is the reason why?

"Don't forget to brush your teeth!" Meg bellows the next morning. "Can't let your folks think we're turning you into gremlins!"

We're only a few hours from parental arrivals and the cabin is frenetic. The girls tumble into the bathroom, nearly tripping over themselves to get a spot at the sink. The conversation once again turns to snacks and food and whose family makes the best cookies.

"Remember, girls, we'll have a big party tonight to share all those treats, so no talking bad about anyone else's mama!" Meg says.

The girls laugh but Meg wrinkles her nose as she ducks back into the counselor room. "They act like we don't feed them," she whispers with disgust, pulling on her striped senior staff shirt. "They get ice cream every day and cookie patrol before bed. Plus three full meals. With dessert at two of them!"

I cluck my tongue in recognition and lace up my sneakers.

"You were never like that," she says.

I snap my head up. I've never heard her say anything like this, or even reference the fact that there is, distinctly, an *us* versus *them—them* being the lifers who pay full price and stay here until they go off to internships and law degrees. And *us*, the staffers trying to escape something, the local girl who's granted free tuition thanks to her parents' jobs.

Sure, there are a few in-betweeners like Levin, but there's no denying the fissure of tension spoken only among those who know spoiled, ungrateful children when they see them. Straddling the line between being the invited and the hired has always been a game of survival.

Meg and I make our way into the camper room and most of the girls are already waiting on the lawn, but Bianca and Jordie are huddled on their bed, unmoving. "I got this," I whisper to Meg.

Jordie's bedspring squeaks with my weight as I sink down onto it. "Everything okay?" I ask.

They look at each other, as if they're having a silent conversation meant only for sisters. But then Jordie clears her throat. "Fran said all the parents bring gifts on visiting day."

"Sometimes," I say.

"We didn't tell Mom to bring anything," Bianca says. "What if she doesn't? What if everyone thinks she doesn't love us?"

My heart nearly breaks for these two little girls who could have anything they want but still think love is given with heaping piles of crap. I want to tell them these dumb visiting day packages mean nothing, that they don't indicate anything about how much their parents love them. But nothing I say will teach them that. Not now.

That old song "Wagon Wheel" blares on the loudspeakers, and I know that's the cue.

"Your parents love you very much," I say. "So, so, so much. Whether they come with piles of stuff or not."

They look at each other like they don't believe me, but I paste on a smile and hold out my hands. They take them, and I lead them out of the cabin, up toward the rest of the girls. They all look well taken care of with combed hair and clean shirts. They look shiny and healthy and safe.

Jordie and Bianca catch up with their bunkmates and stand at the wooden fences near the traffic circles. It's the same place where I waited for the buses to pull in, for Ava and Imogen to come home to me.

All the kids line up, pressed up against the fences, excitement and nerves crackling in the air. The parents are here.

It always starts the same way. Stu and Mellie ride down the hill first in a golf cart with music blasting from the speakers. Soda cans drag behind them like they're newlyweds. Then come the cars. Hundreds of minivans and SUVs and convertibles carrying parents and their care packages. They're all decorated with signs painted with kids' names and funny slogans. Every year, Mrs. Graves from Tenafly, New Jersey, with her bright blonde hair and diamond earrings, runs down alongside the cars like she's carrying the Olympic torch. She's tradition, too, and has had kids attend Alpine Lake for fifteen years in a row. Her youngest is a super senior now, so it'll be her last visiting day.

When each kid sees their parents, they scream and run toward the lawn, which turns into a parking lot for the day. There, they're greeted with tight hugs and sloppy kisses and watery eyes that ask *are they taking care of you?*

I watch from the back, as kids howl upon recognition and skip off toward their families. This is the hopeful part of the day. The hour when all the kids with complicated parental arrangements can dream that maybe things will be easy for one day. Maybe their parents will keep their shit together. Maybe all the hoopla, the celebration, the sugar will make all the other problems disappear.

Ava clucks her tongue. "I hope the stepbitch doesn't expect me to talk to her. She won't, right? She couldn't."

I try to detect worry in her voice but I only hear annoyance. Her dad's new wife lives in some sort of bubble, flying around Ava's world like a lazy mosquito. She's always a threat, a nuisance, but rarely lands on flesh to suck blood.

"And, right on cue," Ava says. I follow her gaze to a silver Mercedes SUV driving slowly down the hill. A handmade sign is taped to the passenger side door. WE LOVE YOU, BIANCA AND JORDIE! A petite bottle-blonde hangs out the window, waving wildly to the twins, who are standing on their tiptoes behind the fence, only a few feet away.

"Guess she hired a driver," I say without even thinking.

But Ava doesn't respond and when the car careens around the traffic circle I can see why. Her dad is sitting in the front seat.

Ava drops her arm from around my shoulder.

"I thought you said he wasn't coming?" I ask.

Ava shakes her head, her mouth hanging open. Imogen rushes over. "Was that . . . ?"

I nod and grab her hand. Together we envelop Ava and try to hustle her over to the tennis courts, but she stops us, her feet defiant. She pushes us away and shakes her head.

"Was that really him?" she asks.

"Wasn't he supposed to be in London this weekend? Wimbledon, right? His fund has a box there?"

"Always. He only came to visiting day that one time because Mom said she'd divorce him if he didn't," Ava says. "He was cheating on her the whole time and then left us anyway."

Imogen laughs and weirdly that seems like the right thing to do, so I let out a snort, too. A small smile spreads on Ava's face and soon she's got a full belly laugh going that shoots through her whole body and all the way from her dark roots to the platinum tips of her hair.

Ava leans forward and rests her hands on her knees to keep herself from falling over. I don't know why but I do, too, and soon we're all balls of tears and laughter and grasping hands and arms.

"Oh man," Ava says, wiping her eyes. "This is so fucked up."

She glances back over at the fence where all the kids were standing, and we see that it's only the stragglers who are left. The kids who come from overseas or whose parents are always late. My heart stings for them and their worried expressions.

Ava straightens her spine and her face is determined, sure, different than it was only minutes before.

"What are you going to do?" Imogen asks.

Ava sighs and looks over toward lower girls' camp where we all know her dad and stepmom are heading for Bloodroot, ready to unpack boxes of treats and smother the little girls with love and affection like all the other parents who've invaded our camp.

I expect her to say something shocking and brilliant, something that would explain the placid look that's taken over her face, something that would indicate she has a plan to make her asshole of a father pay.

But she turns back to us and shrugs. "Ignore the motherfucker."

CHAPTER 38

Then

I only saw Ava get violent once. And it was for such an unexpected reason.

It was the first week of super senior summer, our final as campers. A bunch of us were lounging in the Adirondack chairs during rest hour playing cards and talking about the best dining hall hacks, like how to assemble a makeshift McMuffin.

After a little while, a yellow bus pulled into the traffic circle and out poured the boys—Tommy, Dale, and their cabins, all the guys we had grown up alongside. They were wearing Alpine Lake basketball uniforms, shouting obscenities as they came back from playing another camp up in Maine.

Ava whistled as they walked by. That summer she liked to say that if she got catcalled in New York, she could do the same to the boys here. Even the playing field. Let them know how it felt.

Dale and Tommy looked up and elbowed each other. They broke off from the group and jogged over to us, sweaty and red-faced. A few of their bunkmates followed.

"You guys win or what?" Ava asked, shielding her eyes from the sun.

Both of them looked at Ava, curious, but didn't answer.

"Celebratory parade or pity party?" Imogen asked.

Tommy nudged Dale, who looked at him nervously. The other guys stood behind them, shifting their weight from foot to foot. "Ask her," one mumbled.

"Why are you being so weird?" I asked. There were nerves in the air. The kind of uncertainty that made me want to run.

Dale nodded to Ava. "Met some kids from your school at the other camp."

"Oh yeah?" Ava's voice tensed. It was so slight I'm not sure if anyone else noticed, if *I* would have noticed if I hadn't spent so long learning her tones, her intonations. "From Excelsior? Who?"

Dale started listing off some names, people I didn't recognize or even really hear. Mostly because I kept my gaze on Ava, watching her reaction, her face pale as she tried to keep her expression placid.

"All right, whatever."

One of the other guys behind Dale piped up. "Ask her."

Ava stood and crossed her arms over her chest. She was already so tall then, towering over most of the boys our age, and when she took a step toward them, they all seemed to cower. "Ask me what?"

"When they found out we knew you, they wanted to know if it was true."

"If *what* was true?"

"If your dad was really doing some *Wolf of Wall Street* shit."

"What the fuck did you say?" Ava said.

"Ava, I don't—"

Imogen and I leapt to our feet, understanding what was about to happen, but it was too late. Ava had already pulled back her puny fist and hurled it at Dale's face, causing him to double over in pain.

Ava winced and cradled her fist in her elbow. Imogen and I rushed to her side as Dale cried out.

"What the fuck? I wasn't the one who said it!"

"Talk shit about my family one more time and I'll tell everyone here about the time you flashed me in the Lodge, which is actually *true*."

The boys behind Dale stifled their laughs as Dale pinched the bridge of his bleeding nose.

"Crazy bitch."

Ava smirked. "Someone has to be. Come on." She motioned for us to run after her, toward the rock wall, away from the boys.

When we got out of earshot, her shoulders collapsed and Ava fell to the ground in a pile of woodchips. She brought her knees up under her chin and after exhaling an enormous breath, she let it all out, sobbing into her chest.

"What the hell was that?" Imogen said as we crouched next to her.

It took a while for Ava to catch her breath and when she did, her voice was shaky. "Those rumors nearly ruined my freshman year. Everyone saying my dad was some criminal mastermind. As if half of Wall Street *isn't*."

Imogen gasped quietly next to me.

"We had no idea," I said, rubbing Ava's back.

"You think I'd want you guys knowing that awfulness? It's not even true." Ava wiped her nose with the back of her hand. "I was hoping I could keep it a secret, leave it behind in the city. Mom kept saying it would all blow over this summer, when everyone forgot about it."

"Hate to say it, but she's right," Imo says. "No one will remember in September. There's always new drama."

"But now people *here* will know."

Imogen and I were quiet, huddled around Ava. Her protectors. "We've got you," Imo said. "We'll destroy anyone who tries to talk shit."

"No one fucks with Ava Cantor," I echoed.

Ava offered a weak smile and we sat there together for a while until our group leader came looking for us, letting us know it was time to change for afternoon swim.

The rumor never spread around camp, thanks to the fact that a junior counselor was caught smoking weed with a camper, an *actual* scandal that engulfed camp for a full week.

No one talked about Ava's dad's dealings after that. Not Imogen. Not me. And no one talked about the biggest revelation of all: that after everything Mark Cantor put Ava through, she still came to his defense without a second thought.

CHAPTER 39

Now

Ava's true to her word, and even at lunch—when we see her dad taking selfies with the twins from across the picnic tables—she hides her face from him, curtained behind hair.

"He hasn't come looking for you?" Imogen asks, gentle but concerned.

Ava lets out a puff of air, exasperated. "How many times do I have to tell you, Im? My dad is *not* like your dad. Or yours, Goldie," she says without looking at me. "He's a prick." She stops talking abruptly and I know it's so she won't cry.

"I thought . . ." Imogen says, poking at the potato salad on her plate.

"You thought nothing," Ava snaps. "You have no idea. Both of you, with your perfect families. You've never known what it's like."

She stands in a huff and leaves.

Imogen looks at me, concerned. "What the fuck was that?"

"I have no idea."

"Did you talk to Mark? During cabin time with the twins?" Imo asks.

I shrug. "Not really." It's true. Meg sweet-talked and smiled and patted all the girls' hair, charming the parents until they left for whatever activities their children wanted to show them. I hung back and smiled pleasantly, repeating Heller's email to journalists over and over in my head.

What have you done, Mark Cantor?

"So fucking weird," Imogen says, shaking her head. "Well, let's . . . try to keep them away from her. We'll do a full debrief later."

"Sounds good," I say. Imogen clears her plate and heads over to say hi to some of her campers. I steal a look at Jordie and Bianca, blissed out on parental love. How could their dad not treat Ava with the same devotion? For all she has, for all that is at her fingertips . . . there's no way this doesn't crush her.

But then Mark Cantor looks up from Bianca, who's deep in conversation, explaining the stories behind each of her ten friendship bracelets, and scans the tables. An icy chill shoots up my spine as his gaze lands on me. For a second I wonder if he recognizes me, but when I look closer, it's as if he's looking right through me, a random girl. No one he should concern himself with. Not at all.

Levin gave specific instructions for all of the lifeguards to plaster big-ass smiles on our faces and pretend like we're waiters at a five-star hotel. The usual playfulness and camaraderie have been replaced with fake laughs and hidden eye rolls. But the parents are oblivious, cooing over their children as they watch them flap around in the lake and show off their waterskiing skills.

Stu talks up some of the heavy hitters—parents whose kids are VIPs, thanks to their donations or status. I shield my eyes from the sun and spot him slapping a cable news anchor on the back, chuckling at what must be an off-color joke. I imagine he's talking about how the guy's daughter, some uncoordinated twelve-year-old, is bound to be an Olympic swimmer one day.

Levin snorts next to me. "God, I hate visiting day."

"But you seem normal," I say.

"COD," he says. When I give him a quizzical look, he explains, "Child of divorce."

"Ah," I say. "Well, it always sucked for me, too."

Levin glances at me sideways, almost impressed. "Yeah, I guess Willa and Lou were always working. Musta been weird when you were a camper."

I shrug and scan the waterfront. Ava and Imogen are both up top, on cabin duty, so I'm alone down here. The parents all look alike, with their designer athleisure or their preppy sweater sets. Lots of big floppy hats and sunglasses, handbags that are meant to be taken to Michelin star restaurants, not a summer camp. It's like peering into so many of these kids' futures.

But there's one guy who *doesn't* look like everyone else. Mark Cantor. There he is, walking down the hill, trailing behind the twins, who are dragging their towels along the gravel. His eyes are glued to the phone in his hand, but Bianca and Jordie look free, like they have no cares in the world. They each have one of their mother's hands as they lead her down to the lake's edge. Mark waves them off and sits down on the towel wall. He doesn't look up from his phone.

Instead of freshly ironed khakis, he's wearing the midlife crisis special: expensive-looking joggers and a tight white T-shirt that probably costs more than my winter coat. Thousand-dollar sneakers are tied to his feet. He's got a casual way about him, with gold aviator sunglasses and thick dark hair. He's tanned from spending all his time in Palm Beach, but he doesn't resemble the other high rollers here, the old stuffy guys who are dressed for a golf game.

Mark looks . . . relaxed. And because of that, since he's lazing around here like he doesn't have another daughter on the same property, like he may not have been involved in some massive scam that led Heller to his death, something inside me snaps.

Levin rushes off to deal with a kayak incident and I stride over to Mark, standing in front of him so I block the sun. It takes a beat before he notices my presence. Then he glances up from his phone, his eyes hidden behind those dumb sunglasses.

"Can I help you?" he asks, annoyed.

I'm shocked even though I know I shouldn't be. I've been in his daughter's life for a decade and he still has no idea who I am.

"Goldie Easton," I say. "Ava's best friend." Saying that phrase, those words sandwiched together, gives me a bubble of pride.

His face shows no emotion. "Right," he says, then turns back to his phone.

"You know she's here," I say. "Up by the cabins. And you haven't even said hello."

This gets his attention and I can tell I struck a nerve by the force with which he shoves his phone into his pocket. He stands and crosses his arms, his back toward the water, hiding his face from his family. He pushes his sunglasses on top of his head, and now that I'm so close I can see a few gray hairs sprouting above his ears. A spattering of wrinkles forming at the corners of his eyes.

There's a small deodorant stain near the bottom of his shirt and the knees of his joggers are a bit worn. And when I glance at his watch—a thick, shiny, heavy piece of metal that screams *expensive*—I can see that the pearl-studded hands are frozen, like the timepiece is broken.

A sense of unease hangs over me. Spending time with Ava and Imogen in New York, watching them dissect people in real time, it helped expose some of the cracks in perfectly manicured appearances. A bitten nail so red you can see blood? That means insecurity. A poorly stitched enclosure on a wallet? Yeah, that's a fake from Canal Street.

Looking at Mark now I wonder if his façade is cracking in front of me.

"You know you're Ava's dad, too, right?" I ask. My shoulders tense and I know I'm pushing him.

Mark raises an eyebrow and smirks. "Goldie," he says, looking at me intently. "Ah, yes. You must be the one from Roxwood. The townie."

My heart stings and I wonder where he heard that word. If Ava ever used it to describe me. A moment of betrayal flutters in my heart. "I am," I say, trying to hold my chin high. I lean in and lower my voice. I know I need to take a risk. It's my only chance. "I heard something interesting about your business recently."

But Mark holds up a hand, unconcerned. "With all due respect, Goldie, you have no idea what I do. And you certainly haven't a clue about what goes on between me and my daughter."

Then his wife calls to him from the sand. The twins look at us and wave excitedly. We both wave back, playing the roles of doting counselor and father.

When they turn away, Mark's face falls. I try to think of something else to say, of another dagger to land in his chest. But I can't.

I'm frozen. Mark takes a few steps down the sand before he swivels his head to look back at me.

"Did you know the boy?" he asks. "The one who died here. His name was Heller, right?"

The question shocks me so deeply that the only answer I can provide comes in the form of a nod.

Mark shakes his head and looks back toward his family. "Such a shame." He starts walking toward the water, his gait calm and secure. He doesn't turn back around, doesn't glance in my direction, even when he reaches the edge of the water, gazing out at the lake.

CHAPTER 40

Then

"You had to do *what*?"

It was my second summer at Alpine Lake and all of the girls in my cabin started talking about the ridiculous crap they had to do in order to gain admissions to camp.

Imogen nodded her head aggressively. "I had to send in tapes of my plays," she said. "Of me singing and dancing, too."

The ten kids in my cabin were sitting in a circle, and the other campers piped up, too. One said Stu and Mellie came to her little league softball games and another said they reviewed clips of her gymnastics meets. They all shrugged as if this were no big deal. As if being able to go to *sleepaway camp* should be determined by things like extracurriculars and participation in class.

Everyone commiserated about the test they took to determine their congeniality and how well they might get along with others. Apparently, the thing was divided into multiple choice and essay sections, like a standardized test.

"I thought it was *impossible*," one of the girls said. "My mom kept saying it was harder to get into Alpine Lake than Harvard."

"*My* mom said she'd buy my older sister a new laptop if I failed and she retook it for me!" another one joked, as if this were a badge of honor instead of horribly embarrassing, not to mention immoral.

I hugged my knees to my chest and wondered why I didn't have to do any of that to come here. I secretly hoped it was because I was special—I was worthy of being here without proving anything to anyone. But I knew it was not because I was special. My presence was a glitch. A mistake.

One of the other girls nudged me with her foot.

"You're so lucky your parents work here. I bet you didn't have to do *anything* to get in."

That's when I realized everyone saw me as a charity case—that I was only accepted because of the work, the sweat, my parents put into this place.

I kept quiet but Ava threw her arm around me. "I didn't have to do anything either," she said, smiling at me. "I guess *some* of us are special." Ava wiggled her eyebrows at me, holding her chin high, and I was grateful she was fibbing for my benefit.

Later that night, after flashlight time, I crept into Ava's bed and cuddled up close to her.

"You didn't have to lie," I said. "I know why I'm here."

"It wasn't a lie," Ava said. "I didn't have to do any of that stuff either. No test, no tapes." Her face was serious as stone, as if she believed that some of us *were* special enough to bypass an admissions process that no other summer camp has.

It was in that moment it became obvious to me that because of her parents' enormous wealth, because of all the perks of having a Cantor kid at Alpine Lake, Ava had been allowed in without a second thought. Like me.

That was the first time I felt bad for Ava, that I realized even with all she had, she was still capable of believing in the things that made her feel better, even if they weren't true.

CHAPTER 41

Now

Mark Cantor knows Heller died at camp.

The thought haunts me as we watch the kids say goodbye to their parents driving down the hill. All the moms and dads wave tearfully out their windows as some of our campers sob into Meg's stomach, dampening her shirt.

I pat a few campers on the back as they pout and sniffle. I remind them that there's a whole bunch of candy and treats waiting for them in the bunk. But I can't get Ava's dad out of my head.

As we head to the dining hall for dinner, I glance at Jordie and Bianca, huddled close together, talking excitedly about the books of crossword puzzles their mom left them. They don't have answers. They're nine.

Ava drops into her chair but she's quiet and distracted, pushing a soggy piece of pineapple pizza around on her plate, ignoring requests from her adoring campers. She leaves the dining hall quickly without saying goodbye. Imogen looks over at me and shrugs before one of her girls tugs on her sleeve, asking for help with her high ponytail.

I head back to my cabin and hang with the girls, snacking on homemade cookies and Australian licorice, hugging the kids who need some extra love after an overwhelming day. Later, when all the kids have crashed and the cabin's full of the sounds of labored breathing and a few soft snores, I try to find my own sleep but it won't come. I toss and turn for a while but it's no use. My head is swimming with questions, all of them involving Heller, Ava, and Mark Cantor.

I reach up onto the shelf above my bed and grab my phone. Back in the winter, whenever I couldn't sleep, I'd look at my camera roll to find old images of Imogen, Ava, and me at camp when we were kids. The stills became so familiar over the years. Us in matching Fourth of July outfits. Preparing for a DJ social. Even with everything going on, I wonder if they'll bring me comfort now.

But when I tap over to my photos, I sit up in bed. The most recent pictures are from the clerk's office. Files hidden in a folder in Heller's desk, marked *Camp Alpine Lake*. After discovering those emails, I forgot about all these pieces of paper. I swipe through fast to find they're all spreadsheets, full of numbers that have no obvious meaning attached. I lean back against my pillow and clench my core, full of frustration.

Goddammit, Heller.

None of this makes sense. If he wanted Cal to find this crap, he would have left some indication of what it meant. I flip over onto my side and kick my covers off, restless. How am I the person who ends up with a camera roll full of cryptic spreadsheets? The person desperate to find out what happened to Heller? After what he did, the fact that I'm still searching for answers—for him—makes me want to crawl out of my skin.

I grasp my phone tightly and swipe to exit the photos, but my thumb slips and the next image comes into frame. The composition makes me pause.

On the screen, there's a piece of paper with a bunch of cards scanned onto it, like someone was photocopying them to have duplicates.

I look at it closely and make out that the top one is a debit card with no bank or name listed. And the second one looks like a pre-paid phone card. Below it is a phone number typed in big black numbers, but it's not a US one. Instead, it has a country code, +41.

But the cards aren't what make me stop. It's the fact that at the bottom of the piece of paper, there's something written in pencil. It's not in Heller's handwriting, his loopy cursive that bubbles up and expands. It's small and messy, barely legible at all. Almost like chicken scratch. It looks familiar, like I've seen those kinds of letters before, but I can't remember where.

After I enlarge it as big as I can, I can finally make out the words. *Don't screw this up.*

Tuesday night, there's a frantic energy as all the off-duty counselors head toward the buses for another night out. I try to fight the clawing feeling in my chest, the one that warns me about going to Truly's, about stepping foot into town.

The past few times we've been here, the bar's been quiet, with only a handful of familiar faces seated in booths. But tonight feels different. It's been a month since Heller died, four whole weeks, and for whatever reason, that's a marker—at least to me. It's time for the fair-weather mourners to say goodbye to their tearstained faces, to reemerge into society, and for the truly devastated, the ones whose lives are irrevocably changed, to press on with deep-seated trauma they have no interest in dissecting.

Everyone at Alpine Lake may have forgotten Heller existed in the first place and that this summer started out with death. But in Roxwood, his passing is an open wound.

Howie, the bus driver, pulls out of camp. He ignores the flasks and lights a cigarette out the window.

I'm squished into a seat with Ava but she turns her back to me when we get on the main road. She starts talking to Craig, leaving me out of the conversation. It irks me and I think back to what her dad called me—*townie*—and how much is still unsaid between us.

Imogen pops her head up over the seat in front of me and leans forward, her arms dangling down to tickle the tops of my thighs.

"You okay, Goldilocks?" she says, resting her chin on the top of the seat.

I nod and look out the window.

"Mope city over here," she says.

Her head's cocked to one side, concern furrowed in her brow. My heart softens. "Just a mood, you know?"

"Not a good one."

"Nope," I say.

Imogen reaches for my hand and squeezes and then sits back down with Tommy in front of me. It's one of the things I love about Imo. She doesn't feel the need to make everything better or say trite bullshit. She gets that sometimes shit is hard and you need to feel it.

Meanwhile Ava doesn't even notice something's wrong. I grab her flask from her purse and take a big gulp. Then another.

By the time we get to town I'm nice and buzzed, but I don't feel silly or confident like I usually do after a few drinks. Instead, there's anger and rot floating around inside me.

When we push through the entrance, I'm relieved to find Truly's is mostly empty. I make a beeline for the bar, where I wait for the old guy behind the counter to notice me. It takes a second, but when he finally comes over, he's not there to take my order. He sets down a plastic cup full of something dark, smelling of whiskey.

I must look confused because he nods over to the corner. When I look that way, I spot Cal Drummond sitting on a stool by himself. His face is obscured by a Roxwood hockey beanie even though it's summer, but his eyes are drunk and sad. He raises a beer bottle in my direction and my face flushes, unsure of what to do or say. I take the drink, my insides hard, and sip it gingerly, tasting the offering like it's poison. It's a whiskey and Diet Coke. Heller's favorite.

The taste burns and I'm back in Heller's hut, where the cold crept in through the windowpanes. It's a random November night. Cal and Trina are playing ping-pong and *Goodfellas* is on, the movie cast against a white sheet hanging from the far wall. Ruthie puts on some crappy country-rap song and Heller and I exchange looks like *what the fuck is this?*

We both stifle laughs, sly smiles spreading on our faces. Heller comes up behind me and wraps his arms around my waist, looking out at the party—at the group he invited me into. He leans down, his lips grazing my ear. I can smell his breath, the sweet booze on his tongue, as he whispers softly, "I'm so glad you're here."

But that's not now. That's not real. Heller and that night are memories, ones that means nothing anymore. I take another sip and steady myself against the sticky bar. I squeeze my eyes shut and tell myself the truth.

You're at Truly's. Heller doesn't love you. Heller is dead.

"Whoa, you okay?" Craig comes up behind me and rests a hand on my shoulder, but I flinch instinctively, needing to get away from his touch. "Geez, I was trying to help," he says, holding up his hands.

"Sorry," I say even though I'm not. "I need some air."

Craig takes a step toward the group of counselors and I rush to the back of the bar, which opens up into an alley. I push through the door and step into the warm night. I let it slam behind me and slide my back down against the side of the building, so I'm squatting on my heels. My stupid platform heels that make no sense here in Roxwood.

I inhale hard and try to ignore the stench coming from the trash. I press my hands to my temples. *How did I get here?*

But then the door swings open behind me and I rush to stand, to act like everything's normal and I'm fine. I expect to see an Alpine Laker coming to take a piss after learning the bathroom line was too long, but when I turn around, I run straight into Cal's chest.

"I've been trying to get ahold of you since Fourth of July," he says. Cal's dark eyes are stormy and half-closed, like he's had a lot to drink. But his shoulders are slumped, and all of a sudden it hits me that he's a long-hauler, like me. Someone who won't be able to move on from Heller's death so easily. My whole body softens.

"There's no service at camp."

Cal sighs. "Look, I need Heller's badge back."

"I don't have it on me."

"Bullshit," he says.

I open my purse and dump the contents on the ground, watching as my mascara and some out-of-ink pens roll around on the concrete, no badge in sight.

Cal shakes his head and squats to pick stuff up.

We're both quiet and there's so much between us. So many years of shit unsaid. All of the secrets I kept for him when we were kids. The memories of playing house and fairies and slaying dragons on each other's lawns. The final few months in the fall, when everything seemed shiny and possible, when I became *one of them*, when without words we put the past behind us. When Heller cast his spotlight on me. I thought Cal and I had mended our bond. I thought he would be my *friend* again. But he shoved me aside like everyone else.

"I went there." I bend over and grab a handful of mints, a few beads from the arts and crafts shed that fell from my bag.

Cal crouches down next to me. "What?"

"The clerk's office."

"Did you find anything?" He smells like cigarettes and whiskey, sweat and gasoline. He smells like Roxwood, like winter. I don't know whether to trust him with the information about Ava and her dad. Telling him feels like a betrayal. But omitting the information . . . I'm not sure I can do that to Heller.

"He thought Ava's dad was involved in some scandal," I say. "He wrote a dozen tips to newspapers the day he died."

Cal's eyes widen. "You think she . . . ?"

I want to shake my head. To say absolutely not. But I hesitate, the words stuck in my throat.

Cal starts pacing around the alley, hands pulling at his greasy hair. "Did you see anything there about someone named Sally Burke?"

The woman who worked next to Heller, who Ruthie thought he was *boning*. My stomach flips at the thought.

"They sat next to each other."

Cal takes in this information and furrows his brow like he's trying to solve a puzzle. "Did you ever meet her?"

I shake my head.

"Judah asked me to go through Heller's mail the other day," Cal says. "He couldn't bring himself to do it. I found this."

He reaches into his pocket and hands me a slim envelope. There's no return address, but Heller's name is written on the front in handwriting that looks messy and familiar, like the words on the photocopies of the debit card.

I turn over the envelope and pull out the letter.

In the same handwriting, there are only a few words.

I'm so sorry. Can we talk?
Sally

"What the hell is this?" I ask.

Cal shrugs. "I was hoping you could tell me."

I shake my head and stare at the letter. *What was she sorry for?*

"Hey," Cal says, reaching out to touch my shoulder. "Remember you told me that you wanted me to back you up when you come clean about the accident? About who was driving?"

I nod. That feels like so long ago now.

"I'll do it." Cal's voice is sure and he straightens his shoulders for emphasis. "There's clearly something fucked-up going on. Everyone needs to know the truth. About everything."

A rush of emotion comes over me but before I can say anything else, the door opens behind me. I spin around to find Meg, ambling toward me. She slings an arm over my shoulder. "You okay, Goldie?"

The last thing I need is Meg finding out about whatever the hell is going on with Cal right now. "Fine," I say.

Meg lingers for a second but then takes a step back. "All right. By the pool table if you need me." She retreats but when I look at Cal, there's a puzzled look on his face.

"Who's that?"

"My boss. Meg."

"She looks familiar," he says.

"She's hot and blonde. You probably think they all look the same."

"Oh, fuck off," he says.

"Back at you."

Cal swallows hard and smiles. "Goldie," he says. My name is soft and short on his lips. "I'm sorry," he says.

I cross my arms to hide the tender ache inside my heart. Then Cal says it again.

"I'm sorry."

CHAPTER 42

Then

Ava and Imogen came to visit me in Roxwood sophomore year. They invited themselves after Ava's fall break trip to Malibu fell through at the last minute, and Mom and I spent a full two weeks planning the itinerary for the perfect long weekend.

We would go leaf peeping in the Green Mountain National Forest, get maple creemees at Grandee's, and kayak over to the waterfront. Mom even convinced Stu and Mellie to let us spend an afternoon at Alpine Lake, so they could see camp in the fall.

I was so nervous as I waited for them to arrive in a black car Ava's mom hired to drive them the full six hours north. I sat on the couch in our shabby living room, peering out the window, feeling like I was back at camp, waiting at the gazebo for the buses to pull around the traffic circle.

Our reunion was tender, full of tears and tackled hugs. I was grateful they didn't ask for things they knew we didn't have—like chilled vodka or Megaformer workout classes. They knew coming to visit meant slow-braised meats for dinner, Mom's seven-layer bars for dessert, and movie marathons under my favorite quilts.

The weekend was perfect—all flannel and pumpkins and apple cider donuts—until Ava got bored on their final night in town.

We were sitting in my bedroom, a deck of cards strewn in front of us. I dipped a Wheat Thin in a jar of Nutella and laughed as Imogen tried to recite Cher's opening monologue from *Clueless* by heart.

After Imo's third failed attempt, Ava butted in. "What if," she started, "we walked down to Truly's? See what all the fuss is about before we become counselors next year?"

We hadn't stepped foot inside the bar yet, only heard about it through stories from the older people at camp. But kids in my grade had started hanging out there after hockey games. I had never been invited.

As I was about to suggest we watch another movie, Imogen jumped up and down. "Can we, Goldie? Maybe we can tell your parents we went to get another creemee. We can take a look inside. They won't even know."

I chewed on the inside of my cheek, trying to find the words to let them know that my parents *would* find out because things don't often stay hidden in a small town like Roxwood.

But I let them convince me and even lied to Mom and Dad, who didn't seem to think anything was weird about our little fib.

I could feel Ava's and Imogen's nervous anticipation as we walked down my driveway and made a left and then a right as we hit the main drag in Roxwood.

"There it is!" Ava pointed to the hand-painted sign that hung on the front and I felt the butterflies hum in my stomach.

"Yep, in all its glory." I kicked at the ground with my worn-out sneaker. "Can we go now?"

"Hold on," Imo said. "Don't you want to see what it's like?"

"I heard they don't card." Ava's eyes twinkled, full of mischief, and before we could stop her, she took off running toward the entrance and ducked inside.

I let Imogen drag me over there but when we got to the door, I couldn't do it. I planted my feet. "I'll wait out here," I said. "Do a lap and come out."

Imogen pouted. "Seriously?"

I nodded.

Imo kissed me on the cheek and darted inside. I leaned up against the brick wall and exhaled, watching my breath turn into a little cloud of smoke in front of my face. I could hear Imo and Ava laughing behind the door and squeezed my eyes shut.

"Goldie?"

When I opened my eyes, I saw Cal standing in front of me, his arm slinked around a girl I didn't recognize. He had a big smirk on his face and smelled like weed and whiskey. His pants hung low on his hips, too low, and he looked skinny, like he hadn't eaten dinner—or lunch. I pushed aside my instinct to worry about him. He hadn't wanted me to for years.

"Hi," I said.

He nodded to the girl he was with and she looked me up and down before heading inside Truly's.

"Does Goldie Easton like to party now?" he asked, slurring the words. I watched him sway back and forth, pitying him in a way I hadn't since his mother died. He was like a stranger.

Before I could answer, Imogen and Ava busted through the door, their hands clasped together, laughing like crazy. "Imo stole a glass," Ava said, holding it up high above her head. "Souvenir!"

Cal clocked them and a look of recognition came across his face.

"No way. You must be Ava and Imogen."

Ava stopped laughing then and looked at Cal with a concerned, curious expression. I could sense her taking in his faded, baggy jeans and the too-small winter coat. I could tell she was making up her mind about him, filing him away as no one important. No one to care about. "Our reputation must precede us, Imo."

Imogen laughed and fumbled for the Truly's glass, but Cal's face stayed stoic.

"Great to finally meet the people who made Goldie think she was too good for Roxwood."

We all got quiet then, and I wanted to melt into my shoes, to disappear completely and pretend like we never left my bedroom floor.

"Interesting you say that," Ava said, a smirk forming on her full lips. She stepped toward him so they stood eye to eye. She didn't flinch. "Because one day, Camp Alpine Lake is going to buy the rest of this shithole town and run the pieces of trash like you straight out of it." Ava grabbed hold of my hand and started walking. "Come on, Goldie."

Cal stood there in disbelief, bewilderment in his eyes.

I wonder if he expected me to stand up for him, to tell Ava she had no idea what the people in Roxwood were actually like. But I didn't. Because in so many ways, I believed her.

CHAPTER 43

Now

"Did you hear how they're going to break color war this year?" Tommy asks.

Most of the counselors are moving slowly thanks to last night's adventures at Truly's. After I came back in from the alley, from Cal, someone handed me a tequila shot. I tossed it back and winced before the booze started to numb everything.

It was James's birthday and he kept buying more and more drinks, sending them around the bar until it was time for us to head back to camp. The whole night ended with him pissing himself on the bus. Poor Craig had to clean him up and shove a breath mint into his mouth when we pulled into the traffic circle so his group leader wouldn't notice. But we all knew he'd never get in trouble.

Stu and Mellie ignore these kinds of things, especially when former campers like James are involved. Kids whose parents spent a hundred grand sending their kids here year after year, kids who are desperate to send *their* kids here in a few decades. Those are the cash cows. The lifeblood. You don't fuck with lifeblood.

Now Tommy's standing in front of me in line for the fruit bar. He stabs a strawberry with his fork and takes a bite out of it.

"Where'd you hear about color war break?" I ask, grabbing a banana. Stu and Mellie always try to keep the start of color war a huge secret, but it inevitably slips out once someone like Tommy starts blabbing about it.

"Overheard a bunch of the group leaders talking about it by the coffee machine," he says, nodding over to the hot bevvy area. "I hear they're going to do it after booth carnival instead of movie night."

"They did that when we were Ramblers," I say, more for my own memory than his.

Tommy smiles. "Fuck, that was fun." Then he leans in so close I can smell the booze from last night on his breath. "Sometimes, I swear I wish I were still a camper. Shit was so much easier, you know?"

I look at him with his thick red hair and a smattering of pimples spread out along his nose. What kind of hardships has Tommy Eisenstat faced, really? He was a varsity lacrosse player in an affluent New York City suburb and is headed to Tulane in the fall, where he'll undoubtedly double major in premed and beer pong. If he manages to graduate without tanking his GPA or getting involved in some hazing bullshit, he'll go off to med school and land a sweet residency alongside his father in Mount Sinai's cardiology program. He'll work for a few years in the city so he can meet a wife, and then decamp for private practice in New Jersey, where he'll live five minutes from where he grew up, have babies, and send them to Camp Alpine Lake as soon as they turn eight. He'll tell his pretty little wife, "That's where I used to fuck that movie star Imogen Wexler."

But I don't say any of this to him. Instead, I peel my banana and look toward my kids.

"Gotta go."

On my way, I grab a slice of toast but before I can slather it in butter, Meg tugs on my elbow and pulls me off to the side.

"You can't have toast without . . ." I start to whine, but when I catch a look at her face, I shut my mouth fast. Her eyes are darting around the room and her pale neck is covered in red, like she's super nervous, like something's wrong.

"What's going on?" I ask.

Meg looks around like she doesn't want anyone to hear, but when I scan the room I notice a tension simmering through the air, and for some reason, all eyes seem to be trained on the girls from Bloodroot, on Jordie and Bianca.

They're oblivious, with heads bowed toward one another, matching bows sitting high on their ponytails. They both have Ava's eyes. Her nose, too. They look like Ava did at their age. Determined and smart, but breakable.

"It's the Cantors," Meg whispers. She shoves a piece of newspaper toward me. I unfold it carefully and am greeted with a clipping from the *New York Post* with today's date. An all-caps headline dominates the top of the page.

**FINANCE HERO MARK CANTOR
BECOMES OVERNIGHT ZERO THANKS TO
MAJOR TAX EVASION SCANDAL**

I bite my lip and my heart speeds up. Heller was right. "Has anyone else seen this? It's not like the kids have internet."

Meg clenches her fists and darts her eyes around the room. "News travels fast here, so, uh, yeah."

"Shit," I say again. I look around for Ava. Even though I still have so many questions for her, I need to find her. There's no way she can deal with this on her own.

"Everyone's staring at them like they're zoo animals." Meg looks like she's about to break into a sweat. "I'm gonna bring them to the office with Stu and Mellie. Can you get all the other girls ready for swim?"

"Of course," I say, though all I want to do is find Ava. "Do they know? Jordie and Bianca?"

Meg looks over my shoulder at Mellie and mumbles some sort of goodbye before scooping up the twins and leading them out of the room.

I ball up the article in my fist and head to the bathroom. It's only when I'm locked inside a stall that I lay it flat on the toilet paper dispenser and start to read.

Cantor Assets, founded by Wall Street legend Mark Cantor, has officially gone belly-up. The former New Yorker has been accused of knowingly helping his clients avoid taxes by working with Swiss bankers to allegedly set up illegal offshore accounts. While this activity was legal as recently as the mid-2000s, it's now against the law to maintain these kinds of hidden funds, often used to obscure how much income the ultra-rich actually have. Those found to have hidden offshore assets could face serious jail time.

Sources say Cantor Assets was facilitating one of the largest networks of secret accounts from US residents. Cantor refuses to give up his full client list, but the IRS claims he was working with tech CEOs, celebrities, and foreign adversaries of the United States.

When we reached his attorney for comment, Cantor's lawyer declined to say anything and instead hung up the phone, but not before calling this reporter "a putz." This story is developing but Cantor's future in the financial industry will not be.

Everything I read buzzes around my brain. *This* was what Heller was trying to get out into the world. The sleigh bells ring out in the dining hall and I know that's my cue to bring the girls back to the cabin.

I blow out a puff of air and hustle out of the bathroom, gathering the campers with a hurried gait. I keep an ear out, trying to hear if they're talking about the Cantors, but no one brings them up. These girls are too concerned with swim lessons and the tennis tournament, friendship bracelets and Mad Libs. They barely notice the twins are gone.

The girls rush inside Bloodroot to change for swim, and I pause on the porch, breathing in and out, trying to keep my cool.

"Have you seen her yet?" Imogen appears next to me with frazzled hair and wide eyes.

"Nope," I say, holding my sweatshirt tightly around my waist.

She leans back against the wood railing. "You heard the news, right?"

"Yup."

"I can't believe it came out."

My stomach hardens and I turn my head toward Imo.

"You knew?"

Imogen turns red and her mouth gets small. "A few days before we left for camp, Ava's mom told her she was moving a bunch of assets into more secure environments."

"What the hell does that mean?"

Imogen shrugs. "I don't know but Ava took it as a sign that her dad was up to some shady shit and her mom was trying to cover their tracks, keep their funds safe." She looks around. "I guess those rumors from a few years back didn't start from no-where."

I cover my mouth. Heller was *right*. But how did he know? *Why* did he know? Why did he even care?

"Ava called me crying, totally freaking out. Told me not to tell anyone."

"But . . ."

"The whole camp probably knows by now. Hell, everyone in the city *definitely* knows. Ava's life as she knew it is officially over."

But all I can think about is the fact that Ava told Imogen and not me. And Imogen never thought to clue me in. Is it because I wouldn't get it? I wouldn't understand the high-stakes world they come from and how one bad decision could lead to a million smaller ones that could rip lives apart? If anything, I know that better than both of them.

My eyes start to burn and I bite my lip, forcing myself not to cry.

Imogen looks at me and reaches a hand out to squeeze my shoulder. "Come on, Goldie, don't be like this. We have to be there for Ava right now."

I hate that she knows what I'm thinking. But it's only half of it. If Ava knew about her dad—and if Heller confronted her about it in the dinghy that night—then Ava had a perfect motive to kill

Heller, to keep him quiet. And the idea that Ava could actually do that . . . the realization makes my blood run cold.

"Ava made me promise not to tell. It's not like she was proud of it."

"Yeah, well, I tell you everything." But as soon as the words leave my lips, I regret them.

She looks at me hard then, with knowing, suspicious eyes. "Do you, Goldie? Do you really?"

I take a step back, wondering what she knows as she walks away.

CHAPTER 44

Then

The last time I visited Ava in the city was in early October. Excelsior Prep homecoming. That Friday night, I stepped off a bus that stunk like blue cheese and walked into the bowels of Port Authority Bus Terminal. I spun around, searching for Ava and Imogen, who said they'd meet me there. The stench of sticky buns and garbage filled my nostrils and I blinked, trying to take it all in. Coming to New York always felt like preparing for battle. This time was no different.

It only took a second before Ava and Imogen appeared, wearing silky tops and glitter on their cheeks. They held big plastic bottles of water and were teetering on stilettos, giggling and grasping each other's hands. "Oh my god, there she is!" Ava screamed. She toddled toward me on her heels and nearly tackled me to the ground. Imogen grabbed me by the shoulders, shaking me and pulling me toward her.

They were wasted and giddy, and Ava grabbed my duffel bag, slinging it over her shoulder. "Come on, my favorite pizza's on Bleecker, but there's a passable spot around the corner, and after the night we've had, we *need* pizza."

The exhaustion I'd been carrying moments before was replaced with desire—desire for them, for their night to be one we shared, and for them to forget they had ever been apart from me. So, I let them drag me to a pizza counter, where we wolfed down plain slices sprinkled with parm and red pepper flakes. Ava's phone buzzed, but she refused to pick it up, and instead, she and Imogen regaled me with stories about the party they had been to at the Bowery Hotel, where some kid rented a suite and hired a DJ and there were personal mini bottles of Veuve being passed around like Diet Coke cans. I nodded and laughed and sat on my hands to stop them from shaking. And when we were done, we shoved our grease-soaked paper plates into a trash can and let Ava hail us a taxi heading uptown.

We snuggled in the back, and as we zipped up Park Avenue, I remember thinking, *This is the beginning. This is the start of my new life.*

Ava lives in one of those old doorman buildings that looks like a museum and takes up a whole block. It has its own courtyard, roof deck, pool, and shuttle service that will take you to the airport.

That night, we stepped into the elevator, operated by a white-bearded guy named Nicky, who always handed us peppermint candies from the pocket of his smart gray uniform. We took turns sticking out our tongues until the doors opened on Ava's floor, right into her doorway, since her mom owned the whole floor. It wasn't the penthouse she had lived in with both her parents, but it was only two floors down. It never ceased to take my breath away, how this whole three-sixty view of Manhattan was hers.

The next morning, Ava woke us up early so we could grab bagels and lox before the rush. The fish melted on my tongue and I had my first taste of roe, letting the little orange bubbles burst inside my mouth.

At some point the doorbell rang and Ava squealed. "I have a surprise for you guys."

Imogen raised her eyebrows but gave a knowing look. "You didn't..."

Ava shrugged and skipped to the door.

"What did she do?' I asked Imogen, but Ava returned before she could respond. Behind her was a team of chic-looking people, carrying suitcases. They set them down and unzipped the bags, revealing blow-dryers, hot tools, and more makeup than I'd ever seen outside of a drugstore.

Imogen kicked her feet in the air and leapt off the couch. "Ava, you nut!" But she threw her arms around Ava, who laughed and laughed.

"It's the least I can do since you guys came all this way and we *never* get this kind of time together."

"Wow," I said. "Thank you so much, Ava, I mean . . ." I didn't know what to say, how I could repay her for such an extravagant gift.

But Ava stopped me before I could say anything else. She wrapped an arm around me and kissed my cheek. "How often does Goldie Easton come to New York?" she asked.

I blushed but then Ava introduced Paul and the rest of the members of her glam squad, dropping little details about what fashion shows they worked and which celebrities they attended to. I smiled and nodded as my stomach flipped, the smoked salmon I had enjoyed suddenly sour.

An hour later, when Paul spun me around in the stool at Ava's breakfast bar so I could look at myself in the mirror, I gasped, barely recognizing myself.

I stood up from the chair and padded down the hall to Ava's room so I could show her Paul's handiwork. I peeked my head inside the door, waiting for her to turn around. But she was hunched over in the corner, talking quietly, angrily into her phone.

"What are you saying?" she asked.

I couldn't tell who she was talking to, not at first. But then she rested her head against the bookshelf, weary, and when she spoke, her voice broke.

"Is everything going to be okay, Dad?"

She nodded a few times and then stood up straight. "Will I see you over winter break?" Ava paused and ran a hand through her hair. "Switzerland? Again?" She paused. "Fine," she said, her voice hard.

I took that as my cue and tiptoed out of the room, back down the hall, to where Imogen was running her fingers through her hair. There we waited for Ava to come out, smiling and excited, as if nothing strange had happened at all.

CHAPTER 45

Now

Meg blares a plastic vuvuzela through the cabin.

I pull my hoodie up over my head and groan. I'm perched on Fran Gertz's bed, weaving her curly hair into two tidy French braids. "Shut it down," I say, which causes Fran to erupt into giggles.

"No can do," Meg says, her voice cheerful, so far from how nervous and freaked out she was this morning. Stu and Mellie must have calmed her down. Jordie and Bianca, too, considering they're now playing jacks in the corner of the cabin with some of the other girls.

Meg claps her hands together. "We've got world cup tonight."

I will not be participating in the annual event, where all of the American counselors play soccer against all of the international counselors and force the kids to pick sides, plying their fans with extra cookie patrol in exchange for loud-ass cheers. But I did promise Meg I would be on camper duty all night so she could play—and kick all the Americans' asses, a challenge I firmly support.

She's wearing her Manchester United kit and she's got a Union Jack temporary tattoo slapped on her arm.

"Spirited, are we?" I ask.

"Don't you know it!" She feigns punching me in the gut and calls for the campers to get their asses into gear.

I pull on my sneakers, going about my getting-ready motions like everything's *fine*, but it's impossible not to think about the *New York Post* article and the mess that links the Cantors to Heller. I need to talk to Ava, even if I'm terrified if what she'll say or how she'll react. Because in my most honest moments, I can admit that I'm frightened by what I'll find out, what she's done.

"Hey, you all right?" Meg asks. "You look like you're gonna puke."

"There's a lot going on," I say.

Meg shakes her head but her eyes grow serious. "It's a weird summer, ya?"

I mumble my agreement.

Meg gives me a knowing look. "It's all right, you know." She pauses and pulls her hair into a high pony. "For this place to not be perfect."

I pick my head up. "What do you mean?"

"All you lifers. You act like this camp is the best place on earth. Everything about it. But it's a business, a piece of land."

She snaps her mouth shut like she's said too much, and heads into the camper room, ready to rile them up.

Meg's wrong though. She doesn't get it. This place has to be perfect—especially when there are so many things that aren't.

I peer out the window and see Imogen and Ava walking hand in hand toward the soccer fields. Ava's head is ducked, her platinum hair loose around her face.

I don't know what I see when I look at her anymore.

Is she my best friend, the girl who stands up for me, who would give me the world? Or is she a killer, someone who hurt Heller because he found out her family's biggest secret and threatened to expose it to the world?

All I know is that I have to find out.

Tonight.

The floodlights make the soccer field look like a stadium and all the kids are set up with blankets and pillows, spread out along the grass. The campers who have no interest in the spectacle are deep in their graphic novels, their friendship bracelets, their nail polish. And the soccer fans are pressed right up against the sidelines, face paint displaying who they're rooting for.

I scan the crowd for Ava and Imogen, stationed a few blankets away, sitting in fold-up camper chairs and sipping glass bottles of diet root beer.

I ignore the frustrated buzzing in my stomach and turn back to my group of girls. "Who wants pizza?" I say with a smile.

They all raise their hands, and I ask Tommy to watch them while I flag down a couple pies being cooked on demand at the rented food truck over by the sheds. I bring the boxes back to the girls and watch them dive in, grabbing at slices of steaming hot pepperoni and plain. Slicks of oil drip down their chins. That'll keep them occupied for a bit.

I back away from the group and take small, cautious steps toward Imogen and Ava. They look relaxed—exhausted—arms long, dangling over the sides of the chairs. I wonder if whatever

I'm about to say will blow that up, ruin the unstable peace Imogen's helped Ava find after today's news. But I need to know. I need to find out the truth.

"Rip their legs off, Meg!" Ava calls, cupping her mouth.

Imogen leans back and laughs. "It's no fun to root for America, you know?"

"Never is," Ava says.

I clear my throat, trying to summon some courage deep within me to finally confront Ava about what I know.

"We need to talk." My voice comes out stronger than I thought it would, with more power, more rage. I glance at Imogen. "Alone."

Ava looks up, surprised, and stands. "Alone? Come on, G."

"Fine," I say, trying to keep my voice steady. I lean in so close I can see Ava's pores. "Heller knew about your dad."

Ava doesn't flinch, but I hear Imogen inhale sharply.

"He was coming here that night to find you," I say. "He—"

"Stop it, Goldie." Ava's voice is loud and harsh and she jabs her pointer finger right at my chest. Her eyes are full of fire. There's something different inside her. Something ferocious, ready to protect at all costs. But for the first time, I know that protection isn't for me.

"It's true," I say, matching her tone. "And you saw him that night, didn't you? I need you to tell me what happened because right now it looks like your dad is a lying, cheating, piece of shit and that *you* had something to do with Heller's death."

Imogen gasps and Ava steps back like I've slapped her.

I cover my mouth with my hand. How did that all come out?

"Geezus, Goldie, are you fucking kidding me?" Ava whispers, but it's no use. People are starting to stare.

Imogen jumps to her feet and tries to step between us, but she can't put out the fire I set. There's too much tension, too many years of rage and insecurity, of jealousy and scabs we keep picking at. There's a decade of friendship worn down to the bone.

"Be honest, Ava." I grit my teeth and spit the words out. "Tell me the truth about that night."

Ava towers over me and narrows her eyes. "Tell me what happened on New Year's Eve."

"What?"

"Tell me what happened to Dylan Adler. Tell me what Heller asked you to do."

Her words knock the wind right out of my chest. *She knows.*

Ava steps toward me and grabs hold of my wrist. "We said we'd tell each other everything," she says.

I look at her closely, eyeing her frantic gaze, her thick eyebrows. There's sorrow in her face, disbelief, too. But she's the same as she's always been, open and sharp, ready to draw blood.

"I guess we lied," I say.

A silence stretches between us as Mellie runs up and grips each of our shoulders, steering us toward the horse stables.

"What the hell is going on?" she asks in a voice reserved for the problem campers.

Ava shrugs her off and crosses her arms, tears glistening in her eyes.

I look for an apology. "Mellie, I—"

"You're what? Sorry? You should be," she says to me. "Ava's had an awful day. I'd expect you to be a better friend."

Her words sting, especially as Ava bites her bottom lip, looking off into the distance.

"Go help Christina set up the sundae bar. Cool off." Mellie throws up her hands and shakes her head. "I expected better of you both." She takes off back toward the game, and Ava and I are left standing there, surveying the damage.

But I can't look at her any longer, so I spin on my heel, ready to leave. Before I make it very far, Ava grabs my hand and pulls me back half a step.

"If you have any faith left in me at all, meet me behind the rock wall after lights out." Her voice is urgent, the pain still there, raw and ragged at the edges. "Wait for my flashlight signal."

I rip my arm away from her and stomp off toward Christina. But I know I'll meet her.

I have no other choice.

CHAPTER 46

Then

I wasn't supposed to be at that New Year's Eve party. I wasn't supposed to be in Roxwood at all.

I *should* have been with Ava and Imogen at some gala Ava had invited us to the week before.

Ava called both Imogen and me and didn't wait for hellos. "Open your email."

Imogen saw it first and squealed into the phone. Ava had sent us invites to some black-tie New York City prep school party that took place every year at a posh uptown hotel. Tickets cost a fortune and Ava had bought them for us.

I brought my laptop close to my face and watched the animated invitation blink back at me, champagne glasses dancing across the screen. The words were all in cursive, regal and romantic.

"You guys have to come," Ava said.

"Obviously," Imogen said, without missing a beat.

When I hesitated, Ava sighed. "Come on, Goldie. What's waiting for you there in Roxwood?"

My cheeks flushed and I stammered, trying to find the excuse. I knew they wouldn't understand, me ditching them to hang out with a *boy*. A *townie*. But Heller was . . . everything up here. And we had been together for six weeks, a lifetime. He consumed me.

But I knew he could never compare to the people Ava dated who wore designer loafers and had been to Paris. The boys in Roxwood weren't lax bros like Imogen's classmates. They were . . . boring. Good for a fling. Something to ogle at during nights off at Truly's. Nothing more.

And yet . . . how could I explain that even though we were together, Heller hadn't asked me to spend New Year's with him, not yet? And that I didn't want to say yes to Ava because I wanted to hold out for him? For some stupid house party where there would be cheap beer in a musty basement and shitty music blaring out of a busted-up speaker?

They would never understand why I would wait for an invite to *that* when Ava was offering me a lifeline, an out.

"Goldie, you're obviously coming," Imogen said.

"Of course!"

"Phew," Ava said. She then started talking about what we would wear and who would be performing and how there would be an extremely sought-after photobooth there so our youth and beauty and fire would be immortalized forever.

Imogen encouraged her, asking questions like she would be quizzed later, and all of a sudden, I felt utterly and completely alone, like I was drifting further and further away from the conversation, like we were speaking different languages.

Soon, Imo had to hang up and go to rehearsal for *A Midsummer Night's Dream* and Ava was heading to a yoga class, and I was left with a silent phone in my hand, still hot from being pressed up against my ear.

We continued our regular text banter for the next few days, our conversations peppered with Ava's thoughts on what kind of New Year's hats she would get and if we would need faux fur stoles to brace against the cold. And as the days passed, I grew more certain of my decision. It was the right call. Heller hadn't invited me to spend New Year's with him. The one magical night where everything is lit up with possibilities and the world is supposed to turn shiny as the years change from one to the other. New Year's Eve senior year. It was a *thing*. Right? It had to be. Who you spent it with meant *everything*. And if I couldn't spend it with Heller, at least I could spend it in New York with Ava and Imogen.

Because, again, Heller hadn't asked me what I was doing.

Until two days before.

We were lying on the futon in his hut, his grandmother's quilt covering our naked bodies. It was heavy and smelled like lavender. Heller must have washed it. I nuzzled into his chest and he wrapped me tightly in his arms.

When he released me, he was smiling wide and giddy. "Dylan finally agreed to host New Year's," he said.

"What?" I asked, my heart beating fast.

Heller stretched out beside me, lengthening his calves until they shuddered. He reached for his phone and scrolled through a text chain with a group called *The Boys*, stopping when he found what he was looking for. He cleared his throat and read. "'Fam's heading to Sunapee. Let's fucking rage!!! 9 pm on NYE.'"

Before I could tell him about my plans to go to New York, Heller held my chin tight and pressed his mouth to mine. My body was warm and tingly, open and yearning.

Mine, I thought, running my hands through his hair, over his back, along his forearms. *Mine*.

"You don't have plans, right?" he asked gingerly when he pulled back.

If I had only said *I'm busy* or *You should have asked me last week* or literally anything other than what came out of my mouth next, maybe everything would be different. Maybe Dylan would be in summer training instead of physical therapy. Maybe there wouldn't be this gulf between Ava, Imogen, and me. Maybe we wouldn't have as many secrets. And maybe, just maybe, Heller would still be alive.

But I shook my head. "I'm free."

CHAPTER 47

Now

The air in the cabin is still and all I can see are shadows of the trees dancing on the wall next to me. I'm full of adrenaline, the blood pumping hard through my veins, my senses alert. The tingling sensation in my stomach says *Wait until the perfect moment. Wait until it's right.*

A flashlight clicks on, bright outside my cabin, and blinks one, two, three times. Our signal.

The bunk bed creaks as I sit upright, but Meg is quiet down below, a bag of bones. I swing my legs over the ladder and gingerly slip into my sneakers, their laces loose for this exact reason. I reach for the dark sweatshirt I left hanging on the hook and pull it over my head, keeping the hood up over my face. I pull back the curtain and walk into the camper room, but not before hearing Meg mumble behind me, "Stay safe."

My throat grows scratchy but I keep going, opening the door to the cabin as carefully as I can. When I get outside, I finally realize what I'm doing. If Ava *did* hurt Heller, then what would she do to me, another person threatening to expose a secret? I may be her best friend, but I'm not her family, no matter what we might say.

I let out a breath and take in the night air. It's cold and still, though I can see the big overhead lights beaming down on the fields by upper camp. A breeze picks up and I count to five, waiting for Ava to exit her cabin. It doesn't take long and then a moment later, Imogen appears, too. My heart quickens and I wonder if this is a setup. If they're teaming up against me. But I push all the bad thoughts out of my head.

Believe in Ava. Just for another night.

The three of us walk silently in single file, Imogen leading the way toward the rock wall down the hill.

Imogen stops first, pulling down her hood. We're deep in the heart of the ropes course, the most hidden place on camp, perfect for a hookup—or a fight.

Imogen motions for us to sit and drops down in the woodchips. We do so reluctantly, forming a little triangle, our knees kissing.

Ava looks away, her face hidden behind a curtain of platinum hair, bright against the dark sky. "This is bullshit."

I shake my head, suddenly so confused, so angry. At Heller for turning the one place that meant everything to me into a nightmare. At Imogen for clearly being on Ava's side. At Ava for . . . shit, everything.

I clench my fists in my lap. "Tell me why you were with Heller that night. Did you . . ." I can't even say the words.

"Are you really about to ask me that?" Ava looks up then, her eyes piercing mine. "You really think I hurt him? I *killed* him?"

"You tell me."

Ava shakes her head. "You first. Tell me why you care so much about Heller. Tell us the truth."

The air rushes out of my lungs and I know it's time. Imogen looks at me, concerned. I close my eyes tight and take the leap.

"We were together," I say softly. "In the fall."

"*He's* why she ditched us on New Year's," Ava says, hurt.

"Is that what you're really mad about?" I sputter. "That I missed your bullshit elitist New Year's party?"

Ava's mouth is a hard line. "So that's what you think of me."

"Come on, Ava."

"You can say it," she says. "You think I'm spoiled and bratty and that I'm as big a monster as my father. That's what Heller said."

"So, you *were* with him that night," I say.

"Tell the truth for once, Goldie," Ava says. "You tell your truth and I'll tell mine."

Imogen looks at me, her face a world of hurt. "Come on, Goldie."

It's her voice that breaks me, and the story tumbles out, hot and quick. I tell them about falling for Heller, about following him to the New Year's party and taking the blame for what happened. I tell them about the aftermath—how we drove to Stu and Mellie's house in Connecticut with a box of brownies and asked them to right all my wrongs, even though they *weren't* my wrongs. I tell them about working for Stu and Mellie, holed up in the winter cabin watching old episodes of *The O.C.* as my eyes glazed over, pushing papers around, grading sleepaway camp admissions tests for kids who would one day run the world.

I tell them about school and how I became a leper, how Heller began ignoring me and my whole world collapsed. I tell them about skipping class, about failing, about having my college acceptance rescinded. I tell them about my mug shot on the desktops, about my humiliation, my depression.

I tell them about Cal showing up at camp, about how he knew I wasn't behind the wheel and how his guilt drives his desire to know the truth. I tell them about sneaking into the clerk's office, the ID badge and the emails Heller sent to newspapers. I tell them I first thought Cal hurt Heller—then maybe Jordan Adler—and that both those theories were dead wrong.

I tell them about Sally Burke and how Heller was *with* her, how Cal found a letter from her saying she was sorry—for what I don't know.

I tell them that I've never felt more alone and that I don't know how to come back from this.

I tell them everything I've been holding inside until there's nothing left except my empty chest, heaving and open and laid bare for them to see.

When I finally look up at their faces, Imogen's eyes are wide and watery and she has one hand over her mouth. Ava's face is still and somber, and she blinks a few too many times.

Imogen speaks first. "How could you keep this from us?"

Finding the words feels impossible. How am I supposed to explain that I thought they wouldn't understand? That I isolated myself from them on purpose because I felt like I wasn't *one* of them. And then I found myself in a web of lies so tangled, I knew I would need a knife to get out, and that sitting there, trapped under the mess, was easier than breaking free.

But how do I say all that? How do I tell my *best friends* that the three of us let each other down in ways we're only now starting to realize?

I don't have long to wonder because Imogen launches herself at me and wraps me in a hug so tight it knocks me over. Her sobs are muffled as she cries into my shoulder, her tears damp against my skin.

"Imo," I say.

But then she pulls back.

"I have a secret, too," she says, pressing the heels of her palms into her eyes. Imo inhales deeply like she's gathering strength. "I didn't get into USC," she says. "I didn't get in anywhere."

"What?" Ava asks, leaning forward, resting her palm on Imo's knee.

Imogen nods, tears slipping down her face. "I thought I was a shoo-in, but . . ." She shakes her head. "I didn't apply anywhere else." She looks up then. "I didn't tell anyone. Not even my parents. I told them I got in and was deferring, but I don't have any other options. This is it."

"Oh, Imo," I say.

"It's not as dramatic as what you're going through," Imo says. "But still. I don't know why I couldn't tell you both. I was scared of what you'd say, I guess."

I wrap an arm around her shoulder. But then I look at Ava. She's not crying. Not a lip quiver or a single tear. She's looking at me with a cocked head and a bewildered expression.

"Holy shit," she says quietly.

"What?" I ask.

"This is way more fucked up than I thought," she says.

"Uh, yeah. Imo not getting into USC is absurd," I say.

But Ava shakes her head. "I mean, yeah. But—no offense, Imo—I'm still on the Heller train. Goldie, I *was* with him that night."

I straighten my spine and lean in.

Ava squeezes her eyes shut, then blinks a few times. "You were right. Heller had found out about what my dad was up to." She swallows hard and closes her eyes. "That first night out at Truly's, you must have said Imogen's name because he thought I was you," she says pointing to Imo. "The next day, he boated up to camp in that dinghy, remember? Before Levin shooed him away, he said he had some information he needed to get to Goldie and he thought I was the only person he could trust to get it to her. He said we needed to meet at the waterfront at two a.m. that night."

"Why didn't he come to me?" I ask.

"He didn't think you'd trust him. Told me he'd done something bad to you."

"And you agreed. Without telling me."

Ava clenches her fists. "He said it had something to do with Mark Cantor." She buries her head in her hands. "Obviously I didn't tell him *I* was Ava, Mark Cantor's daughter. I wanted to know what he knew so I let him think I was Imogen.

"Later that night, I snuck down to the waterfront. He started handing me a bunch of pieces of paper, saying my dad was a criminal, that he was depriving Roxwood of life-changing amounts of money. But before he could explain, he started spilling his guts about what happened between you two and how guilty he felt." She grabs my hand and pauses, her eyes locking with mine. "He kept saying he was so sorry and that I should tell you he loved you. He said he was a coward and he always loved you."

My brain is a mess of questions and half-truths as I try to piece together who Heller was and what the hell he was doing. I squeeze Ava's hand harder and try to focus. "What did the papers say?"

Ava tucks a stray piece of hair into her hood. "I didn't even take them. I was so flustered. I never read them." She's looking down and using her hands to punctuate each word. "That's when we heard a golf cart coming. I freaked out and ran up the back trail and bolted straight to your cabin," she says. "I didn't really believe it. Some random kid up in Vermont uncovering a massive financial scandal? It was absurd. Especially since the IRS wasn't able to nail my dad a few years back."

Ava looks up, her eyes red and watery. "In the morning, I went off campus to get those coffees. I thought we could tell each other everything and start the summer fresh. But there were a bunch of hospital nurses at the 7-Eleven in town, talking about Heller." Ava shakes her head. "They said he was found dead at camp. I knew I couldn't tell anyone about meeting him because people would think I had something to do with it. They said it was an accident, so . . ." She pauses. "I don't know. I . . . tried to forget about it."

We're quiet again, mulling over what she's said. "But the main thing is that he was alive when I left him. He was alive."

"So whoever came down in that golf cart could have done it," I say.

Ava inhales as if the idea hadn't occurred to her.

"Do you remember anything about who it was?" Imo asks.

Ava shakes her head. "I got out of there as soon as I could."

"But how did Heller know about your dad?" I ask. "He said he had proof. How?"

Ava shakes her head. "I don't know." She's hugging her knees to her chest as she rocks back and forth.

Imogen sighs, exhausted, and opens her mouth. "Ava," she starts. "I have to ask. Do you know where your dad was that night? Is it possible . . ."

Ava freezes. "I . . . I don't know."

"Could he have been here? Could he have known Heller *knew* and killed him after you went back to upper camp?"

The whole thing sounds wild, but so does Heller *being murdered* at Camp Alpine Lake.

"I'll connect to Wi-Fi tomorrow," she says. "The stepbitch keeps her Instagram so up-to-date, it'll show where they were that night. Probably at a country club in Palm Beach or something equally tacky."

It's a joke but no one laughs.

"How did this summer get so fucked?" I ask, my voice carrying with the wind.

Imogen's hand stops and she squeezes my shoulder. "Because we let ourselves drift," she says. "We forgot that *we* were the most important thing about this place."

Ava inhales sharply. We both know Imo's right.

"We kept secrets from each other. Big ones," Ava says. "We promised we'd never do that."

I nod. "I'm sorry," I say.

"Me too," Ava says.

"Me three," Imogen says but then she shrugs. "Who cares about USC anyway."

We all burst out laughing because she's right. Imogen brings us all in for a hug and I scooch my butt toward them, letting myself be enveloped by them, my friends, the girls who I should have trusted earlier to catch me.

Ava's eyes light up and she smacks her knee. "Oh my god, we're so dumb. The security cameras. The ones at the waterfront. They must have caught everything."

Hope flickers in my heart until Imogen shakes her head. "We

went skinny-dipping that night," she says. "Remember, Goldie? We reset the cameras."

Shit. Without knowing what we were doing, we erased whatever evidence those cameras could have captured.

Ava chews on her lip, then her mouth drops open. "Stu *did* try to talk to me about my dad once this summer."

"When?" I ask.

"The first DJ social," she says, "when you guys were stoned out your minds."

Suddenly I remember. Ava and Stu huddled close near the office, the frustrated, almost furious look on his face as he confronted Ava about . . . something.

"What did he say?" Imogen asks.

"He was bitching about some check my dad was supposed to send." Ava's voice gets small. "Honestly, it was kind of weird. Definitely the most stressed I ever saw Stu. He kept saying that in order to be the most exclusive, sought-after camp, they had to make sure parents kept up their donation pledges. I told him to leave me out of it." She presses her fingers to her temple. "But now . . . I wonder if my dad already knew about the investigation and was hiding his money."

"But haven't you guys noticed that it seems like camp's been cutting back on some things?" I ask. "There's no air conditioning in the office. Christina's spice shipment was delayed. And before the campers got here, Heller's dad was screaming at Stu about messing up their payment."

"This place has more money than god," Ava says, dismissing the idea. "Maybe they were waiting for second session checks or something."

We listen to the crickets, the sounds of the swaying branches, and the breeze passing through the leaves as we try to digest everything we revealed.

Then Ava looks up to the sky. "Crap. The sun."

She's right. Dawn is breaking, which means the kids will be up soon.

We tiptoe back to our cabins in silence, holding hands and squeezing for dear life. When we get there, Ava stops. "We're going to find out the truth about Heller," she says. "The three of us."

Imogen nods solemnly like she's taking an oath.

I shake my head. "This isn't your shit to deal with," I say. "Heller was my mess."

Ava glances toward the sun, which is now peeking over the horizon. We don't have much time. "Yeah, well, clearly my fucked-up family is part of it somehow," she says. "Plus, we're all we've got. We owe it to each other."

Without another word, she and Imogen break off and we all head into our cabins, equipped with the suspicion that there's something wrong with Camp Alpine Lake.

CHAPTER 48

Then

The super raid was tradition. So many things here are. There had been a group chat before camp even started, tossing around ideas about what we could do to prank everyone else during our last summer as campers.

One year, the oldest kids turned the gazebo into a ball pit. Another summer, they took one drawer from each dresser and barricaded the dining hall. Another, they made an American flag out of underwear stolen from the laundry. And one year they used yarn to spin a massive spiderweb around the office.

Ours had to be epic. It had to be fresh.

Ava came up with the idea. She had a grand plan to turn the whole camp into a circus. The dining hall would become the main tent, and we'd spend all night decorating it, so when everyone came to breakfast, they would be greeted with a show. We could leave homemade tickets on every dresser, create signs to hang on each of the doors. When everyone woke up, they'd find us sitting outside the dining hall, dressed up as roustabouts and clowns, running on adrenaline and packets of instant coffee.

Ava spent weeks convincing everyone in our group to participate, even the indoor kids who spent all camp buried in their summer reading and were afraid of getting caught. She set the date and we prepared, making the decorations in secret and hiding them under our beds during Sunday inspection.

When it came time to pull it off, Ava gave everyone tasks and instructions, so we could divide and conquer our beautiful circus.

"You're with me," she said, pulling on my elbow. We had the most dangerous task of all, the one that could *actually* get us in trouble since it involved climbing on top of the dining hall and hanging a big banner across the roof.

It didn't occur to me to say no, to say I was scared or that if we got caught, we could be banned from being counselors—Stu and Mellie's continuous threat.

I grabbed her hand and raced her to the ladder propped up against the side of the building.

We climbed up with ease and found our placement rather quickly. All we had to do was tie the ropes to the dining hall sign, replacing the Alpine Lake logo with our homemade circus one.

But then a beam from a flashlight began shining around, frantic and bright.

"Get down," Ava hissed. "Now."

I let go of the corner of the banner and fell to my knees, waiting for Ava to drop down next to me, behind the dining hall sign. But she didn't. She stayed standing, ready to be caught.

"Ava Cantor, you get down from there," Stu yelled. It was the sternest I'd ever heard him. His voice was full of rage and stress. The way you speak when you hold kids' lives in your hands. Kids whose parents have power. "You're about to break your goddamn neck."

Ava groaned but started to move toward the ladder.

"Who's up there with you?" Stu called.

I held my breath, waiting for her response.

"No one," Ava said.

"Are you telling the truth?"

"Yes."

"Lucky you're Mark Cantor's kid. Anyone else and I wouldn't ask 'em back to the junior counselor program." Stu grumbled but he didn't fight her. He waited until she climbed down, banner in hand, and led her away from me, into the darkness.

His words lodged themselves into my brain and my heart beat fast as I waited until the coast was clear. I was *not* Mark Cantor's kid. I could *actually* get in trouble. Ava had known that before I did.

I ran as fast as I could back to safety, petrified of bumping into Stu or Mellie and being caught in a lie, letting them down.

When I tiptoed into our cabin, still deserted since everyone else was out setting up the prank, Ava was wide awake, looking out the window.

"Oh, thank god," she said, pulling me down onto the bed with her. "I'm so glad you didn't get caught."

"Me too," I said, though we both knew it was only because she had taken the blame for both of us.

CHAPTER 49

Now

Color war sweeps through camp like wildfire, spreading through cabins and laying claim to everything—campers, activities, meals, even the waterfront.

Within a day, the camp is divided into four teams. Lunch tables become safe zones. Tie-dyed T-shirts are replaced by solid primary colors as the kids pledge their allegiance and put on their game faces, ready to dedicate a week of their summer to fighting their friends, winning tug of war and losing their voices as they cheer with vigor.

"Man, do you remember how much we cared about this shit?" Ava asks. We're splayed out on the picnic tables near the dining hall waiting for lunch to start, free from campers and responsibilities for a few minutes. But I can't stop thinking about everything we revealed behind the rock wall only hours before. There was one question on the tip of my tongue but I hadn't had the courage to ask it yet.

Where do we go from here?

Imogen laughs. "I mean, I *should* have been captain when we were super seniors."

Ava swats at Imogen. "You will never get over that."

"I *so* deserved it."

"Obviously," Ava says. "But we know there's some justice in this world because our girl Goldie here not only was captain, but brought our team to victory."

"What can I say? I'm a natural leader," I joke. "Remember songfest that year?"

"We cried for days," Imogen says.

"Literal days," Ava says.

"Well, we *did* write the best alma mater of all time." Imogen sits up on her elbows and clears her throat. "Shall I?"

"No!" Ava and I nearly scream in unison, forcing us all to laugh.

Imo rolls her eyes. "Fine," she says. "Still can't believe they let us be on the same team that year." Imogen looks at Ava. "A Cantor phone call did the trick, I assume?"

Ava smiles but her lips are thin and there's no joy there. None of the brashness from earlier in the summer when she joked about us being in the same group, thanks to some Cantor magic. It's like all the boldness has drained from her and all we're left with is Ava's shell.

Imogen winces. "Sorry, Ave," she says quietly.

Ava straightens her shoulders. Her collarbones are sharp like knives. "Don't feel sorry for me," she says. "Feel sorry for whoever he fucked over." We're all quiet for a sec, listening to the sounds of camp—the laughing, the wind, the high-pitched children's voices floating from the fields.

"Have you heard from him?" Imo asks. "Or your mom?"

Ava presses her lips together and shakes her head.

The bell rings, summoning us into the dining hall. We follow all the kids wearing their teams' colors, singing their teams' songs.

"Beeline for the sandwich bar," Ava calls, and waves over her shoulder.

Imogen and I are left in the hot line, waiting for Christina to serve us tuna melts. But behind us, a loud clanking comes from the dining room. The sounds of plates falling over, silverware crashing against tables, metal chair legs scraping against the floor. Then I hear Ava's voice loud above all the ruckus.

"What did you say to them?" she shrieks.

Imogen inhales sharply and we both bolt toward her voice. When we get there, I see Ava, her stance wide, Jordie and Bianca cowering behind her back. She's leaning down, her pointer finger extended toward some twerpy little kid who can't be more than twelve years old. Her eyes are on fire and her mouth is stretched into an oval, like she could eat him if she wanted to. The room is still waiting to see what she'll say next.

"I *said* your dad's a criminal," he says, his voice indignant, almost gleeful. "My mom told me he's going to jail for a long, long time and no one should talk to Jordie or Bianca for the rest of camp."

Oh no.

Jordie and Bianca whimper behind Ava, but Ava takes another step toward the kid.

"If you talk to them like that one more time, you're going to wish your parents never sent you here," she says through gritted teeth. She straightens her shoulders and looks up, at all the other kids staring at her, waiting to see what Ava Cantor will do next. She spreads her arms out wide and raises her voice. "That goes for everyone here," she says. "If you have something to say about my dad, or to Jordie or Bianca, you come to *me* first."

The room is silent, so quiet you can hear one of the zoned-out Ramblers chewing on the other side of the room. It only takes another second for Mellie to rush toward Ava and the twins, her eyes full of concern.

"Ava," she says. "Let's . . ."

But Ava raises her hands before Mellie gets close. "I'm going," she says. "I'm going." Instead of walking out of the dining room alone, she puts one arm around each twin and brings them with her, outside, away from this mess.

Mellie blinks once, twice, and then clears her throat, summoning her whole *everything's fine* vibe. She smiles wide. "Well, that was fun. Back to lunch, everyone," she says, clapping her hands together. "We'll be updating color war scores any moment now so you'll want to be ready."

The room slowly returns to normal, the comforting sounds of forks click-clacking and kids grabbing at cookies on the buffet, but Imogen and I are both stuck in place.

She starts walking toward the door, but I rest a hand on her arm. "Let me," I say. "The twins."

Imogen nods curtly, but looks shaken. "Hug her, okay?"

"I will."

I follow Ava's path out the side door, ignoring Meg's calls for me to come to the table. When I get outside, I scan the lawn, looking for Ava and the twins. It takes a second but there they are, under a weeping willow a little ways away, off toward the tennis courts. I pick up my pace and hustle over to them.

But when I get close, something stops me. The muffled sounds of sobs coming from both Jordie and Bianca, sniffles escaping their noses. Ava's making shushing sounds, rocking them both against her. She's whispering to them, her voice sweet and low, protective and familiar.

It's not what you'd expect from someone who swore she would never even *talk* to her half sisters. Ava's looking at them like she looks at Imo and me, like she loves them.

"Shh," she whispers into Jordie's hair, her arms around them both. "It's going to be okay. We're going to be okay."

Bianca looks up. "Will you braid my hair again, Ava?"

Ava nods. "Of course. Always."

Jordie sniffles and wipes her nose on Ava's shirt.

The intimacy. I know I shouldn't watch. Slowly I start to back away. But I must step on a branch because Ava whips her head around, looking at me. Her eyes are soft and misty and she smiles a bit.

"Couldn't let you have all the fun with them this summer, I guess," she says.

Bianca laughs, covering her mouth with one small hand. "Ava's the best sister. Besides you, Jordie."

Jordie snuggles up into the crook in Ava's arm. "I know."

Ava shrugs, her lips tugging upward. "Guess I do love them after all."

Ava's outburst is old news by the end of the day thanks to color war, to all the kids running around, hoping to land their team more points, more goals, more wins.

Mellie gave Ava a stern talking-to before our lifeguarding shift. Imogen and I can only see them from afar, but after, Ava barrels down from the swim hut, rolling her eyes. "It was worth it," she says, gazing off at her sisters, sitting with their color war team in the sand. "No one messes with the Cantor girls."

Imogen looks at me, surprised, as if we both can't believe the one-eighty Ava had done on her sisters.

"I checked, by the way," Ava says.

"Checked what?" I ask.

"Where my dad was the night Heller died."

"And . . . ?" Imo asks.

"In Geneva, of all fucking places." She leans back against the towel wall and sighs. "Then they took a luxurious trip to a five-star chalet in Lake Lucerne, according to the stepbitch's Instagram."

"Geezus," I say.

"He was probably doing crimes or whatever, but he was definitely not here." Ava blows out a puff of air. "And get this: I obviously googled him to see what was going on, and turns out he's dead set against giving up his clients' names. It's going to take the IRS years to untangle the whole mess."

"Why wouldn't he spill?" Imo asks.

Ava shrugs. "No clue but that twerp was right. This means he's going to jail for a long-ass time." She rests her cheek on her knee. "Guess he'd rather keep their privacy than watch his daughters grow up. Selfish asshole."

"Ave," I say softly, patting her hair. She leans into my hand.

But no one says what we're all thinking, which is that we still don't actually have a plan to find the answers to all our other questions. Instead, we look out at the lake and watch the kids finish up water carnival, the most anticipated color war event of the summer. They're all huddled on the beach in sweatshirts, damp hair stuck to their skulls, waiting for Levin to announce the winners.

Ava's eyes are trained on Jordie and Bianca, whose sad faces from earlier have been replaced with wide-eyed excitement from all of the kayak races, deep dives, and underwater breath-holding competitions. They knock their knobby knees together, anticipation coursing through them.

"How long?" I ask Ava. "How long have you been hanging out with the twins?"

Ava stares down at the sand, burrowing her toes deep into the ground. "Since they got here," she says. "I started talking to them one day at woodworking and . . . they're cute." Ava laughs. "I don't know. They look so much like me. I wanted to get to know them. Without our parents. Without . . . anyone. Some things are just for me, you know?"

"I get that," I say. And I do. It's why I kept so much hidden.

Ava looks right at me, then over to Imogen. "I guess we don't have to tell each other everything, huh?"

But before we can answer, Levin bounds over to the front of the beach, announcing who's won tonight's events. The losers groan and throw their arms up in frustration, though their gloomy dispositions won't last long. Every year, water carnival ends with the best barbecue of the year, featuring Christina's famous corn on the cob, which she blackens on a big charcoal grill and dips in buckets of butter and chicken fat.

When I get my serving, I plop down on the sand and bite into it, relishing how the grease drips down my fingers and coats my lips. It's best eaten when the sky is a mix of purples, pinks, and oranges, like it is right now. One of those sunsets that buries itself deep in your chest, folding into your memory, daring you to remember it always. I shove my bare feet deeper into the sand, relaxing my limbs, rolling my neck. My lips are chapped from the wind and the sun, and my hair dances around my shoulders. This place, this perfect place. This is how I want to keep it.

I scan the waterfront, gazing out at the white wooden docks, the makeshift boat launch, the inflatable trampoline. How can you look at it all and not think of the *fun*, all the carefree laughter and friendship and breath-holding competitions? All the buddy checks and waterskiing and swim lessons?

But I know how. Because now all I can think about is Heller, fighting for his final breaths as something—someone—held him down below.

We need to find out who was in that golf cart after Ava left.

They'll have answers.

They may have killed him.

I look up at the security camera, the one on the swim hut that we reset. If only we hadn't gone skinny-dipping. If only we had been smarter. If only . . .

I wipe my butter-and-chicken-fat-covered hands on my towel and push myself to stand, so I can throw my corn cob in the dumpster, propped up against a tree near the wooden latrine. No one ever comes over here because it smells like garbage and shit, so the paths are a little more overgrown, but at least it's quiet. That's what I need now. Quiet.

A bird caws overhead and a tree branch rustles. I look up, expecting to find a robin or a chickadee, but there's something else there. Something I'd never noticed before.

A black security camera that nearly blends into the dark wood its secured to. By the looks of it, it's from before they updated the system, which means it wouldn't be hooked up to the rest of the network, the ones we reset that night. But there's a blinking red light indicating that it's recording.

And it's pointing right at the waterfront.

CHAPTER 50

Then

"It's gotta be here somewhere." Mom was rummaging through a metal rack of old tech stuff in Stu and Mellie's winter cabin. It was a cold day in April and she wanted to keep me company while I did some paperwork for Stu and Mellie.

"What exactly are you looking for?" I asked, peering up at her from the desktop. She had taken down an old VCR, a DVD player, a few CD-ROM drives, and even a shoebox full of floppy discs.

"They never throw anything out," she said, elbow deep in junk. "I bet they have it."

"Have *what?*"

Mom stood up straight and wiped her dusty palms on her jeans. "The first summer your father and I worked at camp, Stu was obsessed with his new video camera. It was one of those old clunky ones. But he had this video of Lou and me dancing at the staff party at the end of the summer."

"So?"

Mom sighs. "It's our twentieth anniversary on Friday," she said, smiling. "It would make the perfect gift. Help me?"

She extended her hand and I groaned but grabbed it.

"You take that box, I'll take this one." She pointed to a cardboard box the size of a shopping cart and I started sorting through it with reluctance.

They were all labeled things like *Color War 1998* and *Tennis Tournament 2005*.

Mom turned Queen on the speaker and started singing to herself as we went through everything.

"Do Stu and Mellie ever use this stuff?" I asked, picking up an old Wii system.

"Doubt it," Mom says. "Hoarding habits left over from when they had nothing."

My head jerked up. "What?"

"Back when they started this camp, they barely paid themselves a salary," Mom said. "Ate canned tuna and beans for five years until they hiked up the prices and started wining and dining the Manhattan crowd."

"Huh," I said.

"You shoulda seen their house. The one before the Connecticut mansion. Looked like ours."

Mom turned back to the tapes and we rifled through them in silence until she pulled one out and squealed. "Goldie, come here."

She wiped dust off an old tape and shoved it into the mouth of a small, square TV set with a VHS player attached.

"This thing still works?" I asked.

Mom smiled. "It's barely used."

But then we both shut up because grainy footage of a much younger version of Mom and Dad took over the screen, their faces fresh and free from wrinkles or worry lines. They wore matching

Alpine Lake shirts and jean shorts, and were dancing in a much older, grimier version of the Lodge.

"Say hi, Willa!" Stu's voice said from behind the camera.

"Hi, Willa!" Mom said on-screen. Dad grabbed her waist and twirled her around until they broke into a fit of laughter, kissing each other on the mouth, arms wrapped around each other's curves.

"Wow," I said, in spite of myself. "You guys were kind of cute."

"We were," Mom said, her eyes glazed over with tears. "We definitely were."

CHAPTER 51

Now

"There's another camera." I'm breathless when I get back to Ava and Imogen, who are nibbling at their own greasy corn. "Over by the dumpster. It's an old one, so it's not connected to the main feed, but it must have caught *something* if it was still recording."

Ava drops her corn in the sand.

"How can we see what's on it?" she asks.

I shake my head. "I don't know, but it's gotta be hooked up somewhere." I rack my brain trying to figure out where the hell it might be. "The office?" I ask. "With Pat or something?"

Ava nods, thinking it over. "I mean, that'd be great. She'd let us in there in a heartbeat."

But then I remember that metal cart with so much old gear, the one that's shoved up against the wall in the winter cabin. "I have a hunch."

Imogen and Ava look at me with expectant eyes.

"The winter cabin," I say, quiet.

"We gotta find out," Imo says.

I shake my head. "It's too risky."

We all know it's one of Stu and Mellie's big no-nos. Going in with their permission during the off-season is *fine*, but hunting for contraband footage of a murder during the summer is not.

"We won't be allowed back," Imogen says.

"Kicked out of camp immediately," Ava says.

"Exactly," I say. They look at each other as if they're deciding what to tell me. "What?"

"It's time, Imo," Ava says.

"You guys are freaking me out," I say, my voice frantic. "What?"

"We didn't know how you'd react." Imogen rests a hand on my shoulder.

"What?" I ask again, urgent.

"This is my last summer at Alpine Lake," Imogen says. "It's . . . I want to act. I can't do that if I come back to Vermont every summer." Imogen looks at me with those beautiful bright eyes.

"You too?" I turn to Ava.

Ava nods. "I don't know what I'm going to do with my life, but I'm not going to be a counselor forever." She sighs. "Next summer, I need to start figuring it out."

Tears prick my eyes but I know what they're trying to say: They don't care if they get caught. They have nothing left to lose.

I take a deep breath. Neither do I.

"Okay," I say. "We'll check out the winter cabin."

Levin blows his whistle and everyone starts gathering their kids and packing up their things, a signal that yet another camp tradition is over—at least until next year.

"We can try to get into the cabin tomorrow," I say. "That's when Mellie and Stu have their night off."

I look at Imogen and Ava, their faces hopeful but worried, trained on me. "Are you guys sure about this?" I ask.

Both of them nod without missing a beat. Together in unison, they say, "Yes."

— — —

I leave our little meeting feeling buoyant and hopeful for once. I finally have a plan to find out the truth about Heller and all it took was telling Ava and Imogen every single thing that happened. It shouldn't have been that hard. I should have known they wouldn't back away. We're still sisters by choice because we will always be. I'm a fool for ever doubting that.

"Goldie!" Meg calls. She's rounding up all the Bloodroot girls, counting their heads and making sure they're all here. "Can you go to Willa's shed and pick up a bunch of popsicle sticks?"

"Log cabins before bed?" I ask.

Meg shrugs. "Never understood why it's fun but the girls want them."

"On it," I say. I take the long way to the woodworking shed, listening to the faint hum of lightning bugs as I make my way through camp.

When I arrive, I rap my knuckles against the door. "Knock, knock." Mom is hunched over a two-by-four, refining its edges with sanding paper. Safety goggles are snapped onto her head and she's wearing an old striped senior staff shirt, stained with paint. "Making another cabin sign?"

She stands up and dusts off her jean shorts. "Those things have *got* to stop breaking." She holds open her arms and I dive in for a hug. She smells like sawdust and acrylic paint, woodchips and pine. She smells like our old knit quilts, like Sundays.

"How ya doing, baby?" she asks. "Feel like I've barely seen you."

"It's been a weird one," I say.

"That's an understatement."

She blows on the wood in front of her and reaches for one of the darker stains and a paintbrush.

"Can I grab a bunch of popsicle sticks?" I ask. "Log cabins."

Mom gives a knowing smile. "Of course. They're somewhere in the dresser by the hammer wall."

I rifle through the plastic set of drawers, nodding my head along to whatever soft rock is on the stereo.

But then Mom clears her throat. "Actually, let me help you," she says, scooting the bench back.

"It's okay. I got it." I pull open the bottom drawer and spot the popsicle sticks, but before I can grab them, Mom lunges at me and bumps me out of the way.

"What are you doing?" I ask.

"Nothing," she says.

But then I see her grab a piece of paper, folded neatly, tucked up against the back of the drawer.

"What is that?" I ask.

"It's nothing."

"Show me." I reach for it but Mom pulls it away. "Mom, what the hell?"

"Listen, sweets. You gotta understand I love you. Everything I've ever done has been to protect you, okay?"

My face grows hot and I pull away from her touch. "You're being so weird."

Mom's face changes then. It's hard and sad and full of restraint. "I know, Goldie. I *know*."

"You know *what*?"

"I know you weren't driving Heller's truck that night," she says.

My shoulders tense and everything around me grows still. "What?"

Mom sighs, wrapping her arms around her stomach.

"But . . ." I say.

Mom holds up her hand. "No buts. I know."

"How . . ."

"You don't drive stick."

Mom unfolds the paper she's holding and hands it to me. I scan the page and realize it's a report from Frank's Auto Shop from January.

"I went down to Frank's a few days after the accident to see the damage to the truck. Whole thing was totaled but I made Frank walk me through it, show me every piece of damage. When he got to the console, I saw it's manual transmission."

I'm shocked into silence for a moment but then a realization dawns on me. "You knew I wasn't driving," I say. "Then why didn't you say something when things got so bad? Why did you let me go through that alone?"

"Oh, Goldie," she says, her voice full of sorrow. "I—I . . ."

"Say something!" I'm screaming now but I don't care who hears.

"I went to Stu and Mellie," she says, the words coming out fast. "I called them as soon as I left Frank's and I asked them what to do. But they were skeptical and said to trust you, that maybe it's all a misunderstanding. How could we prove it, especially since you had been so hellbent on giving up everything for that boy?"

"And you never came to me. You never thought, *Hmm, maybe my daughter isn't thinking right and she's going through some shit and I should try to be there for her? I should try to be her mom?*"

Mom closes her eyes and presses her fingers to her temples. "Stu and Mellie said there was no way we'd get Heller to admit the truth. That you probably had good reason for taking the fall and that we should trust your judgement." Mom's eyes are welling with tears and her knuckles are white as she grasps on to the table in front of her. "I didn't expect it to get so bad."

"All this time you knew and you let me *suffer*," I say. The tears fall hot and fast down my cheeks. "You're supposed to protect me."

"We were falling behind on the mortgage," she says, small. "We couldn't afford a lawyer. And Stu and Mellie had figured everything out already. I didn't know what to do."

I shake my head. "I can't believe this."

"Baby, I'm sorry. This whole year's been a mess. We thought you'd spend the summer here and everything would be good again. That a summer here, with your friends, at this place would right all the wrongs and set you back up to get going with your life. But then . . ."

"Then Heller died," I say.

"Heller died."

"I don't have anything else to say to you except I need you to answer this: Do you really think Heller drowned by accident?"

Mom look at me, her bottom lip quivering. She shakes her head. "I don't know."

CHAPTER 52

Then

"It's called a nondisclosure agreement." Judah McConnell was standing over me in the ice fishing hut a quarter mile from their main house.

Heller's head was in his hands and his legs were shaking as he tapped a foot against the floor.

He wouldn't look at me.

He wouldn't speak.

Judah slid the pieces of paper across the small coffee table.

"We know this is a lot to ask of you, Goldie," he said, almost kindly. "And we're willing to compensate you for your trouble."

"Compensate?" I asked.

"Twenty thousand dollars," he said. "It's not much in the grand scheme of things, but it's all we have. Enough to help out with college. You're over eighteen so your parents wouldn't have to know."

I bit my lip. I knew Mom and Dad were worried about money—always had been. If I signed the paperwork and took the cash, Judah was right. I could put it toward school and tell them I received a scholarship or financial aid or something. They could save their hard-earned paychecks to get a new car or repair the generator that blew out during last year's blizzard. Taking this kind of money would help. It would change things. It would make me less of a burden. Judah was right. They'd never have to know.

And besides. I loved Heller.

Heller loved me.

I was protecting him.

Because I knew he would protect me.

I took the pen from the table and pressed the point to the piece of paper.

I would have done it even without the promise of a paycheck.

"Wait," Heller said. "Are you sure? You haven't even read it."

I looked up at his frightened face. It had only been a few hours since the accident, but he looked so much older. His skin was gray and there were deep circles under his eyes.

He needed me.

I grabbed his hand in mine and nodded.

"I'm sure."

Heller let out a shaky breath and squeezed my hand so hard I thought my fingers might fall off.

I held the pen in my hand and signed my life away for twenty thousand dollars.

CHAPTER 53

Now

Songfest drags on way longer than usual. Or at least that's how it feels from the picnic tables in the back, where all of the counselors are trying not to wince as the kids drone on and on, singing about how much they love each other and camp and how two months is never enough time in this place. The sentiments are real. I feel them, too. But I can't think about that now. All I can focus on is this ending so we can sneak into the winter cabin.

Finally, when the last team finishes, Stu and Mellie stand up and applaud, their eyes wet with tears. It's dark now, save for the enormous fire burning in the middle of the circle, illuminating the campers and counselors sitting around the ring. Stu and Mellie hold hands and walk around, looking at the community, this place they built from scratch. The kids are sitting with their designated teams, wearing their colors—blue, red, yellow, green—eagerly waiting for the directors to announce the winners.

Finally they do, and the members of the red team erupt in cheers, hugging each other and falling over as they realize they have finally achieved their dream of being number one.

The other teams deflate and hold one another, reminding themselves, *This is only camp. This is only color war. It's not real life.*

But we all know it is.

Imogen sniffles next to me and Ava elbows her in the stomach. "Softie!"

"It makes me weepy," she whispers, which causes me to stifle a laugh.

"Oh shit, you ready?" Ava asks. She nudges me and we all look toward the center of the circle, where Stu and Mellie are closing out color war with a few more traditions. They make nice with the losing teams and award the winning captains the massive trophy that will sit in the dining hall engraved, now with their names and year on it. If I squint, I think I can see mine. Stu clears his throat.

"And as per tradition, we'd like to invite all of the previous captains up to sing the Alpine Lake alma mater with us." He extends his arm to the counselor area. Pride swells in my heart, even though there are still so many questions about what this place means to me now that it's forever intertwined with Heller's death. But I can't deny that honors like winning color war still mean as much to me as they do to the kids. In the confines of camp, they're everything.

A handful of us stand and we join Stu and Mellie and this year's captains around the fire. I look to my right and left and see Levin, Tommy, Craig, and some of the special events staff. A moment of understanding passes between us. No one else knows how it feels to be victorious, to lead another group of your peers through battle, to feel worthy.

"Join us," Stu says. We wrap our arms around one another and sing the words we know by heart.

I gaze out at the circle and beyond, at this community, constructed out of air and wood and dirt. How did it become something so much bigger than one person? Than one experience? I wonder for how many people here did it become a lifeline? And how, for Heller, did it become a death sentence?

By the time the song ends, there are tears in my eyes. Imogen and Ava approach and wrap me in a hug, their bodies warm against my own. "You ready?" Ava whispers in my ear.

The answer is obvious. "Yes."

Later that night, after the cabin is full of sweet little snores and we're sure Mellie and Stu have gone to the wine bar in town with all the other camp elders, I tiptoe outside to meet Ava and Imogen. Together we make a mad dash for the winter cabin.

I know it better than anyone else in camp. How it always smells of rosemary and cinnamon, thanks to the candles Mellie buys, and how the pillows are refreshed every other year so it always feels new and pristine.

Stepping onto the white wood porch feels like a betrayal, but I know we have no other choice. I enter a series of numbers on the keypad and feel my heart beat fast as the door unlocks.

I lead Ava and Imogen to the back of the house so we can access the office. It's the only part of the cabin that's less than perfect, messy even. There's a combination on this door, too, but it opens when I enter the correct code.

"Right there," I say, pointing to the metal rack full of old equipment. Imogen starts going through it all, pulling out CD players and DVD machines, boom boxes and old-school walkie-talkies.

"What the hell is this stuff?" Ava asks.

"Junk," Imo says, pulling out one random device after another.

We each take a rack and start going through everything, looking for *something* that could be hooked up to the camera by the lake.

"Think this is it?" Ava holds up a square khaki cube that looks like it's from the seventies.

"Nope," I say. "The camera was black with white lettering. I bet its receiver matches."

We're silent, moving aside hard drives and electronics until Imogen pulls out a small black handheld device that looks like a vintage Game Boy but larger. Almost like an iPad but clunkier. The brand name is scrawled in white along the top.

"Eh?" she asks, holding it up.

It looks familiar. "I think my parents had one of those when I was a kid. They used it to make sure the feral cats stayed out of Mom's tomatoes."

"Looks like it needs to be plugged in." Imogen starts searching through a box of wires and dongles, until she emerges with something that fits into the back of the machine.

She shoves it into the wall and there's nothing left to do but wait.

Ava taps her fingers against the table and Imogen's doing some meditative breathing thing until finally the screen flickers on.

When we see the screen, I gasp. It's right there. All the footage from the summer, cataloged by date.

I peer over Imogen's shoulder as she uses the chunky arrow buttons to scroll down. Wind chimes tinkle on the front porch and a shiver slinks up my spine. "Can we go any faster?" I ask.

"I'm trying," Imo says, fear in her voice. For all her and Ava's talk, I know she doesn't want to get caught, doesn't want to feel the wrath of Stu and Mellie's disappointment. Lucky for me, I've already felt it once before.

"There," Ava says, when Imo finally lands on the right date. "Look at the midnight hour."

Imo toggles down and we see the grainy black-and-white footage pop up. The camera's so old, you can barely make out details. No color or shading. Shapes moving around in the dark. But even still, the waterfront is unmistakable. Camp Alpine Lake at night. Breathtaking.

"There we are." I point to the corner of the screen where you can see a few naked butts running toward the water, splashing around in the moonlight.

"Huh, maybe I *should* have gone for Aaron this summer," Ava says. She mimes zooming in on his behind. "Cute."

Imo swats her on the arm and stifles a laugh as she fast-forwards through the tape until there's nothing, just stillness.

"Try the next hour," Ava says.

Imo clicks over to it, and sure enough, when she lands on the thirty-five-minute mark, there's a splash of bright hair peeking out from a dark hoodie. A figure sprints down the beach. It's obviously Ava, whipping her head around, looking for someone, something.

Ava inhales sharply beside me. "It's okay," I say as her eyes stay glued to the screen.

We wait a second, peering at the stillness, but then I notice movement at the top of the frame. A small boat slowly approaching in the water. Heller's dinghy. "There he is."

We watch the scene unfold as Ava said it did. Heller boats over to the beachfront and climbs out of the dinghy so he's standing on the edge of the dock. He steps onto the sand, onto Camp Alpine Lake property.

Ava motions for him to move over to the kayak stand, so they're under cover. At least a little bit. I watch as he follows her to the exact spot where I found his necklace. They talk for a little while, a minute or two, before we see headlights coming from off frame, spotlighting the waterfront. It must be a golf cart. The glow illuminates everything, including Heller's dinghy, tied up to the close dock. The golf cart pauses and the lights flicker off.

On-screen, Ava whips her head around, trepidation in her eyes, and then she looks back at Heller, pushing him toward his boat. He stumbles and I wonder if this is where he lost his lightning bolt. In a split second Ava's gone, hightailing it up the back trail, while Heller runs back down to the dinghy, into the spotlight.

"That's when I came to your cabin," Ava whispers to me.

But before Heller climbs into the boat, he swivels his head around, looking to where the golf cart is off-screen. He freezes as if someone's calling to him, saying something.

I lean in to the picture, like it's going to give me answers. I wish I could turn the volume up to hear his voice, or enhance the image to make out the emotions on his face.

Heller takes a step away from the water. Then he does the unthinkable. He jogs up the beach, past where he stood with Ava. And then he disappears off-screen.

"What the fuck is happening?" I ask, panic in my voice.

Ava's got a quizzical look on her face, her head cocked to one side. "Is he . . . talking to whoever's in the golf cart?"

Imogen nibbles on her lip and fast-forwards. But nothing appears on screen. We can only see the stillness of the water and the beauty of the night.

We search for something, anything that can bring answers. I'm holding my breath and all of a sudden, Imogen gasps beside me.

When I see what she's looking at, all the air leaves my lungs.

No.

A hooded figure appears. Their face is obscured and they have no defining characteristics. One person of average height and weight dressed in dark sweats. Their back is to the camera but then the whole picture comes into view. The person moves slowly, dragging a lifeless Heller—*my Heller*—across the sand by his legs like he's a piece of lumber.

I watch in disbelief as they heave Heller into the shallow end of the lake before running back off-screen.

Heller floats for a bit, the water rippling behind him, until he stops next to his dinghy. A rope catches on his foot, still stuffed into his white sneaker. The moon shines bright, and it looks like he's glowing in the dark, dark water. I want to cover the screen, shield his body from onlookers—from me.

But I can't pry my eyes away from him because if I do, that means he'll be gone for good.

"Who would do this?" Imo asks. Her voice is shaky and scared. No one says anything. No one makes a move. We watch Heller float in the water alone.

Dead.

Ava wraps an arm around my shoulder. "I'm so sorry," she says breathing warmth into my neck. I shake my head against her chest and she pulls me tight to her.

Imogen fast-forwards until we see the sun starting to peek out from the horizon. "There's Levin," she says. He appears on-screen wearing swim trunks. He stretches, all smiles, as if he's about to take a morning dip, but as he approaches the water he stops, frozen, until he drops to his knees. Levin fumbles for his walkie and it only takes a few minutes before Stu and Mellie appear in a golf cart. Imogen speeds ahead some more until the Roxwood police come into view. She stops the tape before we can watch them pull Heller out of the water on a stretcher.

"Fuck," she whispers.

The air is still and quiet as I rack my brain for answers.

"Can you rewind?" I ask. "To the golf cart."

Imo looks between Ava and me like she's not sure if she should, but Ava nods, so Imo presses back until we can see the person from the golf cart appear on-screen. She pauses and we stare at the device, trying to make out who it could possibly be. "I wish I could zoom the fuck in."

"Is there *any way* to tell who this is?" Ava asks.

I break out of Ava's arms and get close to the screen. I point to the bottom corner where you can see their hand grasping Heller's ankle tightly. I fight back vomit.

But it's useless. All we can see is darkness, the shape of a human. Nothing to hold on to.

Imo is about to close out of the file when Ava stops her. "Hold on," she says. "Right there." She points to the person's torso and suddenly I see what she sees.

A striped piece of fabric peeking out from below their sweatshirt.

We'd all know that pattern anywhere. It's an Alpine Lake senior staff shirt.

I shake my head but the truth is obvious now. Heller's killer works here, among us, and has all summer.

All of a sudden, a branch snaps in the distance. "Did you hear that?" Imogen asks, whipping her head around.

Ava's face goes pale and she grabs my wrist. She presses one finger to her lips and motions for us to be quiet.

Voices. A few of them. And they're headed right this way.

Imogen shuts down the receiver and throws it back into a box. We scramble out of the office, but as we're about to head through the front door Ava freezes. Whoever's there is heading right for us. We're trapped. Ava spins on her heel and motions for us to turn around and retreat farther into the cabin.

Panic pounds in my chest and I know we're screwed. So fucking screwed. Imogen and Ava feel it, too.

But I know this cabin like I know my own home. There's a back door off the kitchen. If we can get close, we'll be able to make an escape. The voices get louder and I know there's no time.

"In here," I whisper, motioning to the walk-in closet off the hall. "You two stay here."

"But—" Ava says.

"Go!" I shove them inside and retreat to the kitchen pantry, which is big enough for one. I wedge myself inside, under shelves full of canned soup and jelly jars.

"Ah, I must have left the light on," someone says, joyous and slurry as they swing open the door loudly.

Crap.

I can't quite make the voice out yet but I can tell it's young and male, too buoyant to be Stu, which is odd since I don't know anyone else who has the code to get in.

A woman laughs at the entryway, shutting the door behind her. *Who is it?*

I slide down the wall, hoping to make myself as small as

possible. But as I hit the floor, something vibrates in my pocket. *Shit.*

I must have automatically connected to the Wi-Fi here, meaning a bunch of texts and emails are now coming through. I fumble for my phone and silence it, but not before I see six texts from Cal pop up on the screen, each one with more urgency than the last. The most recent one is frantic.

> Check your fucking email!

I tap over to my inbox and wait what feels like a million years for the messages to load. There's a ton of spam and one from Cal with no subject. The email is blank save for an attachment. It starts to download, but the Wi-Fi here isn't that strong—this *is* Roxwood— so it takes a bit.

Footsteps make their way down the hall and I hold my breath, trying to be as quiet as possible. *Who the hell is here?*

All I know is that there's a man and a woman, and they seem to be helping themselves to Stu and Mellie's bar cart. I hear the sounds of ice clinking against glass and the fridge opening. Whoever it is starts making kissy noises and I roll my eyes. With my luck, it's probably my parents who found the code and use this cabin as a bone pad. Barf.

I glance back at my phone and see that Cal's attachment has loaded. I'm about to open it as I get another text from him.

But then the couple starts talking.

"I can't believe I've never been in here before." The male voice is crystal clear now, unmistakably Levin as he takes a sip from something. Ice cubes clink against a glass. I freeze in place and press my ear to the door.

"That's because you're such a goody-goody." Meg laughs and taps her glass to his.

"You sure it's okay we're here?" he asks.

"Of course," she says. "They told me I could come in here whenever." Comfort spreads throughout my chest. It's Levin and Meg. It's no big deal. But why would Stu and Mellie let her in here?

Levin chuckles then sighs. "I never should have let you go last summer. I'm sorry . . . about everything."

"By *everything*, do you mean the whole asking me to move to New York with you but then freaking out when I got laid off from the startup that promised to pay for my visa?" Meg's voice is sharp and I suck in a mouthful of air. I had no idea that's what happened at the end of last summer. I thought she went back to England.

Levin sighs. "You know I regret that. All of that."

Meg makes some sort of reluctant noise and takes another sip of her drink. "You're lucky Mellie and Stu took me in."

I shake my head, wondering if I misheard.

Cal texts again and I finally look back at my phone.

> I knew I recognized your friend! The British one. Took me a bit to place her, but I definitely saw her one time at Applebee Grocer in the fall. Head down being all secretive and shit. Now this???? FUCK.

I have no idea what he's talking about so I tap back over to the email and open the file. It's a photo of a newspaper clipping with a headline proclaiming something about a small new park over by Grandee's.

But there's also a photo of a bunch of employees standing behind the mayor as he cuts the ribbon with an oversize pair of scissors. It's hard to make out any faces since the photo is still pixelated, all different shades of gray. I scan the caption and find a list of names. My heart quickens when I see the name *Sally Burke* sandwiched between Heller McConnell and someone random. I start to scroll up to the photo to try to see where Heller is and where she could be standing. But it takes a while to load.

"I'll never be able to repay them for helping you out," Levin says. "At least you still could come down on the weekends."

Down? I think. *From where?*

"Until you told me not to come anymore," Meg says, her voice small.

"I regret that, too. It was a shit year."

Finally, the photo comes into focus and I zoom in, enlarging the image as much as I can. But it doesn't take long before I find Heller and Sally. And when I do, I nearly drop my phone.

Because I'd recognize that woman anywhere.

Sally Burke is Meg.

I bring my hand over my mouth to keep from making noise, to calm everything that's on fire inside my body.

How is this possible?

In the main room, the couch groans and it sounds like Meg is walking over to the back door. "At least all that time in Roxwood made me learn a few things . . . like how they keep all the good booze in *here*," she says in a playful voice.

My eyes go wide as I start to put the pieces together, trying to untangle all the things I've just learned:

Meg got laid off and her visa ran out.

Meg came to Mellie and Stu for help and they sent her to Roxwood. But she didn't tell anyone she was here.

Meg changed her name to Sally Burke and got a job at the clerk's office—right next to Heller.

Sally sent him a letter that said *I'm so sorry.*

She betrayed him in some way. Did she . . . want him gone?

And if she did, that means . . .

Meg killed Heller.

A scream bubbles up in my throat but before it can come out, Levin speaks. "You know what I could really go for? A burger."

"I know where Christina keeps the leftovers," Meg says, the playfulness back in her voice.

"Say no more." Levin stands, and I wait to hear the screen door slam as they leave the building.

I stay rooted in place for a minute more, trying to figure out what the fuck happened, but then the door swings open and Imogen and Ava are staring at me, confused and bewildered. Their eyes are wild with questions.

"Did you hear that?" I ask in a hushed whisper.

"Every word." Ava stares at me. "What the hell was she talking about?"

A light blinks on outside. Imogen pulls at my arm. "We have to go. Now."

We rush out the front door, panting as we make our way back to upper camp, not daring to speak.

Finally, when we reach the cabins, we eye one another with reluctance. There's still so much to say. I don't want to leave them yet. But it's too dangerous to be out here any longer now that we know the truth. I pull them to me and hug them tight.

"Tomorrow," I say. "Let's come up with a plan tomorrow."

Ava squeezes my shoulder and Imogen nods solemnly. Then they both depart, disappearing inside their cabins.

I gently pull the door to Bloodroot back, careful to not make a sound. The campers are quiet and everything seems okay—untouched. Once I get into the counselor room, I discard my hoodie and look around. Meg's bed is still neatly made, her little Union Jack bear sitting on her pillow.

I peer at her stuff—her fleece sweaters and hiking boots and baseball hats. *Who are you, Meg?* I want to scream. *What did you do?*

I spot the cabin banner, the one she made all those weeks ago when the campers first arrived, with her chicken-scratch handwriting, barely legible at all. But that's when it clicks into place.

Don't screw this up written on that piece of paper with the debit card I found in Heller's desk.

I'm so sorry spelled out on the letter Cal found from Sally.

Those words were written in the same handwriting as the one on this banner. Meg's handwriting.

My hands move before my brain does and in an instant, I'm rifling through her things, tossing her sweatshirts and socks and T-shirts onto the floor. I need to know if it's true, if she is who I think she is. I need to know for sure. I need proof.

It doesn't take long to find what I'm looking for and when I do, the sobs come suddenly without warning, spilling over onto the fabric in front of me.

I look down into my lap, breathing hard as tears fall from my face onto Meg's striped senior staff shirt.

CHAPTER 54

Then

"Come see us in New York!" Meg said. "Levin's place isn't too far from Ava."

"The Upper East Side is approximately one million miles away from Washington Heights." Levin heaved Meg's duffel into the trunk of his car. "Metaphorical miles, of course."

Meg smirked and punched him playfully on the shoulder. "For real, though. Let me know when you're visiting, yeah? We'll have a proper night out."

It was the final day of camp the year before, and Meg and Levin were the last counselors to leave. After they drove away, it would only be me left at Alpine Lake, the way the summer started.

I didn't want her to go, didn't want to see her drive off with Levin to start her new life in New York working for some tech startup as a receptionist. I wanted her to stay with me, to become one of the in-betweeners, someone who straddles the line of *us* and *them*.

Meg wrapped me in a hug, fierce and tight. She smelled like ginger and peppermint, and her Alpine Lake hoodie was worn thin from being run through the camp laundry so many times.

"Love you, G," she whispered into my hair. "You've always been my favorite. Don't tell the others."

CHAPTER 55

Now

The morning after songfest, the campers are exhausted, drained from having to battle one another with their voices, and are delighted to be free from their teams, back on the same side, the side of *camp*. But I can't focus on their chatter, not even as I braid Bianca's hair, because all I can think about is the fact that Meg killed Heller.

"Breakfast!" Meg calls from the bathroom, shouldering her backpack. She shoos everyone out the door and my chest tightens as I hang back in the counselor room.

Now's the time, I think. *I need to confront her.*

The final kid rushes out to the lawn and when it's the two of us, I reach for her arm.

"What are you waiting for?" she asks. "Come on!"

I stare at her, bewildered at how she can be so . . . normal. How someone I thought I knew could be an actual killer. I want to ask so many questions, yell until my lungs give out. Instead, I say the one word I know she'll understand.

"Sally."

I hold my breath, waiting for her to say something, to acknowledge the truth. She squeezes her eyes shut and presses her clipboard tight to her side. For a second, she looks so young, like she did when she first became our counselor. A baby-faced eighteen-year-old, the same age I am now. A child in so many ways. Now . . . I don't know who she is.

Meg blinks open her eyes and turns on her heel. She pastes a big smile across her face and yanks her arm out of my grasp. "Race you to the dining hall, Jordie!" I watch her jog behind the girls, the perfect Alpine Lake counselor for one more day.

Ava, Imogen, and I are preparing for another session of free swim, lathering suntan lotion up and down our arms, bronzed from eight weeks in the sun. But there's a silent tension between us. I know we're all wondering *what do we do now?*

I bite the bullet.

"Meg is Sally Burke. The woman from the clerk's office."

Ava and Imo freeze. Sunscreen slips through Imogen's fingers, plopping on the sand in a big white blob. Ava opens her mouth like she's going to say something but she doesn't.

"What the hell are you talking about?" Imo asks.

I nod. "Cal found a photo of Sally in the local paper. It was Meg."

Ava leans in. "Are you sure?"

"One hundred percent positive. It tracks with what she was saying last night, too. How she came up to Roxwood after she lost her work visa. Stu and Mellie must have helped her get a job."

"But why would she change her name?" Imogen asks.

"I have no idea." I shake my head. "But I confronted her this morning. I called her Sally."

Imogen's shoulders tense. "And?"

"She freaked out," I say. "Ran off to breakfast." I squeeze my eyes shut and duck my head toward them. "She's guilty. I know it."

"Wait a second," Ava says, pumping her hands up and down. "You think she was in the winter cabin the night Heller died and saw him on that bootleg receiver thing? Used that moment to come down to the waterfront and do it?"

I shake my head. "It sure looks that way."

"Why?" Imo asks. "What was her beef with Heller?"

"I've been trying to piece it together and the only thing that makes sense was that they *were* together. They must have been. She must have wanted to keep it quiet so Levin wouldn't find out. She was desperate to get him back." I fight the pain building in my chest. If that's true it means they *both* betrayed me in more ways that I realized.

Ava clears her throat. "What if . . . what if she knew about my dad?"

She *had* written *Don't screw this up* on that piece of paper with those sketchy cards. Maybe they were connected to Mark Cantor, too.

I nod. "She might have."

Ava covers her face with her hands. "My dad," she says. "He could have paid her to do it. To get rid of him and make it look like an accident."

"Are you serious?" I ask.

"I don't know, but, I mean . . . maybe." She pinches the bridge of her nose. "She needed cash, right? If he thought Heller could actually tell the world about what he was doing . . . I don't know what he's capable of." Ava sniffles. "Fuck. I'm so sorry this all comes back to my garbage dad."

But I cut her off. "None of this bullshit is your fault. We're going to prove it."

"What are you going to do?" Imo asks.

I don't want to admit that I'm all out of ideas. But looking at Ava and Imogen . . . I can't lie to them. Not again.

"I don't know," I say.

Ava pushes herself to stand. "That's why you have us," she says. "We have to stick together today, okay? Everything will be fine. Three on one. That kind of thing."

I nod, grateful for them, their devotion, that all the things I thought could break our friendship turned out to be untrue.

I gaze out at the lake, the sun beating down, bouncing off the surface. Stu and Mellie are down here, too, wading in the shallow end, splashing around and laughing with the little ones. I think of everything they've done to make this place the best, to keep it alive.

Having this come out about Meg would destroy them. It would destroy camp.

"I have to tell Stu and Mellie," I say, nodding to the directors.

Ava sighs. "I don't know, Goldie. You're basically begging to get fired. The whole sneaking into the winter cabin thing?"

I shake my head. "This is bigger than that. They'd want to know if a woman they trusted was a killer, don't you think? If someone else found out, it could bring this whole place down."

Imogen bites her lip, her gaze following the directors as they climb out of the lake and towel off.

"We can't let Meg destroy Alpine Lake," I say.

Imogen bites the inside of her cheek. "We'll come with you."

Ava nods. "Let's wait until after banquet, okay? Jordie and Bianca are really looking forward to it." She smiles. "It's the best night of the year."

Meg avoids me for the rest of the day, which I guess is what I would do if the person I'd been living with for eight weeks found out I was lying about my identity and was likely a killer.

She ditches Bloodroot at lunch to help out with banquet preparation and I spot her running around the kitchen, her arms full of streamers and balloons, a frantic smile plastered on her face.

I don't see her at rest hour, when we're supposed to be helping the teary-eyed girls pack their trunks to go home. And she doesn't show up to afternoon swim, the last chance our campers will have to splash around in the lake they've all come to love.

She's even MIA in the afternoon, when the girls are getting ready for banquet, putting on their fancy dresses and dabbing makeup on their eyelids. I help them pin their hair into updos and twist their braids into crowns. I curl my body around the little ones who are crying, devastated to leave this place. I watch as they sit close to one another, holding hands and complimenting each other's outfits. I take their photos as they hug one another desperately, like it's the last time they'll ever be together. I marvel at Jordie and Bianca, right in the middle of the group, when they had been on the outside only a few weeks before.

None of them ask for Meg. They're interested in only each other, in the friendships now imprinted on their hearts. The other Ramblers pour out of their cabins onto the lawn. Imogen, Ava, and

I stand together, watching the girls. They're so open, so warm. Untouched by the grief that comes with growing up. I want to box them up and keep them this way forever.

Ava rests her head on my shoulder. When I look down, I see she has tears in her eyes. "I miss it," she says softly.

"Me too," Imogen says.

Finally, the dining hall bell rings, summoning us all to banquet, and we follow our campers, their tiny heels clacking against the gravel.

It always makes me emotional, this night. How it signifies the end of summer, the marking of something magical, something that changed you.

I watch as Ava rushes over to the twins and leans down, posing in between them for photos. In another time, another life, they may have shared the pictures with their dad. But I now know they're for them, these three sisters.

Meg is nowhere to be seen. Not outside the dining hall or at the formal dinner, where we eat Christina's steak and potatoes and sip sparkling apple cider. She doesn't appear when Stu and Mellie hand out spirit awards and tennis trophies, or when they make sweet speeches about how this year has been so special, so unlike the others.

I spot Levin sitting at the staff table across from Mom and Dad and wonder if he knows what the hell he got himself into by falling for Meg. If he knows what she's capable of—who she *really* is.

Another DJ social follows and we rush the girls into the Lodge for the final dance of the year. We're still in our good clothes, but the counselors plop down on the couches and watch the awkwardness unfold as usual.

We laugh as the kids jump around, the stilted movements from the first dance still there but less pronounced. They toss beach balls and wear funny glasses, hugging one another as they try to capture all these little moments deep within their hearts.

I keep my eyes on Stu and Mellie, dancing in the back of the room like the loving chaperones they are. But after I get back from a game of Simon Says I notice they're gone, Mom and Dad in their place.

Mom catches my eye and waves, an olive branch. We haven't spoken since she told me she knew Heller was driving and I still don't have the words to discuss that, but I walk over to my parents anyway.

"Care to join me for a father-daughter dance?" Dad says, his voice light. I wonder if Mom told him.

I shake my head. "Do you know where Stu and Mellie went?" I ask.

Dad's mouth turns into a frown but Mom points up toward the dining hall. "I think they ran up to get a tray of cookies for the kids."

"Meg was with them," Dad says.

"Meg?" I ask, a chill running down my spine.

Dad nods. "She looked like she was having a hard time. Must be sad about the summer ending."

I don't hear anything else he says because before I know it, I'm busting through the doors of the Lodge, ignoring my inner voice, the one that tells me to grab Ava and Imogen first. It's too late for that. I have to find Stu and Mellie as fast as possible, before Meg has a chance to hurt them.

CHAPTER 56

Now

I need to get to them. There's no other choice. These are the people who did their best to protect me, to bring me into their world, to give me things I could have only dreamed about.

I run to the dining hall, through the serenity of camp. Without kids wandering about, it's still and quiet, stuck in time. The nets are strung tight, the activities at the ready, like the children will use them tomorrow. But there are signs this summer has come to an end. This place has been wrung out, loved and worn. There are deflated basketballs, limp nets on the tennis courts, mussed dirt near third base. Reminders about what this place is for. How it allows you to fall over and over, always providing a safe place to land.

I'm panting by the time I get to the dining hall but there's no time to regain my composure. I throw open the doors and the room is black, a faint smell of bleach permeating the air. Maybe Dad was wrong. Maybe they're not here at all.

But then I hear something. Hushed, urgent whispers coming from the kitchen where Christina is usually posted up.

I rush to the delivery entrance close to the kitchen and push open the door, nearly stumbling over my heels.

Stu and Mellie are standing behind the warming stations, wearing their fancy banquet attire. They look up in surprise, concerned expressions on their faces. Meg is next to them, her pale skin bright red and her bottom lip trembling like she's been crying.

"Get away from her!" I yell. "She killed Heller."

Meg's eyes go wide and she takes a step toward me.

"Don't come closer." But for the first time I realize how stupid this decision was, how dumb I am for walking into a closed room with Meg hoping to defend people I love with nothing but my brain.

Mellie holds up her hand and Meg stops moving.

"Goldie, what's going on?" Mellie says. She and Stu exchange a curious look and she comes toward me, extending her hand to graze my arm. "Are you all right?"

"Did you hear me?" I ask. "Meg killed Heller. I have proof."

I spill the story as quickly as I can, fumbling over words as I try to explain how she worked at the clerk's office under a pseudonym, how she got close to Heller, how I am so sorry but I snuck into the winter cabin, found the old camera receiver, and watched her drag his lifeless body down the beach and into the lake.

Meg clenches her fists. "That's not true," she says, anger rising in her voice.

"Don't try to deny it," I say. "I saw your handwriting on that letter to Heller. There's a photo of you in the paper with the name Sally Burke."

Meg's mouth drops open. She knows I've caught her. I've figured it out. Stu fiddles with his fanny pack and looks up to the ceiling, squeezing his eyes shut. He must be freaking out, trying to figure out what to do.

I'm about to explain how I found out that Meg and Sally had the same handwriting and how Cal found the photo of her in the

Roxwood Read, when Stu fumbles for something, dropping his wallet. The contents spill out and I stoop down to help pick everything up. There in the middle of the pile is a nondescript debit card. It looks familiar but I can't place it.

Mellie gasps. "Meg, is this *true*?" She reaches for the card in my hand.

But I hold on to the piece of plastic, turning it over. There, on the back, is a phone number written in permanent marker. It starts with a +41.

"What is this?" I ask, the words catching in my throat.

Stu clears his throat. "Here, I'll take that."

"No," I say, my voice hard. "Tell me."

"It's how they get money out of their foreign bank account." Meg's voice is loud and furious as it echoes through the building.

"What?" I croak. "What is she talking about?"

"Tell her everything," Meg says. "Or I—"

Meg's words hang in the air as Stu steps back, bumping into her hard. She should stumble on her feet but instead she falls, and a loud crack reverberates through the room, shifting my organs and causing me to cry out, as Meg's head hits the side of the stove and she collapses to the floor.

I shriek and rush to her but Mellie holds me back, blocking me from her body. I stare at Meg, lifeless on the floor, Stu shocked and frozen beside her.

"Do something!" I scream.

"It was an accident," Stu whispers.

Mellie spins around, her eyes wide with fear and her mouth trembling. "Goldie." Her voice is hoarse from all the singing and cheering that come with the last few days of camp. But there's no mistaking that the rasp is so far from her usual calm. I have to believe Mellie will know what to do. Mellie always knows what to do.

"Goldie," she says again, tears pricking her eyes. "I'm so sorry."

My stomach turns to stone.

"It spun out of control," Stu says, crouched over Meg. He frantically hunts for a pulse. Meg makes a strange guttural sound and Stu glances up. "She's alive," he says. "She's okay."

Mellie exhales and her shoulders slump forward. She presses her hands to her forehead and groans. "It wasn't supposed to be like this."

"Mellie," I say. "What are you sorry for?"

She starts pacing, walking around the room, her eyes darting from the door to the walk-in fridge to the industrial-size dough hook. All of Christina's ingredients are lined up neatly, put away after such a big dinner. Suddenly, I wish she were here. I wish *anyone* were here.

Mellie kicks up her pace, mumbling to herself, glancing at Stu, whose hand is still wrapped around Meg's wrist, timing her pulse.

"Mellie!" I scream. "What are you sorry for?"

Mellie stops and pivots on her heel so she's facing me. All the color has drained from her face and her eyes are glossy. She clasps her hands in front of her chest and opens her mouth slowly. "You have no idea how hard it is to run this kind of camp," she says, her voice pleading and desperate. "The pressure we're under to not only provide the best but *be* the best. The margins in this industry are so thin. You either excel or you perish."

"What are you saying?"

"Campers like your friends—Ava, Imogen, Tommy." She presses her fingers to her temples. "They come from families where things are expected. Demanded." Mellie takes a step toward me and I force my feet to stay rooted in place, to ignore the terror coursing through my veins. "If anyone would understand, it would be you, sweet Goldie. How awful it is when these people look down at us, think of us as *the help*."

I shake my head. "That's not who I am to them."

Mellie looks at me with pity, cocking her head to one side. She raises her hand to graze my chin. "But you are," she says. "We all are."

I'm quiet, sifting through the truth.

"You have to understand," she says. "After the heavy hitters wanted to send their kids here, they wanted to know which country clubs *we* belonged to. They wanted to come to *our* home for pre-summer cocktail parties. They wanted to pretend like we were their equals—not their employees. Becoming that . . . that's how we would make this camp the greatest, the best, the most exclusive. It's how we kept it alive."

Her words don't make sense. "Why are you telling me this? What does this have to do with Heller?"

Mellie wraps her hands around mine. "I'm trying to explain."

Panic rises in my throat. "Explain what?"

Stu pushes himself to stand. "Why we did what we had to do."

I push Mellie away and back up so I'm pressed against the wall. "What did you do?"

"It was just a little at first," Mellie says, her voice trembling. "Upping our salaries. Skimming a few thousand dollars from the

Alpine Lake account here and there to pay ourselves bonuses. And then a loan to build the new house so we could throw parties for the VIP families. It was so little compared to what they had. What they paid."

"I don't understand," I say. "Isn't that . . . embezzlement?"

Shame coats Mellie's face. "We *had* to do it," she says. "We always had the intention to pay it back."

"Did you?" I ask, hopeful this is all some misunderstanding. "Pay it back?"

"We . . . we couldn't. There was too much to do. Parents to impress, appearances to be kept." She runs her hands through her hair and I see tears prick her eyes. "It became clear we had two choices: Declare it legal income and give half of it to Roxwood in taxes or . . ." She looks up. "Hide it."

I press my palms to my eyes. "Wait, so you didn't want to call it legal income because you didn't want to pay taxes?"

Mellie's shoulders slump forward. "Just give it away? It would be a waste."

I shake my head, knowing that's not true. Even a small amout of additional money would have helped Roxwood do things like fund arts programs and senior centers, or provide free school lunch. Those funds could have increased the school budget or paved roads. They could have helped people like Dylan and Cal and Heller, all the kids whose futures were dimmer because of where we'd been born.

I always thought Mellie and Stu were doing Roxwood a favor by being here, but now . . . it was all one big betrayal. And then everything clicks into place.

"You enlisted Mark Cantor." I keep my voice even.

"He was desperate to get Ava into camp. But you know Ava."
Mellie shakes her head. "Poor test scores. No real talent."

I clench my fists.

"It was a fair trade, Goldie. He set up a bank account for us
overseas to hide our little bonuses. Ava came to Camp Alpine
Lake no problem."

"And she didn't have to take the entrance exam," I say, remembering what Ava told me all those years ago.

"You have to understand," Stu says. "It wasn't illegal back then.
Not until after the financial crisis. Then we had to start using those
prepaid phone cards to ask the Swiss bank to put cash on our debit
cards."

"But now . . ." I say.

Mellie turns to me. "Embezzlement and tax evasion? We could
go to *jail* if we were found out," she says. "You know what that
would mean? The end of Alpine Lake. The end of everything we
worked so hard to build. Everything we love. Everything *you* love."

I shake my head. The idea of losing Alpine Lake is impossible.
But so is knowing that Mellie and Stu committed a *crime*.

A gargled groan erupts from across the room.

"Meg!" I rush to her side, kneeling on the ground next to her.
"Heller," I say through tears. I know I need to get the words out.
"Did you kill him?"

Meg looks up at me with hooded, unfocused eyes. A lump is
forming on her forehead, red and round, and she grabs for my
wrist. "No," she says, pointing behind me. "They did."

The rest of my body grows cold as I spin around to find Mellie and Stu standing over us with panic-stricken faces. The realization dawns on me. They have striped senior staff shirts, too.

I clamber to my feet.

"He wasn't supposed to be at camp," Mellie says, panicked. Her eyes are wide and bloodshot and I barely recognize the woman in front of me, the woman I trusted with my life only minutes before.

I try to keep my eye on Stu as he slowly steps toward the magnetic rack of knives hanging on the wall behind him.

"What happened?" I ask, tears falling down my face. "I need to know what happened." My voice is a whisper. "Please."

Mellie's crying now, too, and for a second, I think she's going to deny me the right to know the truth. But she doesn't. She starts talking.

"We got an alert that the cameras were disabled thanks to your skinny-dipping adventure," Mellie says. "So, we went to the winter cabin to make sure everything was okay on that old receiver. When we got there, we saw him boat up to meet Ava."

"But how did you know Heller knew all of this?"

"Mark got a tip that some kid in Roxwood named Heller was digging around about his company."

"So, you went down to the waterfront?" I ask. "To confront him?"

Mellie starts pacing again, frantic. "I thought it would be so simple. We knew he was driving in that accident, not you. We figured we'd say if you expose us we'll expose you."

The truth presses down on me as I remember Mom told Mellie about Frank's Auto Shop. They knew. They knew and did nothing to help. Not until it could benefit them.

Mellie looks at me, her eyes full of despair. "He loved you. That boy loved you. He told us to go right ahead and rat him out. He was sick of keeping that secret."

I cover my mouth with my hand.

"How did you . . . ?" I ask. I have to know.

"It's such a tragedy," Mellie says, pursing her lips together. "He tried to fight. He did. But we didn't have a choice. Stu had his fanny pack on him and I . . . I grabbed the emergency insulin pen. It happened so fast."

All the air exits my lungs and I feel like I can't breathe, like my world is on its side. We all know what happens when you give someone insulin who doesn't need it. Stu would tell us year after year as a warning not to play with his pen. It could put you in a coma no problem. Kill you, too. And it would never show up on a tox screen.

"You . . . you gave him an insulin shot and dumped him in the lake to make it look like he drowned?"

Stu reaches out to the wall of knives and grabs the wooden handle of a cleaver, turning it over in his palm. "We love you like a daughter, Goldie. Really we do." His voice quavers as he walks back to Mellie, handing the weapon over to her.

Mellie looks at the steel blade, then up at me, tears streaming down her face. "But we love this camp more."

I swallow a scream as I brace for impact, expecting her to run toward me, for steel to slice through flesh. But instead, Mellie flees, pulling Stu with her. He stumbles over his own feet and follows Mellie out the swinging doors, into the dining hall. I run after them, but that's when I hear Mellie slide the knife through the door handles, sealing the kitchen off completely.

I run around to the back of the room, looking for the other exit by the alleyway reserved for deliveries. But that one's locked, too.

I pace around the room, searching for a way out. But then the panic subsides. What are they going to do? Keep me in here until breakfast?

Beads of sweat begin to form on my brow and my neck grows hot. Nerves, I think. But then my throat grows scratchy and raw. *Water. I need water.* Smoke begins to fills the kitchen, whisps coming through the cracks in every door.

Suddenly their plan crystallizes. They're going to burn down the dining hall.

And Meg and I'll be in here while it goes up in flames.

An accident.

I try to think fast but my mind is hazy and it's so hard to move. I reach for Meg and pat my hand around her waist until I find what I'm looking for. I grab the walkie from her hip and press the talk button.

"Dining hall's on fire!" I scream as loud and long as I can. "Help!"

I start to cough and I'm seized by fear. It may have been a minute or an hour since Stu and Mellie left us here, and there's no way to know. When I reach up to touch the metal panels on the swinging doors, they're hot. Too hot. I look down and see smoke billowing through the sliver of air in between the dining hall and the kitchen.

I taste banquet steak coming up my throat and soon I can smell the sour stench of bile. The room flips on its side and my vision goes spotty as I stumble to the ground.

"She's in there!"

Ava's voice is desperate and loud, close, but too far for me to feel relief. A window smashes nearby and I try to lift my head to see, but it's too heavy to move. The door breaks open and I roll over, straining to see what—or *who*—is there. Imogen's sobbing but she wraps me in her arms so tight, and I catch a whiff of blueberry, of Ava.

They start dragging me out and I hear other people, loud and scared, rushing in for Meg.

I look up at my friends, my two favorite people in the world, and then, everything goes black.

CHAPTER 57

Now

I dreamt of Heller after he died.

I dreamt we were in a house full of people, of strangers, talking and laughing and pretending to have a good time. Because everyone but Heller knew it was his last day alive. We glanced at each other wondering, *Who will tell him?* But no one did.

I greeted him with a hug and he felt solid and sure. But he was distracted and busy, being pulled between groups and into conversations.

I let him go, knowing the night was long. There would be time to talk, there was always time to talk.

But as dawn peeked through the skylight, he slipped out through the front door. I moved to the window and watched him walk away, down a dark street until he disappeared. There was no more time to talk. Not then. Not ever.

And I turned to the other people in the room, the strangers whose faces had become familiar.

I smiled, at ease. I was ready, finally, to press on.

CHAPTER 58

Now

When I wake up, my throat is sandpaper, raw and scratching. Breathing hurts. So does swallowing. Saliva forms, but it tastes wrong, like my body shouldn't be making it.

I blink my eyes open and all I can see is the night sky, a smattering of stars soaring above me. It's peaceful. Quiet. Profound. But then everything else comes into focus.

The flames.

The ambulance.

The cop cars.

The sirens.

The kids.

The *kids*.

They gawk and stare at the beloved dining hall as dark cloudy smoke billows from the windows. Fire with its blue edges and its radiating heat consumes the place. Some of the campers cry, tucking their chins in each other's necks.

They shouldn't be here. They shouldn't be watching.

Where are Stu and Mellie? They should be shielding them from the scene.

But that's when I remember that they're the ones who did this.

– – –

"She's up," Mom says, her voice urgent and worried. I try to swivel my head but everything hurts. "Shh, sweets," she says. "You don't have to move. It's over now. It's over."

I can hear her choking on her sobs, trying to stay strong, and I sense Dad close by, too. His tall presence standing at her side.

"Can we see her?" Ava's voice is small and wavering but it's hers nonetheless.

I snap my eyes open and see her standing in the door with Imogen. They're both wearing the outfits they wore to banquet, but their faces are covered in soot, ash staining their arms. Imogen's hair is tied in a sloppy ponytail and Ava's platinum mane is a dirty shade of gray.

"You're here," I say.

Ava gasps and they both rush toward me, arms extended.

"Be gentle," Dad advises. "She's fragile."

I shake my head and everything throbs, sending a searing pain through my body. But I'm not *fragile*. I need information.

"What happened?" I ask, tasting smoke.

Mom sighs and looks at Dad, weary. "We heard you on the walkie. Ava and Imogen ran there as fast as they could. And when we saw the dining hall . . ." Mom covers her mouth. "We weren't sure if the fire department would get here in time."

"We got you out before the roof collapsed," Imogen says.

"They saved your life," Dad says.

"Is Meg okay?"

Mom nods. "She's going to make it."

"Stu," I say. "Mellie."

Mom nods. "The police found them in the office in the winter cabin, destroying everything having to do with their foreign accounts."

"Heller," I say. "They killed Heller."

Mom and Dad exchange a look.

"You don't need to worry about that now," Dad says. "You're safe."

I shake my head, nearly ripping the IV from my hand. "Where are they?"

Mom clears her throat. "They both confessed. To everything. You're never going to see them again."

I wake up the next morning, feeling like there's an anvil on my chest. My room is empty for the first time since I've been here. The sun streams through the flimsy curtains. *An amazing Alpine Lake day.* That's what Stu would say over the announcements if this were any other morning of the summer.

I stretch my arms over my head, surveying my body for aches and pains, bumps and bruises. Everything seems raw but intact.

"Get a load of the Brit down the hall?" A nurse speaks casually outside my room, chatting with an orderly.

I lean forward, trying to find out information about Meg.

"Roxwood PD are coming by soon," the orderly says, snapping a wad of gum. "Lucky she made it out alive."

A hitch catches in my throat and I know I need to see Meg. Now.

I swing my legs over the side of the bed and ignore the throbbing that spreads through my body. I inch myself up and out the door, hobbling along as I hold on to the IV drip, trying to forget the fact that my bare ass is hanging out of this hospital gown.

It takes me a while, but I make it to the end of the hall, where the whiteboard hanging on a door says Meg's name and a bunch of acronyms I don't understand. I twist the knob and slip inside, shutting the door behind me. When I turn around, I gasp. Nothing could have prepared me to see Meg this way, bandages wrapped around her arms and forehead, a bright pink gash trailing down her cheek. A tube's stuck into the back of her hand, which trembles when I step closer.

She stirs and cranes her head to see me. "I was wondering when you'd show up."

"Are you—"

"I'll live." She tries to push herself to sit but the movement seems to tucker her out. I slide into the plastic chair next to her bed.

"I—" Meg starts to say.

"It's all right," I say, suddenly feeling very tired. "You don't need to say anything." The words betray me. She needs to say something. Anything. There are still so many unanswered questions. So much I don't know.

I clear my throat and find the courage. "How, Meg? How did this all happen?"

Meg presses her hand over mine. She clears her throat and motions to a cup of water on the table next to her. I stick a plastic straw in it and bring it to her lips. She takes a sip and locks eyes with me. They're full of sadness and panic.

"I got laid off in New York and I knew I couldn't stay in the

States without a visa." Meg looks down at the tube sticking out of her body and starts picking at her cuticles, the skin around them red and raw. "I needed to."

"Levin?"

Meg nods. "I didn't know who else to call. Stu and Mellie told me to take the train out to their place in Connecticut." She gazes out the window at an empty parking lot, the mountains near Alpine Lake rising behind it. "They took me in and said they could take care of my visa if I did some tasks for them. Minor ones. Paperwork, reviewing applications. That kind of thing."

"You worked out of the winter cabin," I say. *Just like me.*

Meg sniffles. "It was so cozy, being up there. I wanted to call you. Desperately. But Mellie said I couldn't. She said we had to keep it a secret while they sorted out all of my immigration stuff." Meg shrugs. "I wasn't supposed to work outside of New York state, so it was a whole thing."

She leans back against the pillows. "But everything changed when Levin dumped me. I was depressed, stuck up there all alone. Bored as hell." She sighs. "Stu came up one day and left his email open. I couldn't help taking a peek."

"What did you find?"

"So many messages to Mark Cantor, asking him when they could make their next trip to Switzerland. They wanted to deposit more money, make a few withdrawals before the summer started." Meg huffs and crosses her arms. "But Mark said no. He was getting paranoid that someone was onto him so he was asking all his clients to keep low profiles."

"Is that why so much shit was weird this summer? The AC in the office? The late check to Heller's dad?"

Meg nods. "They were low on cash."

"Geezus."

"It gets worse." Meg shakes her head. "I didn't want to be privy to any sort of information that could get me in trouble, not when I was trying to stay here *legally* and get Levin back, so I confronted them."

"What did they say?"

"Stu convinced me that by working for them and *knowing* about the accounts I had already become complicit and that if anyone found out, I'd get sent back to the UK immediately. I'd lose Levin for good." Meg clasps her hands together. "Mellie said the best thing to do was to help them. She got me a fake ID, found me an apartment twenty minutes away, and arranged for me to get a job at the clerk's office to make sure no one in Roxwood caught on. But then..."

She shakes her head, sniffling.

"Then you met Heller." His name catches in my throat.

Meg nods and sniffles.

"Were you two..."

"Hooking up? God no!" Meg swats at me. "That boy was head over heels for you. I loved hearing him talk about you."

A lump forms in my throat.

"Broke my heart we couldn't all hang out together." She inhales deeply. "We got close and he told me about how all the facilities in town had gone to shit. How the school needed new laptops. How they couldn't pay the parks department employees so they had to furlough the whole team and shut down Little League. It's not like Stu and Mellie could have fixed everything, but the fact that they wanted to keep everything for themselves... it made me furious." She shakes her head, her brow furrowed. "They take and take from this town, never giving back."

"You told Heller what was going on. Gave him photocopies of the debit and phone cards."

Meg nods. "When it was time for me to come back to camp, I made him promise to wait until after the summer to leak the news. It was selfish but I wanted one more summer at camp."

"One more summer with Levin."

Meg covers her face with her hands. "It seems so stupid now."

"But he couldn't wait. He wanted me to know. That's why he tried to tell Ava."

Meg turns to me. "I didn't know he was there that night. I swear."

I don't know what to say or if I believe her. There's still so much that doesn't make sense. "What about the letter you sent him? You told him you were sorry. Why?"

Meg's lip trembles. "Stu and Mellie found out I told him. They read my texts when I went out for a jog. He wouldn't speak to me after that." She blinks as tears fall down her face. "It's all my fault."

I squeeze Meg's fingers and rest my chin in my hand, blinking back tears. "That's why he said it was a risk to come here after dark, why he gave his ID badge to Cal."

"I'm so sorry, Goldie," she says, her eyes closing as she lolls her head to one side.

"Meg?" She stirs but doesn't say anything. I move my arm toward her but then a nurse enters the room, knocking against the doorframe.

"Seems like she needs some rest, dear," the nurse says. "You should head back to your room."

"But—" I say.

The nurse shakes her head. "Up, up." She pulls at my arm and leads me out the door.

"I'm not—" I start, but she pushes me to the hallway and shuts Meg's door behind me. I walk to my room slowly, trying to organize my thoughts, understand everything Meg revealed. But there's something I can't let go of, a murky realization that's only now coming into focus.

I always wondered *why* Stu and Mellie helped me after the accident. Why they threw me a life vest when they easily could have let me drown. Now I'm curious why they did the same thing for Meg. There's only one answer I can think of and it's not an easy one to reconcile.

They actually cared.

Amid their lies, their acts of violence—Stu and Mellie wanted to champion the underdogs. Because in the end we were like them. Until one of us threatened their very way of life. In another world, Heller could have been one of their charges, another lost soul to take in and make whole again. But in this one, he was someone outside the gates of Alpine Lake. Someone who didn't matter at all.

CHAPTER 59

Now

When I shuffle back to my room, I see it's not empty.

Cal's hopped up on the windowsill, a paper bag with the Café Cloud logo on it sitting next to him.

"Brownies," Cal says. "Your favorite, right?"

It hurts to smile but I do it anyway as I climb back into bed. He hands me one and I sink my teeth into the fudgy center. "How'd you know I was here?" I ask, mouth full of chocolate.

He grabs one, too. "It's all over the news."

"Everyone knows, huh?" I ask.

"That the Alpine Lake owners killed Heller for trying to expose their financial fraud?" He nods. "Yeah. They know."

I take another bite of brownie. "Good."

Cal sighs and glances down. "Judah said he'll find you soon. When he's ready. To thank you."

I sniffle, catching tears in my throat.

"You did it, Goldie."

I look up at him, his eyes rimmed with red. "Yeah. I did."

"Thank you," he says. "Thank you." He wipes the back of his face with his sleeve. "I'm ready to back you up, you know. I'll tell the truth about the accident. Whatever you want."

I start to cry then, the tears falling in big wet plunks on the brownie in my hand, ready to find out what it is exactly that I want all over again.

By the time the doctors are ready to release me, camp is over. The session has ended and all the parents came to get their kids, still in shock from the evil of it all. Ava and Imogen told me all about it. How some families came the very night of the fire, not wanting their children to spend another night in the place. And once word got out, it traveled up and down the East Coast so finally, every affluent parent who had dared send their kid to Camp Alpine Lake knew: its owners were liars. And murderers.

Meg's got a few more days left in the hospital, but Levin's started visiting, sitting by her side. She has to stay in the States a little longer to help out with the Cantor Assets investigation. Cooperate with the Roxwood police, confess what she knew about Heller. But after that she's heading home to the UK to restart her life. Figure out what's next.

My parents' station wagon pulls up to the door and I bend down to see Ava in the driver's seat, Imo right beside her. I climb into the back seat, overcome with gratitude. Ava tosses her hair over one shoulder and glances at me in the rearview mirror. "You okay?"

I reach forward over the console and squeeze her hand. "Now I am. Are you?"

Ava shrugs. "The stepbitch came to get the twins this morning," she says. "Hate to say I'm going to miss those little goobers."

"Think you'll see them again?" Imogen asks.

"They're actually moving to Connecticut," Ava says. "So, they'll be close to me." She pauses. "And Dad. Inmate visiting days and all that."

"Oof," I say. "I'm sorry."

Ava smirks. "I'm not. He deserves to go to jail for what he did."

Imogen rests her head back against the seat. "Remember when we thought our biggest problem would be who we'd hook up with this summer?" she says wistfully.

Ava and I both break out into laughter and Imogen can't help herself either. As we drive down the hill entering camp, my stomach is full of butterflies, humming in time with the sounds of my two best friends, happy, at least for a second.

"Still one night left for Tommy time, Imo," I say playfully.

"Nah," she says. "I'd rather spend it with you guys."

We pull through the gates to see all the counselors who stuck around. They're standing near the fences where the kids usually hang out for visiting day. They all wave and cheer and welcome me back to the place I blew up, the place I saved.

"Well, shit," Ava says.

A sweet little jolt runs through me and for the first time in a long time I feel something I never thought I would again. Hope.

The loudspeaker crackles overhead and I jump at the shock of it. I thought only Stu and Mellie had access to it.

"This thing on?" Mom says, her voice nervous and high.

Ava stifles a laugh and folds a shirt on her bed.

"Clearly never used this thing before," Dad says. "But, uh, all-staff meeting at the picnic tables. Now."

The loudspeaker goes quiet but then someone else speaks far away. "I've got two hundred cookies. Think that's enough?" It's Christina, talking somewhere behind Dad.

"Should be fine," he says. "We'll empty out cookie patrol, too."

"Aw, crap, we left the speaker on," Christina says. The microphone goes muffled and then finally it shuts off.

Ava, Imogen, and I are all laughing then.

We make our way to the picnic tables, and I look out over the manicured grass, the neatly marked field, and the rows of pristine, picturesque cabins—all the things that have kept me going my whole life. I wonder if I'll ever get them back.

There's caution tape around where the dining hall once stood, signaling that there *was* a crime here. That everything has *not* been sorted out. There is still so much to do, so much to uncover. My heart is heavy with each step I take, and I reach up to touch the bandage on my forehead, to remember that it was all real. Whatever happened over the past few days was *real*.

I climb up onto a table and sit with my feet sturdy on the bench. Imogen plops down between my legs, resting her elbows on my knees. Ava sits on the grass in front of her, pressing her back up against Imo, who reaches down to pet her hair.

Everyone else assembles and the staff is quiet and still, trying to pick up the pieces of this place that we all love, that we've given so much to. A few people throw me somber nods. I don't know what they're supposed to mean—*thank you* or *I'm sorry*—but all I know is that it hurts too much to nod back.

Mom and Dad are standing at the front of the group, behind Christina. Mom's got on a vintage Billy Joel shirt and long jean shorts, her woven sandals frayed on her feet. Dad's wearing a

Roxwood Hospital T-shirt and exercise shorts, his hair matted under a backward Alpine Lake baseball hat. They both look like they haven't slept.

I want to run to them, to be sandwiched between them in a hug so tight I can't breathe, but I don't move. Because Dad starts talking.

"This is a dark day in Camp Alpine Lake history," he says, his voice wavering. "I don't have some powerful speech to make everything better or to absolve Mellie and Stu of what they did. All I know is that I have spent the past twelve hours trying to figure out how the hell we can make things right, how we keep the spirit of this place alive while also acknowledging the anger and resentment we feel toward the people who built it."

He rocks back and forth on his heels. "Stu and Mellie constructed camp to be a family. They turned it into one. But then they did everything they could to break it." He swallows his words then and pauses. "It's hard to reconcile that with the people we all knew."

He looks around as heads nod and tears fall.

"We don't have the answer. We don't know what to do. Not yet. But we wanted to thank all of you for making this place what it is. For helping those precious kids get home, and for being *there* for one another."

He starts to cry and turns to Mom, breaking down into her chest. Christina steps forward, ready to pick up where he left off.

She offers a weak smile and holds my gaze for a second longer. "The three of us are going to stay here for the next week or two closing up shop. Whoever wants to can stay and help. No shame if you need to get out of here, if this place is tainted forever for you now. But those of us who want to stay and make it better . . . well, we'll be here to help you do that.

"And yes, there will be cookies!" Christina calls, her voice high above the crowd.

"Who knows what will happen to this place," Mom says with a shrug. "But we're not going to abandon it yet. Take the day to yourselves. Do whatever you like. But if you're still here by break-fast time tomorrow, we'll assume you're sticking around to help. If not, you know we love you always and forever."

I look around the tables at all the counselors mulling over the decision in their head. *Stay or flee?* There's so much history here, so much baggage, so much life. Destruction.

But the answer is obvious to me at least. I have nowhere else to go.

CHAPTER 60

Then

The first time Mom and Dad brought me to Camp Alpine Lake, I couldn't believe such a place existed. I had never seen the lake so clear, the fields so green. The sun was high and bright but a breeze swept through the trees, raising goose bumps on my arms.

It was before the season started, before campers arrived, and they let me run free, untethered, unsupervised, as I wandered around, taking it all in with my tiny legs, my wide eyes.

"Find us when you're hungry," Mom said, patting me on the arm as I set off on my exploration. "It won't be hard."

I roamed the grounds, feeling like I had been given a gift, a slice of independence. That was what camp was supposed to be, I decided—something magical and mine, at least for a moment.

CHAPTER 61

Now

I wasn't sure if the flames were going to scare me, if I was going to be able to look at fire the same way again after what happened in the dining hall. But fire is such an important part of camp. Starting it, maintaining it, feeding it, breathing life into it. It's all a symbol. An obvious metaphor for building something that can so easily take on a life of its own.

Looking at the one in front of me, the one being tended to by the other Alpine Lakers . . . it makes me mad. Stu and Mellie used what I loved against me, and tried to make me afraid of something that has only given me such comfort.

Guarded by stones and counselors who look after it, by friends and caretakers, this fire is safe. This fire is purposeful. This fire is not meant to destroy. It's meant to rebuild.

I settle onto one of the logs and hug my middle, tucking my chin inside my sweatshirt. "Here," Ava says. She approaches with a plastic cup filled with red wine.

"Thanks," I say.

She sits down next to me and Imogen appears on my other side. The three of us stay huddled, staring at the fire in silence. All around us, stragglers appear, taking seats and finding drinks. The mood is so different than it was eight weeks ago when we all arrived, ready to make something great. We had so much hope then, so much energy. Now it looks like everyone has been defeated, like someone popped the bubble that held camp inside of it. They let all the air out and we're left fighting for the oxygen.

"I'm staying," Ava says, her voice steady.

"Same," Imo says.

"Really?' I ask. "Thought you guys would want to get out of here tomorrow."

"Have you learned nothing, Goldie?" Ava jokes. She throws her arm around me. "We're not gonna leave you *now*."

"How'd you know I was going to stay?"

"Was there any other option?" Imogen asks.

"I was thinking about it," I say.

"No, you weren't," Imo says.

"You're right. I wasn't."

"See, we know you better than you know yourself." Ava smirks and takes a sip of her drink. "What do you think they'll do with the place?"

I look across the circle at Mom, Dad, and Christina. They're sitting in fold-up lawn chairs, not saying anything. Staring into the fire with sleepy eyes and deep lines drawn on their faces. Christina reaches into a paper bag at her feet and pulls out a few cookies. She passes them around and my dad's eyes twinkle a thank-you.

"I don't know," I say. "Sell it?"

"It'd be a great hotel," Imogen says. "One of those massive luxury mountain resort kinds of things, you know? With a big auditorium to host visiting theater troupes."

"Or a wedding venue," Ava says. "They could make bajillions."

"Maybe a boarding school," Imogen says.

"Thoughts, Goldie?" Ava asks.

I look up at the endless sky and think about Heller, about how he took his last breath under the Roxwood stars, the ones he loved so much. He died here, at the place that gave me everything and then took it all away. He died loving me. He died knowing the truth about what he did would come out, knowing that was okay. It was right.

"Maybe I'll buy it one day," I say, almost a whisper. "Turn it into something better. Something new." I look at Imogen, then Ava. These girls. The ones who know my every twist and curve and freckle. The ones who know how to break me apart and make me whole.

"We could all come back," I say. "Together."

ACKNOWLEDGMENTS

Thank you to my agent, Alyssa Reuben. I am so lucky to have found you, a person who gets me and all of my dreams—and knows exactly how we can achieve them together.

Thank you to Ruta Rimas, who skillfully edited this book over many Zoom conversations, emails, and phone calls that often started with an excited, "What if . . ." I am grateful for your care, guidance, and enthusiasm. Thank you to Gretchen Durning, whose notes improved this story in so many ways.

Thank you to Casey McIntyre, who championed this book from the beginning and whose support I'd be nowhere without.

Thank you to Elyse Marshall, the publicist of my dreams. I'd pack book mailers all day just to hang out with you.

Thank you to Krista Ahlberg, Sola Akinlana, Michelle Millet, and Abigail Powers for your proofreading and production prowess.

Thank you to Christine Blackburne and Kristin Boyle for crafting yet another bombshell cover that stands out among the shelves.

Thank you to the incredible people at Razorbill and Penguin Teen who make publishing magic happen every single day. I am indebted to you all: James Akinaka, Kara Brammer, Christina Colangelo, Felicia Frazier, Alex Garber, Carmela Iaria, Jen Klonsky, Bri Lockhart, Jen Loja, Shanta Newlin, Debra Polansky, Emily

Romero, Kim Ryan, Jocelyn Schmidt, Shannon Spann, Bezi Yohannes, Felicity Vallence, and Jayne Ziemba.

Thank you to Aaron Buotte at Paradigm for all your efficiency and help.

Thank you to Matt Snow for pushing me to be a better story-teller.

Thank you to the readers, booksellers, librarians, and teachers who get so excited about YA thrillers, especially mine. Thank you for allowing me to continue doing the work I love so dearly.

Thank you to Laurie Elizabeth Flynn, Kit Frick, Kathleen Glasgow, Liz Lawson, and Courtney Summers for lending your extraordinarily kind and generous words to help get this book out into the world.

The Counselors would not exist without the friendships I made during my own transformative summers spent at sleepaway camp. To Jamie, Julie, Liz, Marissa, Marley, Mia, and Zoe: thank you for the inspiration, the brainstorming, and above all, the memories.

Thank you to Halley, Ben, and baby Luke for so many mean-ingful moments spent together after a year with so few.

Thank you to my parents, who have always supported me, no matter how lofty my goals may seem. Thank you for knowing, even before I did, that camp is where many children find indepen-dence and self-worth, and that I would find mine there, too.

Thank you to Maxwell. I'm so glad we made it official.